CU00869269

BROTHER BROKEN

Cecile Beaulieu

Includes Excerpts from the
Journal of Denis Beaulieu

 FriesenPress

One Printers Way
Altona, MB R0G 0B0
Canada

www.friesenpress.com

Copyright © 2023 by Cecile Beaulieu
First Edition — 2023

All rights reserved.

No part of this publication may be reproduced in any form, or by any means, electronic or mechanical, including photocopying, recording, or any information browsing, storage, or retrieval system, without permission in writing from FriesenPress.

ISBN
978-1-03-916529-8 (Hardcover)
978-1-03-916528-1 (Paperback)
978-1-03-916530-4 (eBook)

1. *FIC045000 Fiction, Family Life*

Distributed to the trade by The Ingram Book Company

DEDICATION

to the boys

AUTHOR'S NOTE

All major events in this story are factual. Some are drawn from the author's memories and some are recalled by other persons. Details may not be accurate and may be contrived and expounded to facilitate flow and story development. Select names have been changed or omitted to protect the identity of individuals.

EPIGRAPH

A brave man once requested me
To answer questions that are key
Is it to be or not to be
And I replied, "Oh why ask me?"
Mike Altman and Johnny Mandel
M.A.S.H. theme song:
"Suicide is Painless"

I wanted to use words from the song 'Suicide is Painless' in the title of the book, but it seemed absurd and inappropriate, considering the piece was meant to be the "stupidest song ever written" (Robert Altman).

As M.A.S.H.'s movie director, Robert Altman wanted it sung during the staged funeral of a medic who had faked suicide. The director's son, 14-year-old Mike Altman, wrote the lyrics in under an hour and it became a No. 1 hit in the UK. Music lovers obviously didn't consider it a stupid song.

The lyrics are brilliant, the tune is catchy and when it gets in your head, it won't leave. That's how it's been the whole time writing this book. There is something soothing about the piece and I wanted to mention its significance.

TABLE OF CONTENTS

PART ONE

CHAPTER ONE — IMPERVIOUS

I once had the eyes of a child, but I've slowly gone blind
And now I'm reaching around in the dark and don't know
what I'm gonna find
Big Sugar
"Bump on the Head"

I'm not a nice person. If you could read my thoughts, you would know this is true.

On first meeting, I may project the image of a rather pleasant, well-mannered person. Our conversation could revolve around a variety of interesting subjects, none of which reveal anything tangible about me. You would provide most of the dialogue and I would prompt you with lead-ins so you'd think you were controlling the conversation.

I wouldn't interrupt your rambling. As long as you did all the talking, I could avoid sharing.

Without bringing attention to myself, I'd scan the room to avoid eye contact with you and note anything I could use to distract from our discussion. Eventually, the tedium would get to me, and I'd find any excuse to break from the harsh hell called *small talk*.

Please don't take it personally. I treat everyone the same. My family is no exception, and I love them very much. Monopolizing my attention feels like an attempt to invade my isolation. That's something I can't tolerate for very long.

The sound of the phone ringing assaults my calm, its whining screech triggers panic. I get spooked, like a doe startled by a predator's approach. I won't answer anyone who attempts to reach me this way. I'll assess the message left and consider whether to reply.

A text message is more likely to be acknowledged, but only if a response is necessary.

I don't do social media.

If you ring my doorbell, you'll be left standing outside. I'll ignore the pressure to open the door. Unless you break it down, you won't obtain access to my home . . . or me.

I'll avoid you if there's a chance we'll run into each other.

Grocery stores are especially challenging. It's an art to shop while scanning the aisles to dodge accidental encounters. One advantage to public locations is that no one notices other people's movements unless they are consciously paying attention—which is what I do. My mission is to get the crap I need and get out, unobserved.

Sometimes, hostility builds inside me and I itch to get in someone's face. I look to release some of the agitation I've repressed. I dream of planting a golf club through a windshield—preferably that of a very nice sports car whose driver has perturbed me. It pacifies me to imagine swinging a club and landing it somewhere wicked.

I don't golf, but I could find a golf club . . . if I were to try.

But mostly I brood behind closed doors, and only dream of confrontation.

I know why I wake up most mornings with acrimony in my bones. I have nightmares. Actually I have the same nightmare, over and over again. It goes something like this.

I'm the lone traveler on a raft that's been set adrift down a slow-moving river. The river is carrying me further from the dock, and it's the only dock in the world. I see silhouettes of three boys—only sometimes, they are men. The trio are standing near the edge of the dock. I recognize them.

"Hey, can you throw me a rope?"

They ignore me.

I call out: "I'm sorry, I'll change!"

They look at me with disdain, and show their backs to me.

I begin to panic as the river's flow quickens, moving me fast away from the dock. The man-boys walk away together, paying no mind to my distress. They are the only ones able to save me from being swept out to open sea. Instead, they abandon me.

The dream ends, and I learn why I can't redeem myself. It's because I've caused them pain. I've been a bad sister, and they're done with me.

I'm done with me. I can't seem to fix me.

Want some advice? Stay away from me—protect yourself.

Here's a reminder: I am not a nice person.

Just so you know, I wasn't always like this.

CHAPTER TWO — THE DUCK HUNTER

> First thing we'd climb a tree and maybe then we'd talk
> Or sit silently and listen to our thoughts
> With illusions of someday casting a golden light
> *The Tragically Hip*
> *"Ahead By A Century"*

It was summertime. I was barefoot and trailing after John, though I didn't always manage to keep up with him. He was, after all, my big brother, older by two years. I selected him to be my guardian, whether he liked it or not—and only because I didn't want to be left behind, especially by him.

John could venture farther than I was allowed. When he was off somewhere beyond where I was permitted to roam, I would be stuck at home with my little brother Mitch, whose babyish interests provided me little intellectual stimulation.

John was worldly. He had been exposed to ways far beyond the one-block radius of my confinement. I craved his independence, and I needed to tap into his vast experience. He held the secret to living freely, outside the perpetual scrutiny of parents.

At five years old, he had already managed to establish a wide network of social contacts who depended on him to drop by for regular visits. Granted, most were senior citizens. They were wrapped around his little finger. His intensely inquisitive eyes drew people in, and women envied the abundant curls of his baby-soft hair. He carried charm in his back pocket, and doled it out generously. He knew whose allegiances he could secure, and he had it pegged where to score the best treats.

John had all the companionship he could want. Perhaps he thought being shadowed by a little sister might cramp his style. Then, one day, for no particular reason, I became John's ally, which meant my role was his sometimes-partner-in-crime, the easy target of his pranks, and his potential scapegoat, lookout person, and holder of the bag.

Eventually, Mom relaxed the range of my boundaries, and I was finally permitted to tag along with John when he ventured about town. I was pumped to keep up with him, step for step. His route was tried, tested, and true, and it encompassed the village's entire six blocks.

At any given time, the population of our village never exceeded a hundred. It occupies a very small piece of ground in Northwestern Saskatchewan. The community sits on the edge of northern boreal forest. Farming is the area's main industry. Our village borrows its name from the Cree language. The word is *Makwa,* which translates to "loon." Most would agree that the name Makwa holds a nicer flavour than its English counterpart, especially since "loon" holds two meanings. One is an aquatic bird that frequents the nearby lakes. The other is a term describing a state of mind, inferring insanity. Strange things can happen in Makwa, so in either sense the name fits the village. For what it's worth, Makwa exists on the opposite side of the bush-line from normal. Being normal is boring, and Makwa was anything but boring.

If it truly takes a village to raise a child, we were in the perfect setting. There was a shared intimacy, and people respected each other's space—usually. As a rule, people looked out for one another, and my parents had no need to fuss over our whereabouts every waking moment.

John could be gone for an entire afternoon. Sometimes, he didn't show up for mealtime, which initiated *the search*.

"Go find Johnny."

Within fifteen minutes, because our village was small and John's habits were predictable, someone would locate him.

"He's having supper with Mrs. McGuiness."

It wasn't uncommon for Mrs. McGuiness to feed the strays who appeared at her doorstep. She was an elderly widow who lived by herself and looked forward to company. She welcomed him into her household: "Come in, Johnny."

He was comfortable with her, and made himself at home at her table. She was genuinely happy to see him, and lavished him with good eats. John was the welcome visitor who saved Mrs. McGuiness from another evening dining alone, though him showing up at her place on that *particular* night may have had something to do with it being liver night at our house.

Dad was a WWII vet. He had served in the Royal Canadian Navy. After the war, he pedalled a bicycle four hundred miles north of his parents' home in Gravelbourg, Saskatchewan. He bought land and started a farm.

Dad caught the eye of my mom with his drop-dead good looks. She was the cute little farm girl whose family lived nearby. She stole his heart, and they married in 1949.

Marguerite and Jean were their names, but most people called them Margaret and John, the Anglicized version of their French names. They were French-Canadian Catholics, expected to populate with more French Catholics, so they started *une famille*.

Their first-born was my sister, Pauly. After Pauly came Rod, Denis, John, me, Mitch, and Gus. Two parents, seven kids. My family calls me "Céc," which sounds like "pace," not "peace."

My brother John was born in January 1957. Within a few months of his birth, Mom and Dad had worked up a worry— there was something wrong. John wasn't progressing the way they thought he should. It was somewhat obvious, but not drastically apparent. My parents needed reassurance. Instead, doctors validated their concerns.

The fix was surgery to repair kidney blockages. Mom and Dad took him to a hospital hundreds of miles from home. John's stay amounted to weeks of stress. His tiny body bore scars like railroad tracks on each side of his little torso. I imagine a 1950s operating room scenario—a surgeon with a cigarette dangling out one side of his mouth while manipulating tiny organs, and a nurse offering assistance or an ashtray.

Maybe surgical practices weren't quite so scary. John recuperated, even though the recovery room was a grim place to occupy. Patients weren't comforted with physical touch. They were mostly left on their own, laid out on hospital beds, receiving occasional care and attention from a nurse. There was no warmth of human contact, so John rocked himself to sleep bruising his little temple against the unforgiving rungs of the hospital crib. That was how Mom found him when it came time to bring him home.

I wonder how he reacted to being held lovingly during the five-hour trip home. Did Mom's caring embrace provide comfort, or was it a strange unrecognizable sensation of closeness, warmth, and containment? Did Dad's tenderness affirm an immediate sense of belonging and security, or did it take a while for John to get accustomed to it? Did he relish the attention his older siblings gave him, or did he take it all in stride? However it played out, he quickly became a favourite in the family.

John may have been a little slow out the gate, but once he launched, he was revved to full throttle. There was no stopping John from plucking the best out of every moment. His little legs would take him any direction his curiosity pointed.

Ma famille lived on a farm until 1958, which was slightly before my time. Dad decided to move off the farm and into town for his kids to have more advantages. He kept on farming, though he had to commute an extra eight miles every day.

The modified granary that served as my parents' first home had become inadequate to meet the needs of a growing family. There were limitations on how much Dad could adapt a single-room dwelling to accommodate six individuals. It was a constant effort for Mom to keep babies and toddlers away from the woodstove used for heating and cooking.

Every crack and gap of the poorly erected structure extended an invitation for cold to enter. During winter, frost formed like crystal gauze growing up the walls. Beds were situated along the perimeter of the room, and frost fused with almost anything it touched. My parents spent many mornings peeling frozen blanket fringe from the wall.

A suitable home for the right price became available in town, so my parents loaded up the truck and moved. Our new home had been used as a rooming house. It was built during the first decade of the twentieth century. By the time my family acquired it, the house was run down—but still a marked improvement from the granary. The main floor had a lobby, an eating area, a kitchen, and living quarters. Guest rooms and primitive bathroom facilities were on the top floor.

Along with its many worthy features, the house had issues. The space was larger than my parents' previous home, meaning it required more wood and coal for heat. Dad explored other heating options, and before long, he had a forced-air furnace installed in the cellar. It burned fuel oil. Floor ducts were piped to the furnace, a thermostat was attached, and heat was dispensed with the flick of a switch. Only my parents could fully appreciate the value of an uncomplicated heat source. The distribution range was limited to the main floor, though, due to the furnace's restricted capacity and Dad's determination to curtail heating costs.

The lobby served as a telephone office. Before my parents bought the place, it had provided phone service to the entire village. By obtaining the home, my family also acquired a home business. Mom became the new telephone operator for the village. Actually, we all became telephone operators as soon as we were mature enough to reach the switchboard, operate the hand-crank, and follow simple instructions.

Mom put us through the training and showed us how to facilitate a call. We started with a clear, concise inquiry: "Number, please?" Meaning, *to whom do you wish to place the call*? When the caller provided the info, we jammed a phone plug into the proper jack and rang up the number. We had to spin the hand crank to trigger the buzzer on the receiver's end and wait for a response. When someone answered, we flicked a switch and freed the call so they could have their little chat. By the age of five, John and I were old hacks at the job.

Our move into town didn't deprive us of living the farm experience. Grandma and Grandpa, my mom's parents, remained in the country where they farmed for a living. John and I spent time there—not the jail kind of time, but the fun kind. There were adventures waiting to be had on the farm, and John made it his mission to leave nothing unexplored. If there was potential fun lurking, he discovered it. If there was mischief to craft, he attended to it. If there were chores to be done, he found ways to avoid them.

I relished stays at Grandma's house. Her hugs were wonderful. She crushed us against her ample bosom, which was like being smothered in marshmallows. She smelled of lavender—a pleasant essence that lingered.

It remains a wonder how Grandma survived the melee of both John and me for extended periods. Our visits were rare—and maybe for good reason.

The farm held so many possibilities in a seemingly limitless amount of space. The layout of the farmstead could have been inspired by a snapshot of an African savannah. A tire-packed dirt trail along a fence-line led to the farmyard from the main road. A line of scrubby trees paralleled the trail, and grassy pasture filled the leftover space.

All the farm buildings looked tired, as if on triple-time sentry assignment. The rain had long ago scoured away any remnant of whitewash, exposing bare wood to caustic elements. Except for the green of trees and grass, grey was the prominent theme. Only childlike imagination could dress it up with splashes of colour.

Grandma and Grandpa had three sons who lived with them. The men helped run the farm. Emil, who was one of the sons, was handicapped. As a baby, he had suffered brain damage due to a severe fever. The injury marred his intellect and comprehension. He could never be self-reliant.

Uncle Emil was a large man with the mind and innocence of a child. To us, he was like another fun kid to play with, though much bigger. His size, we thought, we could exploit. It couldn't hurt to have a perceived bodyguard on our side. In reality, Emil was the one who needed protection, and no one understood this better than our grandmother. Even though Emil looked like he could take care of himself, it didn't take much prodding to reveal his childlike vulnerability. We weren't allowed to tease him, which was something we could hardly resist. It took but one encounter with my grandmother's wrath to eradicate the temptation.

We grew to respect our gentle uncle. We resented it when someone outside the family made fun of him. His unique ways helped us learn to accept differences and understand the value of simplicity. He had one name for all his nieces and nephews—"*petit* boy"—only his vocabulary was mono-syllabic and "*petit*" came out sounding like "tsee." So we all became "tsee boy," and to us, he became "tsee Mil."

Grandma encouraged John and me to communicate with Emil in French. Uncle couldn't understand much English, but I think she said it so we wouldn't lose the language of our family. She recognized the pressure that was coming for us to abandon our culture.

Most people that I knew spoke Saskatchewanese, which is particularly handy for anyone living in Saskatchewan. We used words like *gibbled*, *Vi-Co*, and *chesterfield*, and didn't think the lingo caused confusion for anyone. I didn't even know our dialect was distinct from the rest of the world.

My family was also well versed in *Saskatchewanese en français*. Apparently, the word we used to refer to the toilet was actually borrowed from the Queen's English. We called it the *bécosse* (bā•kuss). The English referred to it as the "back-house." French people adopted the English word, added their own distinct flair, and it came out sounding like *bécosse*. In much the same way "cut the grass" became *mowdelawn*, and *tro-up* translated to vomit.

The trick is to speak rapidly and merge the words using a French accent.

Mornings at the farm often started with Grandpa's buffoonery. He had a habit of teasing Grandma. He poked fun and agitated her, usually while she was preparing breakfast. Their three sons, including Uncle Emil, didn't help the situation with their laughter.

Grandma worked in a frenzy to get everyone fed and out of her kitchen—a deliberate effort to suppress the ribbing and restore calm. We still don't know how Grandpa got away with taunting her. Perhaps it was because of Grandma's innate goodness.

We were in Grandma's charge while the men tended the farm. She had Uncle Emil watch us when she was busy doing other things. Uncle tried to navigate us away from potential monkey business, which was a full-time job for him.

Grandma's wrath was something any sensible-minded grandchild would normally avoid—unless you were the kind of kid who, like his grandpa, preferred to poke the bear. As well as being very protective of Uncle Emil, Grandma held the highest degree of modesty.

So, when Uncle's biological functions kicked in, his own modesty obliged him to go privately around the side of a building to "water the horse." John couldn't resist chasing after mischief. He raced around the opposite side to catch

Uncle doing his business. My brother's raucous laughter called attention to himself. Grandma heard him and investigated. John wasn't prepared for Grandma's deafening shrieks at his inappropriate behaviour.

She bellowed at him, "*Maudit—tsee merde!*"

Grandma also employed gentler methods to teach us the virtues of propriety. At home, our parents weren't so strict about us cloaking the need to do our business, although we knew to keep our body parts concealed. We were innocent, and oblivious to things others might consider inappropriate. So, we intended no breach of protocol in hounding someone for an answer to a question while they were comfortably seated on the toilet, mid-dump.

It was easy to figure out whether the person on the can was adequately settled by checking the position of his feet beneath the curtain. Perhaps bathroom doors hadn't yet been invented—ergo, the need of a cloth curtain for privacy. We parted the veil with the gentle swoop of an extended arm. The spooked squatter blinked wide eyes at us. We asked the burning question and anticipated basic feedback. Instead, we received another swift reaction from Grandma—though this time she explained in a manner that was more composed.

Uncle Emil had many qualities of a child's favourite playmate. His body was plump, like a cherished teddy bear. His big hands could have been fashioned after the Friendly Giant's own hams. He borrowed Santa Claus's cheeks and nose, and his eyes had a puppy quality. Uncle Emil was hardly ever irritable, and hanging out with him had huge advantages.

If we had a notion to climb a tree, and the bottom limb was too high to reach, Emil offered a boost. Then, when we were done climbing, he'd give us a hand down again. If we wanted to know the time, we'd ask him, "Tsee Mil, what time is it?"

Uncle would look at his watch, wind it, and check the time. He'd tell us it was "four cluck." According to Uncle, it was always "four cluck."

The watch was one of the few objects he valued. He also prized his pen and notepad. Uncle thought himself a scribe, and was always eager to put pen to paper. If we came upon a noteworthy situation, we would tell him, "Uncle, write that down."

Being charged with the task of note-taker made him feel important. Like a hungry journalist, he'd pluck the pencil and notepad from the breast pocket of his shirt and scribble some squiggles on a blank sheet. When he was done writing, he'd place them back into his pocket.

Uncle helped us access crawlspaces at the top of granaries. We searched for new cat litters, and were often rewarded with the discovery of at least one family of fur-balls. Sometimes, we had to make crucial decisions, like what to do with the remains of runts who hadn't survived. We settled on providing proper cat funerals in the corner. We covered them with wood chips and mouthed a little prayer to acknowledge their passing. These were notable moments, so we had Uncle document them.

At milking time, mother cats abandoned their babies. They gathered at the barn, lined up in a row, and waited for Grandpa or one of the uncles to give them a milk squirt from a cow's teat. John and I tried our hand at milking, but our grips weren't strong enough to draw milk. We had to watch to make sure the cow's tail didn't work free and whack us in the head.

As long as a cow didn't kick over a bucket, all the collected bovine nectar went to the house. Grandma ran the milk through the cream separator, which made the porch smell like baby barf. I wondered how long it took before milking cows twice a day stopped being fun.

One day, Grandpa parked the tractor in the farmyard after driving it home from the field, where he and two of the uncles were clearing bush. The men stopped to have lunch and a smoke break.

John and I had just finished collecting eggs in the chicken coop for Grandma when Grandpa came outside and found the tractor had gone missing. He was annoyed, but not overly worried. How far could anyone get stealing an old tractor in boondocks Saskatchewan?

Grandpa kicked a loose stone with his shoe and muttered, "*Tabernac*, if I catch *de* stupid bugger who took *de* tractor I'm going to let *imm avv* it." He turned to my uncles and said, "We walk."

I couldn't understand why Grandpa would give someone the tractor if he was so mad about them taking it in the first place.

John and I followed as Grandpa and our two uncles took a shortcut across the yard, past the barn, through the corral, and over a barbed wire fence. Beyond a small crop of trees, a clearing opened up to the field. They met Uncle Emil, who was walking toward them, leading two horses. One of the uncles asked him, "Where are you going with the horses? We still need them to help with clearing."

Emil smiled, patted the roan, and handed over the reins. The horses were Emil's pets, and I suppose he didn't think leaving them in the field through lunch was a very responsible thing to do.

Grandpa scanned the worksite and spotted the tractor parked next to a brush pile. He scratched his head and wondered how Emil had managed to start the tractor and drive it. It wasn't something he had ever been taught to do.

John and I remained occupied and entertained while at the farm. We filled our days with things besides exploring, like helping Grandma in the garden, feeding chickens, and ironing tea towels and handkerchiefs. Summer days could seem endless. The sun didn't set until late, and when Grandma called us in to bed, we responded with debate: "But Mémé, it's only four cluck."

A trip to town marked the end of our farm visit. My grandparents deposited us back home so Grandma could catch some proper rest. Before leaving, she gave us each a warm, smothering hug goodbye.

When I started tagging along with John, we often visited the elderly brother-sister pair who lived next to the post office across the street from us. We made them proper social calls with no intent to cause mischief.

They were generous with their hospitality and eager to invite us into their tiny, neat home. John was relaxed straight-away—like he'd done this a thousand times before, which he practically had.

"Hello, Johnny," they greeted him.

John extended the courtesy of introducing me: "This is my sister."

Mr. T was the younger, more fit brother of Mrs. B, whose frailty was pronounced. Blocky shoes and support hose did nothing to boost her mobility. Because he was a decent kind of guy, Mr. T appointed himself the go-to person for his older sister. Mrs. B was likely to remain seated in an armchair during our visits, while Mr. T who seemed very tall, played host.

There was a warmth about them that made me feel welcome. The wrinkles on their faces were etched there like permanent smiles, and their eyes had sparkle. The tops of their heads were the colour of woolly snow—soft and bouncy. We did our kid-cuteness thing, they did their good-natured old people thing, and we got along very well.

At first, I was somewhat timid with them and maintained a close proximity to John. But over time, they drew me out like a feral chipmunk emboldened to feed from an outstretched hand. Their home was safe. We had permission to relax and explore.

Mrs. B's collection of miniature dolls caught my eye. I wandered over to get a closer look. Each doll was clothed in a lace-frilled dress, crocheted and starched stiff. They were perched on a shelf behind glass, for display only, which didn't limit my admiration of them. Mrs. B understood my fascination of all things pretty, and together, we appreciated their daintiness.

There was one thing John and Mr. T had in common: a penchant for playing pranks. They forged a partnership out of a shared drive to chase after fun. The novice and coach developed a harmless conspiracy. What better way to train the trainee than to pull a gag on the new kid? It didn't take long for them to initiate me into Sitting Duck City. They made a plan and lured me into a trick.

The opportunity presented itself on our third visit. John and I made a regular stopover, we got comfortable, and my guard was down. We were at the kitchen table when Mr. T took something out of the fridge. I anticipated a treat. The rascal offered me a heaping spoonful of cottage cheese, which I accepted with relish. My chops closed down around it. The squishy mush filled my mouth. It was cool and creamy, soft and spongy.

My palate did a double take. Mr. T had said it would taste like ice cream. It didn't.

My grimace did nothing to hide the disappointment. The tricksters sniggered and gloated without remorse. I couldn't spit out the cottage cheese with them watching, so I swallowed.

John's participation in Mr. T's antics didn't come without reward. Sometime later, Mr. T gave John a gift, though it wasn't his birthday or Christmas.

John was boastful as he showed off the toy truck, still in the package. His glee was apparent, and I envied his good fortune. But then John announced, "There's a present for you, too." He paused for a moment, then added, "Yeah . . . it's a stick, and he's gonna hit you with it."

Of course I believed him. Why would he lie? So I made it my mission to avoid visiting our elderly friends.

One day, Mr. T noticed me from across the street. He tried to coerce me over to receive the gift. Like any sensible kid, I kept my distance. I knew better than to go across the street. I wasn't going to let him hit me with a stick.

It didn't make sense that I should be punished—I hadn't done anything wrong. At home, Dad was the disciplinarian, but he seldom used his hand to make us mind. His sternness was enough to keep his kids in line. Mom loved us into being good. We wanted to please her because she deserved it. We knew our boundaries. We couldn't claim ignorance as a reliable defence, and the rules of conduct were basic: treat others the way you want them to treat you. So why did Mr. T find it necessary to smack me?

Mr. T must have gotten tired of waiting for me to come get my "gift." I suppose he determined he had no other choice than to bring himself over to our house. I caught wind of this development and decided to make myself scarce. Dad retrieved me from the hiding space deep within my bedroom closet. I considered Dad's complicity a betrayal. I needed to appeal to his sense of loyalty, and I wanted to cry out to him, "An old guy wants to hit me with a stick, and you're OK with that?!"

Dad carried me to the porch entrance, where Mr. T stood waiting. The old guy had one arm behind his back, obviously concealing something. I knew what it was, so I braced myself for the blow.

Mr. T smiled at me, which I thought was arrogant. I turned my gaze downward and wondered how things had come to this. Why was I the one made to feel like I had done something wrong? I waited with dread and quiet surrender as Mr. T approached me. He swung his arm out from behind his back in a motion that made me wince. I expected a crack against my backside. Instead, he handed me a great big doll.

John had his usual route for dropping in on friends. Maintaining a network of contacts was key—a rule he could have taken straight out of a salesman's handbook. I wasn't far behind as he made the rounds. Old Man Max was near the top of his list. Max's limitless supply of mints was definitely a worthwhile attraction.

Just like Mr. T and Mrs. B, our visits amused him—though there wasn't much in the way of conversation between us. I don't think Max was used to receiving company. He didn't keep his house tidy, and it smelled a little like our porch before the slop pail was emptied. Dirty dishes on the table probably didn't help improve the aroma. Max chuckled when I pinched my nose to abate the smell.

We sat on chairs too large, happily dangling our feet and sucking on mints in easy silence. Max packed the inside of his bottom lip with snuff, turned the volume down on the radio, and didn't say much either. The inertia eventually got the best of John, and he couldn't resist meandering across the room to expose a hidden portrait of a bare-breasted pinup girl. Max concealed his pin-ups behind large calendars, a trick John easily figured out. Max gently scolded, but John could hardly conceal his glee.

Up to this point in my short life, I had never set eyes on the nakedness of an adult woman. Our visits, in a way, were educational. Before Talking Barbie and Malibu Barbie were introduced, my exposure to shirtless females was limited to the no-nipple Barbies. The pinup portrait taught me proper anatomy, and put to bed one more burning question.

In addition to dropping in on neighbours, we had other matters to tend to, like building stockpiles of candy. We couldn't spend all our free time as goodwill ambassadors. John was cunning and creative. He developed ideas to increase our dwindling supply of treats, though his methods sometimes crossed the line. Apparently, not everyone appreciated his talent like I did.

Normally we hunted empties—cashable bottles to trade in for candy at the Hotel Café. We walked alongside the ditch and gathered as many as we could find. The proprietor didn't accept dirty beer bottles or sticky pop bottles, so if the bottles were grimed up, we washed them. Acquiring enough booty took effort. Some days, our findings might only result in a lone dead soldier. One beer bottle empty couldn't generate enough swag to buy enough candy to satiate both our cravings, so John came up with a plan.

It was a good plan that would save us a lot of hunting time. We collected bottles the normal way, cleaned them, brought them to the Café, and traded them for treats, like usual. The hotel owner stored the redeemed bottles in crates outside the back door of the hotel. Perhaps from there it was easier to load them onto the transport truck. There didn't appear to be any kind of surveillance where the crates were stacked.

John scanned the area to be sure there were no snoopy eyes on us. We crouched low and snuck over to the stash, avoiding detection. John picked out the same bottles we had exchanged earlier, and we skittered away with our catch. We brought our loot through the front door of the café and stood the bottles up on the counter. The server greeted us. "Back again, eh? That was quick."

We pointed out our treat choices, and she handed them to us in a small paper bag. John grabbed it, and I followed him outside. We put some easy distance between us and the café before we stopped to scarf down the second helping of candy.

The plan had its merits. A recycling program this savvy held potential.

But the scheme bombed on the second sting.

The inquiry went something like this—

"Can you identify the perps?"

My humourless parents and the proprietor pressured a confession out of us, with no regard for the ingenuity of our method. We were forced to put our innovative practice into early retirement.

We learned two new words—"busted" and "grounded." Incarceration wasn't all bad. We watched episodes of *The Friendly Giant* and *Chez Hélène*. We feasted on brown sugar sandwiches and made numerous round trips down the old coal chute, sliding from the porch into the cellar, where we dropped like toppled dominos. We occupied the sandbox in the backyard building roads and bridges for toy vehicles. When the weather was rough and we couldn't play outside, we rummaged through the "rag room."

The rag room was used for storing anything that could be salvaged or reused. To make a deposit into the room, you had to carefully open the door, toss in your contribution, then quickly close the opening before anything could fall out.

Going into the rag room was an adventure we relished. Our imaginations soared, and we filled afternoons in that space, discovering abundant treasures. An ordinary object could trigger serious reflection. A rediscovered Barbie doll head filled me with questions about the mysteries of physical disadvantages. How could Barbie, who shared a birth year with me, have inherited a substantial rack without having gone through puberty? I could easily wear a bra inside out or backwards, and it might never be noticed, so how unfair was that?

When we tired of the rag room, we made up games to play in the phone booth, which was in the same room as the telephone switchboard Mom manned for the village.

Our telephone booth wasn't like the ones occupying street corners. Ours was a wooden, boxy structure with a glass window on the door. The telephone company set up the booth at the same time they installed the telephone equipment. It was positioned in the corner of the room, next to the switchboard, and it provided callers their privacy.

We used the booth as if it were a jail. The kid whose turn it was to play the bad guy remained inside until his sentence was up. Most times, I was the prisoner, and John bossed me around: "You stay here until I tell you. I'm the police, so you have to do what I say."

The booth wasn't such a nasty place to do time. I brought books or a favourite toy to make lockup more enjoyable. I suppose my parents could have used it to rehabilitate us after our bottle-cashing scam, but I think they considered that option a little excessive.

To be sure, we didn't get bored. Mom found us small jobs to do around the house, like helping on laundry day. John and I were fascinated by the wringer washer. We imagined the wringer to be some kind of hungry predator, and we were responsible to feed it. Mom showed us how to direct wet garments into the wringer and gave us the cautionary speech about keeping fingers away from the rollers.

John always pushed the limit of how close he could get to the mouth of the monster. Mom's back was turned when he got his fingers caught. He felt the pinch and yelled. He tried pulling his hand back, but the wringer held it tight. Mom couldn't hit the release lever quick enough, and John's hand went through the rollers.

It's alarming how flat the wringer could make his hand. For a few days, John lost the use of his fingers, so I took it upon myself to spoon-feed him meals.

This wasn't John's first or last mishap. He fell out of a vehicle when he was only a tot. The car had suicide doors, which swing open from the front, unlike most vehicle doors, which swing open from the back. An air gust from forward motion caused the door to open unintentionally. Fortunately, the car wasn't going very fast. John suffered a minor head wound requiring a few stitches. There was no need for a hospital stay that time.

There were other close calls, too. Next to our house, there was a structure made of wood cross beams, framed into a cradle to hold a water tank. The tank was propped four feet off the ground, and collected rainwater runoff from the roof—as much as 250 gallons. The wood beams formed a cage-like enclosure beneath the tank. We used the space as a hangout and spent a lot of time there. Then, one day, the stand collapsed from the weight of a full tank of water. Mom did a swift headcount to ensure none of us had been caught in the wreck. When a new stand was built, Mom pointed to the empty space under the water tank and told us, "You're not allowed to go there." We listened.

I wasn't allowed to follow John the day he started school. I wanted to go with him, but Mom held me back. I had a difficult time being left behind. Going to school was hard for John, too.

The school was run by nuns, even though it was a public school. The nuns taught Grades 1 through 12, and attendance peaked at about 120 students. Most students were bussed in from the country, which meant John met new kids.

School administrators had an ass-backwards way of staffing teachers. Grade 1 students should have a kid-friendly teacher, but that was not the way schools operated in Northern Saskatchewan. Perhaps it was done on purpose, to have the strictest nun initiate the new students—a sure-fire way to pre-establish order in the school room.

John told me a bit about his first day of school. It sounded like he approached the classroom and lingered in the doorway. The teacher nun was waiting inside to greet all the new kids. She told John where to go sit, but he wasn't ready to sit down. He wandered the classroom curious to investigate his new surroundings. The nun narrowed her eyes and spoke to him sternly: "Sit down."

The teacher wore the nun's official black habit, which gave her stunted frame the illusion of magnitude. Her skirts were starched stiff. They rustled and crinkled as she walked, betraying her sneaking-up game. A polished silver cross hung from a braided cord around her neck. The cross radiated where the sun's rays caught the metal, and it looked like lasers were shooting out of her chest. The white hood of her veiled headpiece fit snug against her wrinkly little face, making it hard to determine if she had any hair. She used her put-down eyes to compel obedience from her students. Her manner was not tender, which bolstered her reputation as a hard-ass teacher.

On another day, John explained how he got into trouble without even trying.

"Monsieur Jean Luc," she chided him, "do you have ants in your pants?"

A commotion outside the classroom had drawn John's attention. He heard the sound of laughter and a ball bouncing down the hallway. Students were going outside to play soccer, and he fidgeted in his seat, resisting the urge to join them. The nun realized he was focused on the door instead of on the lesson. She said to him, "Maybe you would like to spend some of that energy cleaning chalkboards during recess."

John said she had to have been in a good mood that day for her to be so lenient. When it came to discipline, cleaning chalkboards was the equivalent of scoring A on a spelling test. Unfortunately for John, the usual penance was a yardstick to the backside or a leather strap across the wrist.

The rigid structure of school didn't fit well with John. He hated giving up freedom, so it was no wonder he adopted a dislike for academics. His teacher singled him out to suffer the brunt of her bullshit during his first year of school. Perhaps there were things she saw in John that reminded her of things she didn't like about herself—John was small, French, and Catholic. Moreover, John was free-spirited—and maybe that's what drove her crazy.

Grandma crocheted strips of plastic cut from bread bags into useful items, such as rugs and hats. She also crafted book bags to get kids excited about going to school. It worked for a while, until the routine set in. The bag helped with bringing home books, but nothing could improve John's attitude toward school.

He dropped his book bag inside the back door when he got home. It would have stayed there unmolested if I hadn't opened it. I couldn't resist the lure of books, and was thrilled to nose through his. I flipped the pages and browsed colourful pictures unveiling a simple story. I pestered my older siblings to teach me to read, and soon learned about the exploits of Dick, Jane, Sally, and Spot. Perhaps John wasn't charmed by the characters the way I was, since he showed no interest in completing his homework. Then, he was held back to endure another year of first grade.

I was finally able to follow John to school after he completed his second round of Grade 1. Before class on my first day, John gave me a quick tour. We walked the hallway that separated the east side of the school building from the west side. I saw rooms with school desks facing blackboards. I learned where the girls' bathroom was. John pointed out the library, which fascinated me with its tall shelves filled with books. The auditorium was the biggest room of all. It was where students gathered for assembly. The principal's office was next to the auditorium, hidden at the end of a short hallway. We weren't allowed to go in, so John described it to me. He knew the layout very well.

John led me to my new classroom, which was also his. Grade ones shared the same room as grade twos, so we'd be together all day long, though we sat apart.

The old nun stood at the front of the class, motioning with her hands for all the students to stand for prayer. Kids—most who I had never seen before—surrounded me. Out of the corner of my eye, I located John, and relaxed, knowing I wasn't alone among strangers.

It didn't take long for me to see how the nun treated my brother. More than once, she ridiculed him, calling him "Johnny-on-the-Spot" instead of using his real name. All the other kids thought it was funny. Sometimes I forced a laugh to fit in, but I didn't like that it made me feel like a creep.

John's infractions, for some reason, brought out the worst in her. I remember her riding him. I was useless as his ally. Only on our way home after school, far from the nun's earshot, did we brave up a sass at her. John quipped, "Hey you old crow, why don't you go fly a kite?!"

"Yeah, fly to the moon and get cheese!" I added with a slam.

At home, John reverted to his old self. What happened at school stayed at school. Being young and carefree, he didn't hang onto the negative tag the old nun attempted to stick him with. He set his sights on better things. When he walked off the schoolyard, he reclaimed his old life. At 3:30 p.m., there was plenty of daylight left, and he wasted no time chasing after fun.

I never stood up for John in class. I was just there like a spectator, not able to stop the show. Where the nun left off, other kids were quick to further torment him. I don't remember her ever picking on me the way she harassed John. Eventually, the first years of school passed, and teachers improved.

Walking to school wasn't always pleasant during winter. I wished I had learned to play sick on mornings that temperatures dropped below minus thirty degrees. The school principal considered attendance more important than the risk of frostbite, even at minus forty.

Bedrooms were situated on the second storey, and scant heat transferred from the main floor, so we often slept in the cold. I preferred spending winter mornings snuggled under blankets. And always, there was a menace squall churning outside. Lying in bed, I could hear the sound the cold made— it wailed, as if pushing air through a hollow.

The sun couldn't be counted on to provide heat—it didn't rise above the horizon until almost 9:30 a.m. If we were lucky, school might be cancelled, so we wouldn't have to wrench ourselves out of bed so early.

On those days, the furnace ran non-stop yet couldn't achieve a comfortable room temperature. The shivers caused my teeth to clack a snappy rhythm. First thing each morning, my siblings and I raced to claim a spot at the heat register in the kitchen. The warmth it generated was barely enough to appease a couple of kids, so Mom turned on the oven. She opened the oven door to release heat into the room, and we pulled our chairs close. We sat facing the stove and rubbed our hands between our knees, creating more heat with friction.

We didn't have indoor plumbing, and it was the boys' responsibility to keep the water pail in the house amply full. They fetched water from the town pump situated across the street from us. During extreme cold, the shaft on the pump might freeze. In that case, snow would have to be collected and melted. As John grew, the responsibility became his, too.

Mom never complained about manning the telephone switchboard on those days. The room it occupied was further away from the heat source, but she seldom let on that cold coursed through her. Often, she couldn't catch a break between calls, which caused her feet to chill-up a nasty sting.

Apart from ice skating, tobogganing, and building ice forts, nothing much appealed to me about winter. I looked forward to the springtime warmth. It would have been nice to rip the January and February pages off the calendar sooner. Even so, winter helped build character and fortitude.

School expanded our circle of acquaintances. Other than cousins and siblings, we didn't have many kids to hang out with. Most students lived on farms and didn't come to town very often. School became an essential venue for developing new relationships.

The nuns didn't allow us much time to fraternize. They kept us strictly focused on the lesson. Recess, which didn't start soon or last long enough, was the only time we could practise making friends. Lunch break would have been the opportune time, but town kids like us were required to eat at home, while the bussed kids ate together in the auditorium. Loyalties grew quickly given half a chance, and lunchtime opportunities bypassed us.

At recess, I waited for a turn to use the swing. There were too many other kids in line, so I sat on one end of the seesaw. A bigger kid took the other end. Instead of riding it up and down, the way seesaws are supposed to work, he kept my end elevated. My feet dangled in the air, and I bounced my bum with force, but failed to lower the seat. Then, he jumped off his end, and I came crashing down, landing hard on the ground. I would have called him an asshole, but I didn't know the word yet.

A girl who had snatched some chalk from a classroom drew a hopscotch on the sidewalk. A few others waited to play, so I joined the queue and found better reception. I asked one of the girls, "What's your name?"

She handed me a button to toss into the first square and said, "It's your turn. Hurry up before the bell goes."

I was on the third square when the bell rang to mark the end of recess. I kept playing until I missed landing my button into the next square. I was late returning to class. The nun made me stand in the hallway with my nose to the wall. I surmised that making friends was a complicated matter.

I missed Catechism class that day. I was like a non-Catholic who spent free time in the library, except I was in the hallway learning about penance. I wasn't too heartbroken about missing Catechism lessons, which stressed that females seek to join the choir and become nuns and males become altar boys and enter the priesthood. That's about all any of us ever picked up from the lessons besides learning that we displease Jesus with almost everything we do. We were encouraged to go to confession often, because evidently, we had much to confess.

"Forgive me Father, for I have sinned."

"Tell me your sins, child."

"I did adultery."

"Do you know what adultery means?"

"Yeah. I had a sip of beer, like my grandpa."

Mom and Dad marched us off to church every Sunday, so it wasn't like we didn't know how to be Catholic. We prayed, we knelt, we genuflected, we made the sign of the cross . . . we had all the moves down pat.

My family followed the liturgical calendar somewhat religiously. Shrove Tuesdays meant pancakes for supper. Fish Fridays were observed unless there were no fish, and then our meal option defaulted to pancakes. During Lent, we abstained from chocolate treats and participated in the occasional family rosary recitation.

Our attendance at Midnight Mass on Christmas Eve was compulsory, but we didn't mind. We could open our presents right after Mass and fill up on a hot meal of Christmas food, including tortière and roast turkey. Mémé gifted us each a small paper bag filled with peanuts, ribbon candy, and a Japanese orange. Mom sewed us new pyjamas for Christmas. She tailored them out of thick flannel to keep us warm at night.

I don't remember ever witnessing nuns attend Mass at church. They probably had their own service at the convent. Afterward, the priest presided over the commoners. I didn't have to bother with singing in the choir on Sundays—no nuns were present to herd us up to the choir loft. Apparently, choir was for special celebrations only.

Boys didn't get off so easy. There was always a demand for altar boys. John did his duty, but was never enthusiastic about serving. He stood obediently at the altar, holding his hands in prayerful posturing, anticipating the end of Mass— which couldn't come soon enough.

Once outside the church doors, we made a beeline for the general store. It opened briefly on Sundays to accommodate churchgoers, and we spent our nickel allowance on treats we'd been craving all week.

The store had a party-like atmosphere as patrons caught up with news and humorous stories. Most days, there was standing room only. People talked about the weather—a conversation choice more predictable than the weather itself. Some long-winded debates kept people gabbing way too long. The store owner had to herd people out the door so he could get on with his own Sunday plans.

Sundays were a favourite day of the week, though the favourite part didn't start until after Mass. On hot summer days, the beach beckoned. We each grabbed a towel and water toys, and put on a swimsuit. Mom packed the food, Dad drove the car, and we headed to Makwa Lake.

Dad barely had the car stopped, and we jumped out and made a beeline for the beach. We forgot our tire tubes in the trunk of the car and had to run back to get them.

My breath quickened when the first cool splash hit my body. I waded in, holding out my arms, trying to adjust to the cold chill of the northern lake water. I bobbed in the waves, working up the nerve to dunk my head. But then, John came up behind and pulled me backward into the drink. I caught a foothold and stood up, swinging my arms for balance and coughing up lake and sand. I pushed wet hair away from my eyes and went after him. He blocked me with splashing. I tried running away, but my legs were drunk and sluggish beneath the water's surface. I hooked a floating tire tube in my arm and made like a motorboat, kicking distance between us. I laughed as he tried keeping up with me.

We could only stand the lake's cold for so long, and then we had to get out. Coming out of the water, the shivers rattled us worse than a fast trip down a bumpy road. We wrapped ourselves in terrycloth towels and sat on the sand, trying to glean the sun's warmth. We gazed across the lake's wide expanse and pondered its personality.

The lake had a temperament you could read like a mood ring. Beneath cloudy skies, its swells rippled the color of cold steel. On those days, the lake was a surly hostess, inhospitable to its visitors. I preferred to sit at a distance and admire it rather than wade in its icebox shallows. Its disposition warmed on sunny days, though. The surface softened to lush satin, luring beachgoers into its watery playground. But beneath the sensual veneer, the lake concealed a frigid secret. My toes scarcely kissed the surface before budding goosebumps raced up my arms, looking like a reverse run of falling dominos. Regardless of hue, the water was too far north to hold heat.

Sand along the shore was mottled, the colour of oatmeal. It was coarse and felt prickly sharp on our feet, like walking on tiny shards of glass. The sand's texture wasn't great for building sandcastles. Kids grew frustrated at their failing efforts to form one.

I was ten years old the first time Dad took us fishing. John, our little brother Mitch, and I had one fishing line between us. We cast the line from the top of a bridge into the river that fed Makwa Lake. It was early spring, supposedly peak for good fishing.

We didn't know about the patience required for the sport. The afternoon dragged by without so much as a bite. I considered that we might be going about it the wrong way. Some boys from the nearby reservation were fishing off the riverbank. They caught fish, one right after the other, using a wire snare at the end of a pole. Their method was slick and effective, and offered a lot more reward than ours.

We were about to give up when a tug on the line caught our attention. John had control of the fishing rod, so Mitch and I joined in to help. We fumbled with the pole and fought a clumsy fight with the fish. The reel was either jammed or just plain slow, so we grabbed the line with our hands and hoisted our slimy prize up and over the rail.

We crowed with manic pride as our catch flopped itself gritty in the dirty sand. We had hooked a sucker fish in the eyeball, and not one of us wanted to touch it. One of the fisherman boys said it wouldn't be very good eating—muddy taste and wormy. Dad slipped him some cash for a couple jackfish so we wouldn't arrive home empty-handed.

A few years later, Dad bought a motorboat. He purchased it on a whim. John and I were over-the-top excited when Dad announced the news. I envisioned myself waterskiing across a glassy surface, winning the favour of skiers I had once envied from a dry place on the shore. John anticipated long, lazy days fishing, cruising Makwa Lake.

The day of the launch couldn't have arrived fast enough. We piled into the car. Dad pointed it toward the lake and drove it to the small cove where our new craft awaited its maiden voyage.

Words failed to describe my amazement at the sight of our new boat. I could neither force my gaping jaw closed nor take my eyes off it. In a trance, I followed Dad's lead, climbed into the boat, donned a life jacket, and sat myself down. We pushed off and floated away from shore.

Slowly, I began to register the reality of our dream boat. It was made of wood and painted reddish brown, likely to conceal the rusty nails that barely held it together. The number one consideration before climbing into the boat should have been its seaworthiness. Since we were already boarded and drifting away from the shoreline, we could only hope the oil-dank life jackets would serve their intended purpose.

Dad attached the gas line to the outboard motor and primed the line. He tugged on the cord to start the engine, fiddled with the carb, and tugged some more. He adjusted the choke and worked the throttle. The motor sputtered and coughed but did not spark. Dad tried again, though his efforts amounted to squat. We drifted.

We drew the curiosity of boaters cruising past us in their sleek machines. Their stares made me want to jump ship. Perhaps if our vessel sank it would be a godsend. But I had no such luck, so I remained seated in the boat with my family, adrift on a wreck that was more comparable to an anchor than a boat.

I speculated on how Dad had obtained our *bateau*, and pondered the closing of the deal. The boat was likely abandoned on the shore, where some guy had claimed to own it and offered it to Dad for a trade. I'm guessing the transaction cemented on the exchange of the boat for a half-empty bottle of Canadian Club.

Dad was on the losing end of deals gone bad many times. One summer, he had an idea to run a business. He invested money toward the rent of an old gas station. The shop had one gas pump and a service bay for auto repairs. Our best customer was a kid with a dirt bike who only came around after hours, when the station was closed. He drained gas from the pump hose into his bike tank when he thought no one was looking. It was enough to give him miles of cost-free riding.

No one ever told Dad about the importance of location, location, location. In rural communities such as ours, farmers typically bought their fuel in large volumes from a bulk station. Many village residents were seniors who didn't drive, and the scant likelihood of travellers stopping for a fuel-up ensured that the only entrepreneur benefitting from gas sales in town was the station owner, collecting his rent cheques. Dad chalked it up to experience—and a valuable lesson in economics wasn't wasted on his progeny.

We spent part of our school vacations picking rocks at the farm for Dad. John and I were too young to figure out that rock-picking wasn't fun, so we became quite proficient at it.

It would have been more profitable for Dad to manage a rock farm instead of a grain farm, in my opinion. Frost heave caused stones to perennially emerge at the surface—seeding them wasn't necessary. Had I been able to extract geological insight from my future self, I would have encouraged Dad to buy land with water-laid glacial deposits of rich loam instead of the crappy ground moraine that constituted his fields.

The rock-picking crew consisted of my brothers Rod, Denis, and John. I pestered Mom and Dad to let me join them, and the boys didn't argue against having an extra pair of helping hands. I was eight years old, and wanted to be part of the work party to earn some cash.

Dad asked me, "Céc, are you gonna be a crybaby if it gets too hard?"

I raised my shirt sleeves and showed him my muscles.

He rolled his eyes and gave in.

Rod was the head of our little crew. He was old enough to have a driver's license, and would have preferred cruising the streets in a muscle car, picking up girls to overseeing his siblings' work. He didn't own a set of wheels. On the bright side, there was no shortage of girls vying for his attention.

Rod knew how to operate machinery. He drove the tractor that pulled the stone boat. A stone boat is made with wooden planks attached together, same as a barn door, thick and wide. It's dragged on top of the ground like a sled. We walked alongside, stacking it with rocks. I gathered stones that were larger than my fist and smaller than a lunch pail. My brothers did the same. If a rock was too big for us to pick, Rod got off the tractor and helped out.

John found a boulder that couldn't be lifted. Rod proposed to blast it with a stick of dynamite. Dad hesitated at first, then determined that it had to be removed—otherwise, it would damage farm equipment. While the two brainstormed, we enjoyed a break from rock-picking.

Dad instructed Rod, "You'll need to dig around and underneath for a place to put the dynamite. If you can find a split in the rock, that's the best spot to put it."

They worked the plan.

Dad told us to lay down on the ground behind the tractor. It was parked a long way from the boulder, so there was little risk of us getting hurt from the blast. Rod was high on adrenaline. He lit the fuse and ran clear of the site. The fuse was long, and it took about a minute for the dynamite to blow. We couldn't watch the explosion, but when the dust settled, the rock was jarred loose, with a piece broken off. Dad and Rod rolled it onto the stone boat, which marked the end of our recess.

John and I were compensated for our time picking rocks. Dad paid what we considered a fair sum of loot—twenty-five cents per day. Rod and Denis got more because they were older. I wasn't concerned with the disparity, since the pay was five times my ordinary weekly allowance. Bottle-picking was actually more lucrative. Collecting empties on mornings following a dance at the parish hall provided John and me enough swag to last a month.

The real benefit to rock-picking was the stop off at the swimming hole afterwards—Dad's little Shangri-la. The place wasn't so much a swimming hole as a giant, beautiful bathtub. It had crystal-clear water and a gentle, sloping basin of silky sand, surrounded on three sides by thick vegetation. We swam and played until our fingers and toes pruned up. We could have continued all night, except that our bellies growled from hunger, so we put on dry clothes and headed home for supper. This little arrangement worked out well for Mom—she didn't need to fuss over scrubbing the grime off us.

Simple pleasures like going for a nice swim made up for years of scraping by. The promise of steady income from farming didn't come without risk. During the fall of 1959, the weather turned especially bad against farmers. Dad wasn't able to harvest a crop for two consecutive years because of excessive rain.

The grain was ripe to pluck, but the elements repeatedly delayed his attempts. The labour of his hands—the coaxing, the bribing, the tending and nourishing of seeds sown more than three months previous—represented an entire year's sustenance for the family. His role was to be a provider, but the sky's merciless onslaught crippled his ability to perform in that capacity.

Neighbouring farmers felt the same strain. Their crops couldn't be salvaged either. The outlook wasn't good for getting through the upcoming winters of 1959 and 1960. Then, the government stepped in and arranged free food distribution to producers in the area. Families received cases of canned pork. Spam helped sustain them through two years of harvest failure.

During that time, there were few menu options, owing to limited content in the kitchen cupboard, so Mom practised creative cooking. Meals for dinner, supper, *or dupper* (a non-negotiable substitute for dinner and supper) might have included main dishes such as fried Spam, roast Spam, boiled Spam, Spam soup, Spam kabobs, Spam stir-fry, Spam stew, baked Spam, slow-cooked Spam, Spam casserole, breaded Spam, or grilled Spam sandwiches. Poached eggs and Spam might have worked well for breakfast.

In addition to farming, Dad managed the family finances. The stash was meagre, but what little we had he regulated skilfully. He was a natural at stretching the food budget, a craft he exercised daily. Flour was cheap, and Mom baked a lot of bread to help reduce food costs. Dad's catchphrase became "are you gonna eat bread with that?"

His kids knew to take the suggestion seriously. Any time we indulged a craving, like a lone slice of bologna, a pickle, or a spoonful of peanut butter, Dad grilled us: "Are you gonna eat bread with that?"

Harvest time pitched our family's routine on its side. While Dad was busy combining, Mom planned, prepared, and transported meals to sustain him through the long days of harvest. She packed meals into a cardboard box, which was the closest thing to a picnic basket available. A couple kids usually assisted her with the task. At the farm, Mom arranged a place setting on the end gate of the truck and waited for Dad to make his next come-around with the combine.

When the combine rolled in, Mom brought out the food. Dad situated himself at the table set for one, and we watched as he devoured a meal that radiated delicious flavours.

"That sure smells good. Kin I have a bite?" John asked, but the adults ignored him.

Mom had us fill up on food at home. Even so, the ambience of the outdoor feast caused us to gape, salivate, and pine for Dad's portion. Dad managed to ignore our pathetic performance, and continued to feast unapologetically while we watched.

At harvest time, it was easy to understand why a person would choose to be a farmer. Autumn was filled with wonder, and the season captured our imagination. We stood watch beneath a canopy of trees bordering the field. Adorned with colourful, desiccated leaves dancing in the breeze, clapping and fluttering at a perfect tempo—the trees performed for us a boreal symphony. We appreciated the vast openness, the gifts of nature, the taste of absolute freedom. We knew these were invaluable treasures not found within the confines of town.

On special occasions, my grandparents hosted celebrations. Our ever-expanding clan of cousins, aunts, and uncles crammed into Grandma and Grandpa's home.

Their farm house was old and crude. It received scant flair for design when it was built—all pomp was given up for practical use. Grandma used handcrafted pieces to make her home pleasant. Crocheted doilies, knitted afghans, and patchwork quilts supplied a folksy touch. Every piece was an expression of tenderness designed to make us feel secure and loved.

Fragrant traces of woodsmoke and pipe tobacco permeated every room. Worn out, oversized wood furniture added rustic charm, and kids paired up to occupy single seats at the table. Framed portraits of deceased ancestors and religious images hung from the walls. We ignored the eyes in the faces of the pictures as they gawked at us while we ate.

Gatherings took on a festive mood. It started with food—a sit-down meal full of flavours plucked from the field, the garden, and the barn. Helpers in the kitchen bustled to the music of laughter. They set the table and prepared the meal, creating the delicious aroma of roast pork and baked pies. Our mouths watered in anticipation.

Soon, we were busy with the task of eating. Moms spoon-fed babies, toddlers struggled in clumsy fights with forks to get food into their bellies, and everyone else vied for attention with tales and jokes between bites.

Grandpa told us the story of a salesman who came to the farm.

"*Diz* guy, *ee* shows up *wit* books. Not just one book, but a bunch of *dem*, and *dey* all look *de* same. And *dey* are *evvy*, like bricks. I *tells* him, *de* cows don't read, and maybe *ee* should go find a farm *dat* got smarter animals."

Everyone laughed at his story. Grandpa didn't know what encyclopaedias were, so some laughed even more. I didn't, because I didn't know what they were either.

We filled up on more eats, news, and quips, and then pushed our chairs away from the spread. Adults lit up smokes, kids dispersed to play, and washing dishes was delayed for a bit.

An impatient challenger dealt and re-dealt a deck of playing cards, expecting a quick shift of focus from meal cleanup to a game of rummy. Dirty plates from the table were swapped for brown bottles. Players gave up chores in exchange for sport. The laidback part of the day settled in.

Us kids occupied the periphery until we lost interest in the adults' obsession with their cards. We took advantage of their preoccupation to pursue our own forms of amusement.

John and I found our fun at the top of the stairs leading to the attic, away from the disapproving eyes of grown-ups. We rummaged through the contents of a big glass dish that sat on top of a dresser. Inside it were wooden matches and a lone stalk of straw. We couldn't resist lighting one of the matches. We watched it burn down. John blew out the flame when it inched too close to his fingers. He lit another match, and we ogled it until the flame burnt out. John thought it would be fun to light the straw, so we did that, too, and we were even more captivated by the burning straw.

"Hey, let's go light a bale on fire," John suggested, as if the notion supported a natural progression of events.

For a short moment, I was tempted to go along with his scheme. But then the premonition of a severe scolding ran through my thoughts, so I told him: "No!" I didn't want to chance getting into trouble, so the plan was quashed.

Later on, someone noticed a murky upsurge rising from behind the granaries, like a ghost object fanning its tattered remnants. A darkish billow veiled the sun. My cousin blinked to make sure his eyes weren't playing tricks on him. The blaze became obvious when a glowing flare flicked its golden tongue.

In a panic, he rushed into the house, tripping on his way up the steps.

He choked on the words as they came out of his mouth: "There's a fire!"

The card players looked up from their game. It took a few seconds for the news to register. They hurried outside to investigate what had spooked our frantic cousin. They saw rolling clouds of smoke rising skyward, forming a dirty canopy overhead.

Grandpa barked instructions, and moms gathered kids close.

"Get the animals out of the barn!"

"Move that tractor!"

"Where's Johnny?"

Uncles evacuated animals from the nearby barn and placed equipment at a safe distance. They worked quickly to minimize the destruction. Fortunately wind wasn't a factor, and the fire remained contained to the stack of bales. The flames lost their intensity, and the blaze slowly petered out. Wisps of dirty smoke slinked skyward from what looked like a mound of charred building blocks. The loss wasn't significant.

The next I saw John, Dad was carting him by the back of the pants toward the house. I would have felt sorrier for John if he hadn't looked so comical, hanging like a limp rag doll on the end of Dad's fist. I suppose the humiliation would have been enough to reform him, but John's reprimand was swift and harsh, and he learned the lesson.

The following spring, Grandma and Grandpa, along with Uncle Emil, moved to town, which put an end to our farm visits. They took up residence in a house next door to us, and that was just fine by me. It was time for them to step back from farming—their bodies were tired from the strain of hard work. The two uncles took over the farm, which helped my grandparents transition to an easier way of life.

After the fire incident, John shifted his attention to activities that wouldn't get him into so much trouble. He couldn't change his spots at the flick of a switch—it was simply too much to ask. He needed to satisfy a yen to play pranks, so he put on his thinking cap and came up with less harmful gags.

The telephone switchboard in our house became the next lure to tempt him. He dreamt up ways to create mischief with bells, plugs, switches and other gadgets. Surely there could be no limit to his new ideas.

There were advantages and disadvantages to our home being the centre of communication. We sometimes received visitors in the middle of the night, which was one of the drawbacks of being the village's communication hub. The beer parlour was down the street from our home, and the odd patron sometimes found himself in want of phone service at the end of a boozy night.

Transportation was a concern for some. Getting to the pub was never especially difficult, but getting back home was. It wasn't unusual for a guy to be abandoned after last call without a lift home. Sometimes a phone call was the difference between being stranded for the night and making it home to a warm bed.

Dad was usually the one who opened the door in response to knocking. If I was awake, I'd sneak out of bed and watch from the kitchen. John was usually there before me, checking out the action.

When the knocker entered, his speech was sometimes slurred. Other times, the message was clear, but always, the late-night visitors were on the same mission: "I need to make a phone call."

Dad arranged the call connection, accommodating them with privacy in the boxy phone booth. My parents understood the responsibility of providing telephone service. It was a twenty-four seven obligation to the public. Access to communication was an assured right. In this case, it boiled down to getting another drunken sop out of the house so we could get back to bed.

For some of us, the telephone switchboard fed an impish itch for fun. I followed John's lead as we indulged ourselves playing pranks on other kids. One of our strategies was to have a kid place the telephone plug in his mouth. He or she usually required some convincing to do it.

"Just put the plug on your tongue."

We were gifted at crafting reasons why a plug to the tongue was a good thing.

"It's fun," we'd say.

Sometimes, we had to persuade by demonstration, so we'd show them by illustrating with a mouth full of plug.

"See? Wike yiss."

It took some doing, but we eventually persuaded one wide-eyed patsy to try. He opened his mouth as though to receive a communion wafer, and we dropped in the plug. Timing was key, and before he got a chance to change his mind, one of us worked the hand crank.

The surge of electricity never caused his hair to frizz, but watching his eyeballs bulge was satisfactory. Our friends never fully appreciated the gags, nor did they fall for the same trick more than twice.

John told me to fuck off.

The way he said it felt like a slap. All I wanted was to have a turn riding the bike. He pushed me out of his way, jumped on our banana bike, and rode off. I watched him as he pedaled away. He didn't once turn around to look at me.

Where did he have to go that was so important? He wasn't volunteering that information. He'd say it was none of my business. Fine, then. Maybe I'd go somewhere and not tell him where I was going. I wondered how he'd like that.

Another day, he came home snarly as a rabid dog. I left him alone—otherwise, I'd risk facing his fury. I don't know why he was getting so miserable all of a sudden. Maybe puberty was coming, and it wasn't sitting well with him.

Perhaps the teasing was getting to him. It seemed to escalate the older he got. Kids at school turned it up a notch, finding nastier ways to get under his skin. The verbal taunting turned physical, and one thing was for sure: it was relentless.

There was never a particular reason to tease him—kids simply latched onto any excuse. Just like there was no call to shove him out of their way, take his stuff, spit on him, or humiliate him. I think it fulfilled their inherent nature to be assholes. It wasn't enough for them to simply pick on John. They found I was an easy target, too.

Things became more complicated when the hockey player bullies moved to town. The only non-threatening places left to us were home, Grandma's house and anywhere inside the perimeter of our property. We faked courage, standing at the edge of the yard, staring down the jerks who dared us to step out of our safety zone. We had no intention of stepping out— we were scared, not stupid.

We could have given into rock-throwing, but we'd already gotten into trouble once for breaking a window that happened to be inline with a stone's trajectory. We maintained a ceasefire in silent discomfort while our intimidators sneered.

Then along came our baby brother Gus—a toddler toting his favourite lamp.

Things you need to know about Gus:

He was a most beautiful child.

He was very friendly.

He was obsessed with all things electrical.

As a three-year-old, he had no concept of animosity among peers.

The word *bully* was not in his vocabulary.

If he ever had a cherished blanket or stuffed toy, it was quickly forgotten in favour of electrical appliances. Gus valued playthings that ran on alternating current, though he wasn't allowed to connect them into electrical outlets. Even as a toddler, he respected the rules of safety concerning electricity. Fortunately, our house was full of dilapidated chairs.

There were holes in chair legs where wooden rungs had broken off. The openings were the right size to fit the plug of a cord. Gus figured out that if he couldn't plug into actual outlets, the plug-sized gaps left from missing rungs would suffice, so he connected chairs in series with extension cords throughout the kitchen.

When company came to visit and their concept of conduction was limited, they might have been nervous to occupy a seat that looked as though it was wired to electricity. Some may have recalled shocks to the mouth via a telephone plug. None mentioned discomfort while occupying a space at our table. Perhaps they didn't want to provoke the controller of the switch. It remained open to debate whether Gus was destined to become an electrical engineer or an executioner.

Gus and his lamp went everywhere together. It was an ordinary desk lamp, and he was proud to show off its many fine features—especially the electrical cord attached to the base. The lampshade had been discarded long ago, after Gus had deemed it to be a non-essential, unwired adornment without practical function.

He sauntered over to show the bad boys his treasure. We watched in petrified horror as he ventured beyond the boundary of safety, like a sacrificial lamb approaching an unforeseen demise.

John and I called after him: "Get away from those guys! Come back here, you little turd!" But he was too preoccupied with his task to mind us. All we could do was imagine the comely features on his face receiving a lift and rearrangement.

Remarkably, the menaces exhibited a measure of decency. They didn't lay a hand on Gus. They just stood there, amazed by the little kid's bravery. They listened intently and lifted the occasional eyebrow in feigned fascination. It turned out Gus's complete account of the lamp's many fine components wasn't entirely lost on them. We breathed a deep sigh of relief.

It became increasingly difficult to avoid getting picked on. No matter where we went, someone got their jollies by being a jackass. We couldn't avoid the harassment walking home from school, so we tried to beat the rush and get ahead of the line, or stall and be stragglers. Sometimes we took an alternate route just to get a break.

After-school recreation lost some of its appeal. A visit to the ice rink attracted too much attention from the hockey players, who had their sights set on the NHL. Our presence gave them the opportunity to practise body-checking and puck shot accuracy, though we were never actually struck by a puck—which might explain why the NHL wannabes never made it past the junior league.

Regardless of temperature, the outdoor ice rink beckoned us. Our worn-out, hand-me-down skates didn't provide good support, so our feet angled outward at an awkward slant. It looked like we were skating on our ankles. We glided along for hours, playing shinny, until frostbite drove us home. Then we spent the better portion of an hour crying until our digits thawed. The next day, we ran back to the rink to get more of the same.

We set ourselves to play a game of shinny with other kids—kids who were less inclined to pick on us. John was fast on his skates, and he stick-handled with good form. What he lacked in size, he made up for in performance. And we were enthusiastic at play. One time, my gusto landed me a crack to the head against the ice, and I saw stars spinning, like in a kaleidoscope.

We played other games on skates, too, like Crack the Whip or Red Rover. Some contests could get quite vicious. When no one was up for a game, we skated laps around the ice. If snow fell, we didn't hesitate to take up a shovel and help clear the surface. Snow removal was a big job for a caretaker who received little compensation for his efforts.

One year, lights were installed so we wouldn't have to skate in the dark. By mid-winter, daylight made its exit by 4:30 p.m. The caretaker's responsibilities extended to turning on the lights early, and shutting them off at 9 p.m.

Breaks to warm up became more frequent as temperatures dropped outside. A shack alongside the rink provided shelter. Its walls and roof were sheeted with plywood, which didn't provide much insulation from the cold. The only durable part of the shack was the door, since it had to withstand constant opening and closing. A barrel stove occupied one corner, and we kept the fire stoked with wood. The caretaker maintained a stockpile of timber that he bucked up and stacked just outside the door.

The shack had a summer purpose, too. A bunch of us kids gathered inside to play poker in the offseason. We didn't have money to play, so wagers consisted of physical zingers like knuckle grinds to the top of the hand, arm punches, pinches, and other such modes of abuse.

"Show us your cards, or I'm gonna punch you anyway."

It seemed weather was rarely the focus of talk around the table.

Our arms and hands were marked by bruises and welts by the end of an afternoon. The abuse was worse if the tough-guy hockey players joined the game. One time, they brought a pair of red boxing gloves and wanted us to fight. It was one thing to have our arms take the abuse. It was another to expose our whole body to it.

They made us form a ring and decided who was going to box. We weren't allowed to back out. Their idea of fair was to put me up against their younger brother. It didn't matter that he was bigger than me, and itching to put on the gloves. My spindly arms couldn't compete with a brute who could glut himself with a pound of chuck roast for breakfast.

One of the hockey players dressed my hands with the gloves and tightened the laces to my puny wrists. The gloves wobbled on the ends of my arms like dangling fish bowls. They put me in the middle of the ring, and I faced my opponent. I felt especially small and alone, surrounded by kids anticipating a feisty bout. I held up my arms the way I'd seen boxers do on TV. The gloves smelled like feet, so I tried keeping them away from my nose.

They wanted me to throw the first punch.

"Come on, hit him."

I didn't. I stood there, frozen in my boxer pose.

Brute nudged me gently with his mitted hand. He was taunting me to fight him. He pushed me a little harder, and I had to take a step back to maintain balance. He shoved me again, and I nearly fell, so I chanced a swing at him and missed. He came back hard with a punch to my stomach and one to my head. It knocked me to the floor. I stood up and decided that was enough boxing for me. I dropped my hands and the gloves flew off. I ran out the door to the sound of the bullies laughing.

I wished John had followed me out, but he didn't. I don't know what kind of ordeal he was put through. I didn't want to watch, and it wasn't like I was able to help him out anyway. I found a place to hide for the rest of the afternoon, and didn't see John until suppertime. He peered at me with eyes that seared with fury. He had nothing to say about his afternoon, but I saw dirty tear stains dried on his face.

The only thing nastier than the hockey star wannabes was their dog. It was a terrier mix, mean and solid. Stalling after school posed the risk of meeting up with the mangy mutt. I recall its fifteen pounds of skittering muscle closing in as I raced to stay ahead of it. While the dog achieved some gain, almost nipping my heels, I could hear the jerks egging it on with my two least favourite words: "Sic 'em."

The dog met the canine Grim Reaper one wintery day. I saw it panting for air as it lay on the floorboards of an old shed. The boys were trying to coax it back to its feet. They could have poked it with a revive-stick and applied pooch CPR for all the good it did. Eventually the dog croaked. The next afternoon, I ambled home, brandishing a smirk.

The bullying never seemed to let up. To add insult to injury, John was held back another year in school. It couldn't have been easy for him, dealing with the humiliation of being in the same grade as his little sister. One day, something new came along—a distraction, a chance to broaden our narrow perspectives and take our minds off of dealing with jackasses.

The Rabbit River Honkies were a group of young adults who relocated to our area from the city of Saskatoon. I think they were university graduates looking for a simpler way of life, so they came to work and live off the land. They established a bit of a homestead near our town, and built a dome-shaped house, different from any structure I'd ever seen.

The Honkies were quite the spectacle. Strangers wanting to live among us—that didn't happen every day. But these weren't ordinary times. They brought innovation and culture, and triggered our curiosity. Other influences arrived with them, too—like the kind that mellowed you after a couple tokes. I was intrigued by their carefree way of living.

They didn't come to live somewhere out of the way to remain by themselves. They were committed to being part of the community. They invited friends from the city who were professional entertainers. They put on free shows for kids. One time, a well-known children's entertainer came to amuse us.

Chairs were lined up in rows in front of the stage at the dance hall. The performer sat on the platform while the kids who made up the audience watched from the main floor. The guy's plan was to entertain us with songs and stories.

We were new at this sort of thing. No one had ever put on live shows for us before. We weren't given any specific instructions on audience etiquette. We understood things like school performances, which meant we were the ones up on stage, acting out some kind of Christmas pageant for adults, not the other way around. An event with live music always involved dancing, but we couldn't dance, because there were chairs on the dance floor. The only other live spectacle we had ever witnessed was church. At church, our part was to passively stare forward and not fidget.

When the entertainer took the stage, we opted to play the churchgoer role. His lively performance was met with distant stares from us kids. At the end of the show, we each stole a nervous glimpse at the kid next to us. The unspoken question lingered: *Sooooo, do we clap? Or what?*

We didn't clap. Instead, we stood, lined up, and filed out quietly, in the same way we always left church.

The next event, a few weeks later, featured a live band— Humphrey and the Dumptrucks. They put on a spirited performance of country folk music. Again, we watched with reserved interest and mild amusement. They waited for some kind of acknowledgment from us, and we responded with the same indifference as the last event. They ogled us and we gawked at them for what seemed like an hour. Then, we got up and left.

If the point was to bring festivity to our mundane routine, the live concerts didn't quite hit the mark. We figured out that the real party happened at the beer parlour after the gig. We weren't allowed in, so we stood outside the entrance trying to glean some of the fun. At the door, we spaced out our purchases of pop and chips to garner more peeks inside. If the adults genuinely wanted to expose us to new experiences, they should have opened the barroom to us.

Humphrey and the Dumptrucks was the last of the live performances for awhile. Then the Honkies got a new attraction. They bought a building across the street from the bar and called it the Honky Hall. They threw parties where anyone could bring an instrument and help make funky music. There was even a go-go dancer with long braids, wearing a floor-length granny dress and hiker boots. She moved in slow motion, which made the scene even more trippy.

There were banjos and fiddles and an upside-down washtub with a piece of twine and a stick attached to it. Some guy had his foot on the washtub, twanging the string with his fingers. Another guy was so desperate to play along that he raided the utensil drawer and drummed in rhythm with a few spoons.

At first, we weren't allowed to attend these shindigs. Our parents probably thought the parties would turn us onto drugs and we might become potheads. There was no chance of that happening. The Honkies were glad to show us a good time, but they weren't going to share their weed with us.

As a young teenager, I attended a party or two with my friends, and we kept pretty much to ourselves. We were too young to participate in much of the folly and felt weird hanging out with adults.

I watched people dance to sluggish country music and made a comment: "I wish they could play rock and roll."

"Yeah, this slow stuff is getting on my nerves, too."

We went home when it got late and decided that next time, we would explore other interests.

During winter, we sometimes got to watch hockey at the arena in Meadow Lake—if we could find a ride. The Meadow Lake Stampeders always offered nail-biting excitement.

We squeezed ourselves into the narrow seating space of a friend's car. His vehicle reached its transport limit with the horde of hockey fans filling it. Some offered their laps to help pack in more sport enthusiasts. Unlike our trips to the drive-in, we didn't need to hide friends in the trunk to gain them free admission.

It was a party on wheels, that's for sure. We got worked up for the action, like a travelling pep rally. We were stoked to cheer on the Stampeders, and they didn't disappoint.

The seats in the arena were hard and cold, but the excitement of the game kept our minds off the discomfort.

"Check out those girls hanging out at the players' box."

"That's why I should have stayed in hockey . . . for the chicks."

The guys never quit talking about that.

Meanwhile, the uptown girls sneered at us. They didn't like "hicks from the sticks" invading their turf. The same thing happened if we went to dances out of town. It was like we had some kind of disease they didn't want to catch, so they kept their distance. There was trouble if any of their boyfriends took a liking to one of us. Usually, the fuss played out in the girls' bathroom, so we never went in there alone.

Other than sharing a few road trips to watch hockey, John and I didn't often socialize in the same circles. On occasion, we attended bashes together, but mostly we went our separate ways. There were conflicts between us, and we were always too stubborn to give in to the other. We were spiteful, and fought over petty issues, like a seat on the couch, whose turn it was to do dishes, and what music to listen to. The disagreements got increasingly physical, and I remember yelling at him, "Just stay the hell away from me!"

I intentionally avoided him, since our interactions always seemed to trigger a fight. Getting my head in the game of softball or volleyball kept me from stewing over our latest spats. I played out-of-town tournaments whenever I could. John didn't do sports, so it was a convenient way to keep the distance between us.

In high school, we became more concerned with our looks, hair, clothes, and the opposite sex—the kind of things that made us self-conscious. John was particularly distressed about his hair. Long hair was the sought-after look for guys in the seventies, and John's mop top was determined to remain set in tight little curls. The longer he attempted to grow his hair, the frizzier and kinkier it became, and the more he tried to brush it straight.

While other people were paying big bucks to get the afro look, which was also a hot trend in the seventies, John was bent on taming his obstinate tresses beneath a snug-fitting cap. But when the hat came off, there were no fewer curls. It would take him a few years to appreciate the no-fuss care of his naturally beautiful locks.

Girls confounded John. He didn't have a good sense of how to relate to them. He was awkward, and none of his attempts to make a move on a girl ever seemed to work out. The girls we grew up with considered him little more than a supplier of beer and cigarettes. They were happy to have him around for their own selfish motives, but never as a potential boyfriend.

Girls from out of town would eye him up, but his lack of confidence would derail any chance of a connection. They soon found other willing partners, who didn't harbour such insecurities. The frustration drove him further into himself, and he began to avoid the pursuit of female companionship in favour of alcohol.

By the time Mitch hit puberty, he had surpassed all our brothers as the wild child. Little brother should have had my place in the family line, next to John. I wasn't much of a defender against harassment, but Mitch didn't put up with that shit. He was badass from the get-go. The two of them could have been stronger together to defy the antagonizers. Unfortunately for John, Mitch was a few years too young to be of much support—but that soon changed.

Mitch had some catching-up to do, and he was hellbent on hanging out with John as a best friend and brother. The big brother role often flipped, as Mitch sometimes watched after John instead of the other way around. Mitch was just becoming a teenager when he took the lead finding ways to kickstart his social life and join the party scene. And John was right next to him, sharing in the fun.

I wasn't included in their out-of-town excursions—not that I had a yen to go. My absence was simply a casualty of our diverging interests. Occasionally all three of us would attend the same party, but as a rule, we didn't hang out together during our teenage years.

I remember one party in particular because of the music. A tune by Thin Lizzy was playing, "Whiskey in the Jar." The song drew John's attention, and he wanted it played repeatedly. He and Mitch partied hard, dancing and singing along to the tune blasting out the speaker of an old record player. Everybody joined in to make it an epic rendition.

There is no telling what happened while the boys were having their fun away from home. I remember Dad having to rescue them a couple of times from trouble, like when their car broke down.

"Where are you this time?" Dad grumbled into the phone after dragging himself out of bed in the middle of the night.

"At the Rec Centre in Loon Lake. The fan belt's broke."

"Use pantyhose."

"We don't wear pantyhose."

Dad rolled out the family car and headed west to collect the boys. It was late, everyone was tired, and the fixing of their ride would have to wait until another day.

In high school, my brothers were notorious for getting into trouble. I didn't always witness their antics, but some of the stories were legendary, like the time Rod and his buddies found a frozen pig on their friend's farm. They propped the pig outside the window of the principal's office. Its snout was pointed toward the principal nun, as if it could watch while she worked at her desk. She ignored it, knowing a reaction would only instigate more of the same. It was harmless folly, and not enough to cause a rift. The farmer came to collect his pig, but not before we all got to see it.

I had an opportunity to measure up to my brothers' talents, but it only proved that I didn't have their moxie.

"You know the nun's watching us, right?"

We stood inside the boundary of the schoolyard, passing a lit butt between us. I was being a rebel along with my two friends. We shared a cigarette and blew smoke in the direction of sky. I wanted to be badass, to put on the illusion of toughness. The ploy was sort of working. Then, the nun approached us.

Her silence and cold stare sent a shiver through me. After a long minute, she spoke, but it sounded more like a barb. "Are we having fun? Having a little smoke?"

No one offered a reply, though we found it kind of funny. I wasn't the only one cracking a cocky smile.

She probably considered the three of us and surmised I was the weakest link of the bunch. She bore her eyes into me, ignoring the other two. "How would you like it if I slap that smirk off your face?"

She didn't have to. I cowered immediately. My friends maintained their arrogance, and got away with it.

I was trying to be tough, but it didn't work. I stopped trying to pull off those type of stunts, and I never achieved the status of bad-ass.

It was the mid-seventies. Adulthood was creeping up on John and me. I don't think we were prepared for it, yet there was no turning back. We chased after the usual dreams of young adults, trying to make a place for ourselves in a world that was quickly changing. Conflicting messages of what was expected of our generation didn't help us determine a plausible path. We were inundated with choices that hadn't been available to our parents, and all they could do was shake their heads and watch as we wandered haphazardly in the wrong direction.

The pre-launch to adulthood held few triumphs and many disappointments. A general decline in confidence established itself early, and gained momentum in high school. We tried to fit in, but it just didn't work. I was interested in sports, until nepotism became the prevailing rule of participation. John failed in academics and girls, so his interests moved to the brown bottle. We both looked for temporary fixes. I drank to party. John drank to drink. We travelled the same path, leading nowhere. Our other preferred destination was *anywhere away from here.*

There was an anger in John that came out when he drank. It was dark and formidable, and it made me want to hide. He used his anger against our family because it was easy. We weren't able to intimidate him the way outsiders could. The best we managed was to avoid the epicentre of his rage. Some nights were long and nerve-racking as we waited for the storm to pass.

John never completed high school. He dropped out and left to work on the rigs. He came home between work cycles and during spring break-up. Though the bullshit of his troubled youth was behind him, complications never seemed to let up. A snowmobile mishap nearly cost him his life. It happened one night in January 1977. The accident was relayed to me by the driver of the machine.

John was the passenger on a powerful Polaris sled. His friend, the operator, drove at a fast pace through fields and bush. A barbed-wire fence was directly in their path. The driver noticed the wire too late to change direction. He ducked to avoid the line, and John caught it in his neck.

John was snared, pulled back, lifted off the machine, and dropped into the snow. His body landed in a slumped heap, and blood coursed from a gash located somewhere beneath his chin.

In desperation, the friend collected John and rushed him to the nearest hospital. A doctor, not happy to be called in for a late-night emergency, stitched him back up.

The doctor came out of the examination room and said, "That is one lucky young man. It looks like a barb came within a fraction of an inch of his jugular."

John reclined on the table where the doctor had tended his wound. His hospital stay was brief. The sutures held. Time would enable healing.

Doc's parting words were, "Take him home, and tell him to stay off snowmobiles."

John brandished a scar that was permanent and quite distinct. His ordeal became a memory that faded faster than the mark on his neck.

A few years later, during a work shift on the rigs, John caught a pipe across the mouth and lost his four front teeth. He always seemed to be on the receiving end of unpleasant things. He was tough and resilient. He'd just keep going, like a boxer who refused to stay down, even as the bell rang to indicate the tenth and final round.

While John worked on the rigs, I finished high school and got a job out of town. In January 1978, while working as a telephone operator in North Battleford, I met a guy. He was a gas station attendant.

I had stopped for a fuel-up in the car Dad had loaned me for the week. The guy filling up the tank asked me all kinds of questions, including, "Would you like to join me for a cup of coffee?"

I hadn't made many acquaintances since moving to the city. The only two girls I knew had decided to quit their jobs and move back home. I was homesick, and any interaction with another person was a welcome change.

"So, tell me about yourself." He was curious.

"Like what? The music I listen to?"

"That's a start."

Rod Stewart was singing a tune on the radio. "I like Rod a lot."

"Well, isn't that interesting? We have something in common."

Turns out Buck was quite a talker. He freed me from having to say much about myself. I think he especially liked the sound of his own voice, which, in truth, wasn't too hard on the ears.

Buck wasn't particularly handsome, but he had a self-confidence that demanded attention. I learned he grew up on a farm, knew how to work hard, and had big ambitions. He worked extended hours at the service station and boasted that he often ran the place while his boss took days off fishing. He liked fast cars, though he didn't own one.

On our second coffee date, I blurted out, "I'm pregnant."

He looked at me, stunned. He slowly sipped his coffee and spoke: "Well, that was unexpected."

The cashier needed Buck's attention. He left to help her, so I quietly sat at the table, holding my empty cup.

When he came back, he asked, "So who's the father? Is he around?"

I stared at him blankly. I wasn't volunteering that information.

"Well, I know it's not me. Last time I checked, coffee can't make you pregnant."

He refilled our cups from the coffeemaker behind the counter. When he sat down, he leaned in and pressed, "So, what are you going to do?"

"I'm moving back home soon. I can't stay here alone. I really don't know what I'm going to do after that."

Within a couple months, I had left my job and returned to Makwa.

I had outgrown the family home, and my return was awkward for everyone. My brief exposure to independence made it hard to fit back in. There were fewer individuals in the household—Pauly, Rod, and Denis had long ago moved out on their own. John's overwhelming presence made up for the disparity. At this point, our home sheltered six of us, including John, his rage, and his alcoholism. The walls strained to contain it all.

There was a growing divide between John and me, and it continued to widen as our conflicts escalated. On one occasion, we had a disagreement about music. John had been drinking and was feeling no pain. He wanted to put on some tunes, but I couldn't tolerate the clatter. I wanted the music off.

"Mind your own fucking business. I want to listen to Seger." John pushed past me to reinsert the cassette.

"Then go back to the bar and listen to it there." I pressed the stop button.

Our heated exchange continued until things got physical. Out of frustration, John kicked me in the stomach. It knocked me off balance, but I didn't hit the floor.

I yelled at him: "What the hell! You didn't have to kick me, damn it!"

Mom was in the other room when she heard the commotion. She rushed in and lit into John like I had never before seen.

"Stop! Stop it! Get out, you don't need any music!!!"

We were used to John's disturbances, but this time Mom held him to account. Things got out of hand when John kicked me in my pregnant stomach. But Mom didn't know John hadn't put any force behind the kick. The scuffle had sounded far worse than it actually was.

Mom's reaction astounded John. She seldom revealed that side of herself. She established a truce between John and me, and sent us to separate locations to cool off.

That was the last serious confrontation I remember between John and me. Mom's intervention and powerful display made us pause to consider the potentially destructive nature of our actions. Out of a bad situation, something positive emerged—it was a turning point for John and me, and it put the worst behind us.

I kept receiving letters from Buck. I hardly knew the guy, but he was determined to keep in contact with me. He wrote often to suggest that I move to the West Coast with him, where opportunities were abundant. The idea of a fresh start in a new location intrigued me, and I gave it serious consideration.

A few months after having my baby boy, Alex, I decided it was time to stop being a burden on my family. I planned to leave home, and hoped to make a decent life for the two of us. I contacted Buck and took him up on his offer to move west.

He said, "My uncle has a house we can move into. The best part is it has a pool."

How could I say no to that? We made a plan to leave before winter. We set a date, and Buck came to Makwa to help me move. He met my family and presented himself as confident and responsible. His big presence filled whatever room he happened to occupy. He was strong-willed, which may have been a little much for some, but his take-charge attitude was exactly what I needed at the time.

On the day we were set to leave, Mom planned a farewell. It was a simple celebration, with food, drink, and stories. My family supported me on whatever path I was determined follow. They might not have felt comfortable about my move, but talking me out of it was pointless.

Perhaps it was rash of me to partner up with Buck so quickly. I hadn't put much thought into the plan. I told myself that I needed to stand on my own two feet and get the hell out of town. I had hidden apprehensions, but potential consequences were an irritant I avoided considering.

The party progressed. We talked, laughed, and filled our faces. I hadn't expected John to hang around for the duration. I assumed he would be relieved to see me go. He considered family functions and farewells too boring—or so I thought. Instead, he hung around and socialized. He approached me— his demeanour was thoughtful, and his eyes had a look of concern. He put one hand on my shoulder and gently stroked Alex's cheek with the other.

I tried to remember the last time we'd had any kind of gentleness between us. Nothing came to mind. It seemed we were always picking at each other, widening the divide between us. His tenderness was an unexpected gift.

We were face to face and awkward, like a couple of strangers meeting for the first time. So much of our childhood connection had been lost. Neither of us was sure how to navigate the moment. We were clumsy. He took my hand in his, like a handshake—which was the closest thing to a hug he could manage. I realized he was trying to say he cared for me, despite the troubles of our past.

Deep down, I wanted to strip away the years and reclaim my place as his forever ally. I wanted to say to him, "Play me a prank, so I can feel normal again." But normal had left a very long time ago, and wasn't expected back.

He was throwing me a lifeline, and all I needed to do was recognize it. He might have been the only one who truly understood the bad decision I was embracing. In my heart, I stored the few moments we shared for future reflection.

The inevitable was fast approaching. It was nearly time to hit the road, and goodbyes were in order. John's display of emotion nearly derailed my composure. I almost changed my mind about leaving. But I couldn't back out now without losing face. I suppose it was pride that caused me to press on. I failed to acknowledge the risk I was willing to take. I pushed forward deliberately, ignoring the voice inside trying to warn me. I had my mind made up, and I was moving toward independence.

My family followed as I carried Alex to the car. They took turns holding and kissing him. The separation was very difficult for them. How could I simply move away, taking with me the little boy who had stolen their hearts? It was a trouble-some question, so I delayed thinking about it.

Soon, it became time to leave. I embraced my parents one last time and sat down in the passenger seat of the car, with Alex on my lap . . . and we left.

It turns out our trip west translated to a trip south. The idea of Nanaimo, British Columbia switched to the reality of Moose Jaw, Saskatchewan, and the house with a pool turned into a one-room apartment near the downtown. I might have been more upset if I hadn't been so preoccupied tending to my baby. I learned that what Buck communicated was not always based on truth. I became indifferent to his fables because it was easier than initiating conflict. I needed to focus on creating a future for me and my child, and I chose to pursue that from within a precarious household.

The phone rang in the middle of the night. It was John. He wanted to talk and find out how I was doing. He was a little intoxicated and sounded cheerful. He filled me in on local news and threw in a couple jokes. I held the phone close to my ear to capture every word. The deep resonance in his voice was comforting.

"How's my little nephew?" he asked. "Think I could borrow him, so he can drive his Uncle John home from the pub?"

I laughed and gave him an update. "He's great. He just started walking. I don't think he has a driver's test coming up soon. How about if he walks you home from the bar instead?"

We talked until we ran out of topics, and still we delayed hanging up. His phone call was the best sleep interruption I could have hoped for. After that, John continued to contact me once or twice a month. I looked forward to our talks like a kid anticipates Christmas. But our conversations came to an abrupt halt when Buck cursed him over the phone and told him not to call anymore.

Buck's outburst brought to mind a time when he came unglued on my young cousin. She was a firecracker, five years younger than me. And she *loved* my baby boy. On our trips home, she always came to see us and fuss over Alex. For some unknown reason, Buck felt threatened by that.

He found her at the café in Makwa one afternoon, having a sit-down visit with some locals. From outside, he called to her: "Leave us alone. Stay away from my family."

His exact words were more colourful and less civil.

For the life of me, I'll never understand why he feared a pretty little high school girl who only wanted to hang around us, although she may have irked him once or twice calling out his lies. Buck's grand scheme was to isolate us, and he almost succeeded.

My cousin stood her ground at the door, snarled at him, and bellowed, "Make me!"

I'll bet Buck felt his balls shrivel. I was in awe of her bravery, and couldn't help but admire that kind of spunk. I thought I could harness some of her spirit against the rudeness he spewed toward John. I took a stand and confronted him for shutting down my brother.

"You didn't have to do that, you fuck!"

He met my blow-up with a smirk and an apathetic shrug. My guts quaked with hostility, and he stared me down as if to say, "So what are you going to do about it?"

And then, my courage deflated. I backed down like a pathetic dog realizing it wasn't the alpha. I kept my mouth shut while my guts twisted into angry knots.

It was always my job to concede.

For the sake of peace, I had to internalize my fury. Compromise had taken a back seat in this once-convenient relationship. It made its exit right about the time I acquired the role of loser. I was losing my family, my freedom, my dignity, and my will to keep going. The change was subtle, creepy and devious, like the boa wrapping itself around Mowgli in *The Jungle Book*. It severed my link to John, and I regretted deeply that he'd been caught in the ugliness of my situation.

A few years passed before I became free of the bullshit. I hope I never learn the art of controlling people. It must be exhausting keeping track of others plus yourself. What's the draw to imposing your will on someone else? Why dictate who a partner talks to, what they say, where they go, who they spend time with, what they buy, how they dress, what they watch on TV, what they read, even what they think? Seriously, can't a person have their own mind? What is there to gain from that? It's a recipe for disaster, and most controllers eventually lose what they so desperately try to hold.

By the time I was free of Buck, I had learned more than a few life lessons.

Autumn descends on Saskatchewan with stealth and intent, encroaching on the prairie, leaving traces of colour. Beneath a cerulean dome, golden landscapes are dappled with orange and burgundy. A cool crispness emerges, like an itch that worsens with each passing day. Dropping temperatures quicken as time launches toward the season of frostbite, spurring a fundamental drive to prepare for winter.

Massive flocks of migratory birds obey an instinct to fly south. They converge on the skyline as the sun emanates the first and last rays of daylight. Feathered creatures descend in near silence. The faint whisper of wings fluttering announces the arrival. The birds navigate clumsy landings on a pond as their tail feathers skim across water, cutting a tiny wake.

In sharp contrast, their departure is a spectacular display. The push and rush of an aerial stampede becomes a moment worthy of the wait. Throngs of game complete the annual journey across the continent, and hunters lay low in the reeds to catch them in their gunsights.

Duck hunting was for John an escape to a quieter place, where things made more sense. He could contemplate life and find solace while lurking among the cattails and bulrushes, waiting for a cue from above. He fit in this space, inside a realm of contentment. Gone were the cravings for libations, even if only temporarily. At the end of a hunting session, he embarked on his own migration, back to the world of people.

John didn't use specialized hunting gear. He pursued his craft with an old shotgun, shells, and grit, and he seldom arrived home skunked. My family anticipated the return of the duck hunter, his easy smile and stride announcing a good hunt. He carried home a string of dead birds tied together with rope. The birds dangled, slung from his shoulder, as he walked.

He dropped his kill to the ground and retrieved a razor-sharp hunting knife from its sheath. His skilled hands removed the choicest portions of the bird and presented them, ready for the roaster. Mom prepared a wild duck feast that satisfied cravings we didn't even know we had.

Two forces grounded John—hunting and Mom's love. Both provided a semblance of stability. He could be confident in her unwavering loyalty. Their relationship was solid, and it balanced on mutual respect. John ran errands for her, helped out around the yard, and performed repairs. It was his way of showing appreciation. Even though he sometimes pushed the limit of her patience, she was always willing to give him another chance.

Living in a home with someone who struggled with addiction had its challenges. Dad couldn't get his head around how complicated the matter was. He offered John monetary bribes to clean up his act. Of course, such a simple solution could never work.

John and Mom probably never had a deep conversation. Perhaps they couldn't find words to convey what was between them. Silent companionship may have been enough to assure them.

John had a gruffness about him. He couldn't shake his awkwardness when it came to showing affection. Then, he discovered that greeting cards could do that for him. He shopped for cards that dripped with sentiment. He was especially particular with the ones he picked out for Mom. She treasured all the Mother's Day cards he had given her. The fact she kept and stored them as keepsakes was a testament to how much she valued his hidden tenderness and devotion.

There was no doubting the unshakable solidity of their relationship. Mom was John's rock and anchor. She kept him somewhat stable when things got turbulent. I believe his time away from home and on the job was more bearable knowing Mom held his best interests at heart and that she always kept a place reserved for him at her table.

John made good coin as a "rig pig." He laboured as a roughneck on the oil rigs, and his duties were physically demanding. The risk of injury was high, handling tools like chains, tongs, and pipes. He kept his head about him while working on the rig floor. Twelve-hour shifts gave him little time to consider leisure activities other than eating and sleeping.

It wasn't a pleasant career choice, but he garnered enough green to amply pad his wallet.

The camp jobs were usually dry, so he was good and thirsty by the time he completed a hitch working the rigs. Often, he would head straight to the nearest drinking establishment when his time off started.

He surprised me once by announcing his intent to visit Alex and me on his next break. I was excited. It was April 1986, and it had been a few years since he had last attempted to come see me. It would be his first visit since I moved with my son to a new town in Alberta, three hours' drive from home in Saskatchewan.

John seemed better able to manage his addiction. He didn't stop drinking, but he became a happy drunk, instead of confrontational. Perhaps that was the best I could hope for.

He planned to arrive on a Thursday afternoon. I worked until 5 p.m. that day, so we arranged to meet at my house afterwards. I was restless for my shift to be over. My job as a research technician in agriculture kept me buried in projects, which made the hours pass quickly.

I left work, picked up nine-year-old Alex from the sitter, and hurried home to prepare for John's arrival. I had supper planned and ready and only needed to pop it into the oven. As supper cooked, we watched the clock and waited for John. He must have been running a little late.

"When's Uncle John coming?" my son's impatience was showing. "Mom, I'm hungry. Can we eat now?"

Two hours had passed, so I decided we should get on with supper. We ate without our guest. By 9 p.m., I had cleaned up the kitchen and prompted Alex to get ready for bed. John had yet to make an appearance, and I wondered how our plans had come to nothing. By 11 p.m., I gave up the watch and called it a night.

About 2 a.m., I woke to the sound of persistent knocking. I opened the door to my severely inebriated brother. I was more relieved than annoyed. He apologized profusely, slurring his words. "I'm sorry . . . I'm sorry . . . ."

I tried to reassure him. "It's OK. Don't worry about it. It's late, and I have to work in the morning. Come in. Get some sleep. We'll catch up tomorrow."

I led him to the couch, removed his shoes, and covered him with a blanket. He was near passed out by the time he laid down. As I made my way back to my own bed, I could hear him mumbling more apologies into his pillow.

The next morning, Alex and I left the house without disturbing John. I expected he could use the whole day to sleep it off. I left him a note with instructions to help himself to food and anything else he needed. By the time we returned home, he was gone. I hoped he'd be back soon. I delayed supper again, expecting him to turn up.

Again, I answered the door in the middle of the night, this time to two wayward souls. My brother, who had obviously been assaulted, was assisted by a drinking buddy, who was the likely guy John had stood us up for.

John's buddy and I each took an arm and helped John to the couch. John looked rough, but not so battered as to require medical attention. His eye was blackened and the side of his face bruised, but he was otherwise intact. Oblivious to his injuries, John kept expressing remorse for his tardiness. Again I assured him: "We'll make it right tomorrow."

Saturday morning, we slept in. John tried hard to make himself presentable. He was hurting badly from the previous night, the strain obvious on his face. We struggled to have a conversation and managed to keep it somewhat upbeat. Everything seemed to go relatively well until early afternoon, when John announced he was ready to go home.

I didn't want him to leave. I tried stalling him. "Why don't you stay? We've hardly had any time to visit. You can rest here all day. If you're tired, you can lie down on my bed. We can hang out at home. We don't have to go anywhere. We can do stuff tomorrow, when you feel better. Please stay."

He made excuses that he needed to tend to business. I asked what kind.

He said, "My business."

He was hellbent on going, so I persisted. "I can do your laundry. I have a washer and dryer now. I don't mind, and that way, you won't have to bother with it when you get home. Don't go."

My words fell on deaf ears. He was adamant to catch the next bus east, and there was no talking him out of it. In his stubbornness, he left me no choice but to deliver him to the bus depot.

John stood quietly outside my car, holding his duffle bag, while I fidgeted for keys in my pocket. I opened the hatch for him to place his gear inside. Alex brought our pet cat, and John reached over to stroke its head. The cat sensed he was going for a car ride, too, but he wriggled free of Alex's grip. John and Alex climbed into the car for the run to the terminal.

We arrived at the station, and John approached the ticket counter to purchase a one-way trip to Saskatchewan. The bus wasn't due to leave for another half hour, so we found a table in the restaurant. We ordered coffees and a soft drink. The mood was heavy, and we sipped in silence.

As we waited, I struggled to find words that could change his mind. A rip on the front of his coat caught my focus. I wanted to yank the jacket off him, mend it, and erase traces of the assault. Seeing him beat up and knowing he was running away made me want to protect him. I was afraid for him. It felt like he might not come back.

I didn't want him to leave on such a low note, and I suggested we talk. He turned his face away, as if the notion pained him. He wasn't about to share his struggles with his sister. That's not what men did. He was bound to protect the shell he'd spent years building, and nothing anyone suggested could ever change that.

A clerk announced the bus was ready for boarding, and we followed a line of people out the door. John spoke: "Thanks for putting up with me."

I extended a final plea: "You can still stay."

His eyes grew stark and he gaped skyward, as if to keep tears from forming. He walked with obvious exhaustion, but braced himself, determined to leave. He boarded the bus, and I watched him find a seat by a window at the back. He turned his face toward us, and I waved. The bus lurched once and propelled its load eastward, toward Saskatchewan.

During summer breaks, Alex stayed with my parents in Makwa while I worked long hours at the research station. Summer was my busy season working in the field, setting up and maintaining plots for soil and crop testing. The arrangement worked well for us. Alex loved staying with his grandma and grandpa, who enjoyed his company immensely. They gave him space and security. He had the run of the entire town, and he filled his days with play and adventure.

Sometimes Alex's stays coincided with John coming home between hitches from the rigs. John dropped his gear at the back door and entered the kitchen, smiling and tired. Mom put together a quick meal, in case he hadn't bothered to put anything into his stomach that day.

"How was work?" Mom asked him.

Between bites John told her, "We moved the rig. Working close to Drayton Valley now."

Alex asked him, "How much money did you make?"

"Lots, but I could still use more." John looked down at his plate and paused. "Alex, can you bring me ketchup from the fridge?"

"Sure."

Mom asked John, "When do you have to go back?"

"I'm off for seven, so I'll have to leave on Thursday."

By nine o'clock, John wandered over to the pub. He settled back into a routine, which didn't involve staying sober for very long.

The next afternoon, John was slouched in a chair in the kitchen when Alex came in from outside. He watched as John sat up, using his elbows to steady himself at the table.

"Uncle, what's wrong with you?"

John's reply to the question came out slurred and slow, with a garbled chuckle: "Too many barley sandwiches last night."

"What's a barley sandwich?"

Alex waited, watching as John tried to light a smoke. But the shakes made it difficult. The little spectator wasn't going anywhere. John cocked an arm to rest his forehead in his palm. He tilted his head slightly and stared, glossy-eyed, at Alex. They ogled each other for a silent moment. Then John raised his eyebrows as if to convey the burning question, *What?*

"Can you give us rides on the trail bike?"

"Do it later, 'kay? I got skull cramps." He reached for the ashtray, turning his attention away from his nephew.

Alex went outside to the backyard, where his buddies sat waiting.

"He can't. He got skull cramps."

"He got what?"

"Is that like when you get the shits?"

Dad was making himself a fresh cup of coffee, trying but failing to ignore John, who was hunched at the kitchen table nursing a hangover. The sight upended Dad, and he couldn't help but pose the question.

"Can't you stay off the booze for a while?"

"Oh, for shit's sake." John didn't want to hear another lecture. He spewed whiny sarcasm: "Well, I'm not drinking now, am I?"

There was no point getting into it again, so they quickly dropped the exchange.

Tension always mounted the morning after. Dad couldn't ignore the boy's drinking. Mom was better at sidestepping arguments. She understood there wasn't a thing she could say or do to mend his ways. It had to be John's doing and John's alone, and a change didn't seem to be coming anytime soon.

Grandma died in May of 1987. She suffered from stomach ulcers complicated by diabetes. Doctors couldn't contain the blood loss, and she passed away.

It was hard to read Uncle Emil's reaction to her death. We lost Grandpa in 1968. He died in a car accident, and the effect on Emil was concerning. I remember watching him try to hoist a suitcase up his bedroom wall, like he was passing it to someone. Grandpa's death had pained him, and the family was anxious about how he might respond to losing Grandma.

Grandma had lived as a widow for nineteen years with Emil. Another bachelor son, my Uncle Dan, also lived with them. Without Grandma, Emil was dependent on the care of Dan, who wasn't as attentive a guardian. This meant Emil was left on his own for most of the day, with little guidance or supervision. He was free to eat as much as he wanted, smoke as much as he wanted, and stay up as late as he wanted. Grandma had imposed restrictions on Emil he no longer needed to observe, and his health began to suffer.

Emil made bad choices. His diet was poor, and he was careless. His body size fluctuated between plump and gaunt. He took to wandering from household to household, looking for companionship. I'm not sure whether anyone ever turned him away, and I choose to believe most welcomed him.

Wandering was better than sitting home alone while Uncle Dan socialized at the local pub. Emil expressed his grief and sorrow largely through his actions—loneliness wasn't something he could articulate. Only the people closest to him could offer a semblance of comfort while he adjusted to his new reality.

John started having late-night barbecues in the backyard. He'd cook up a steak or hamburgers for himself after arriving home from the pub. On occasion, Emil would come by to keep him company, so John threw on an extra portion for him. Soon, it became a habit—Emil watched for John to come home from drinking, and John prepared a feast for two.

Emil's company kept John from looking for distractions that could otherwise bring nasty trouble. It wasn't uncommon for John to get intoxicated, set his drunk ass down behind the steering wheel of his car, and drive around town like a bonehead. Traffic was non-existent late at night, and there was no police presence. The nearest RCMP detachment was ten miles away, and they rarely patrolled beyond their immediate post. Only a phone call voicing a complaint could bring them out.

Instead of sitting down behind the steering wheel, John put himself in front of the grill. He and Emil were safe in the backyard, perched in lawn chairs near the barbecue. They brought no attention to themselves there, in their tranquil haven. The yard became a sacred spot for them, shielded from the intrusion of meddlers.

Two guys, breaking bread, sharing space. They occupied the choicest seats on an observation deck, beneath the expanse of a dark lid stippled with tiny diamonds. Silence was their other companion, though it was sometimes interrupted by the sound of a dog barking in the distance.

There was comfort in the wordless companionship John and Emil shared. They found a brief escape from loneliness and isolation. They filled their emptiness with the connection of kindred spirits.

At that time and in that space, all was well in their respective universes.

CHAPTER THREE — THE FIRST TIME

Three angels set the table for me, tonight
They know my face, they set a place, it's for me, tonight
Headstones
"Three Angels"

At the age of twenty-one, I decided I had seen and experienced it all. There was nothing left to look forward to. I was ready to take my leave. Such was the culmination of my short, sweet journey on this planet.

I was trapped in a toxic relationship with a partner who maintained rigid control over me. I saw no avenue of escape. His pattern of abuse was to isolate and berate me. Temporary abandonment was another nasty trick he enjoyed playing on me.

I'd had enough.

I didn't think I could win the struggle against his domination, and there were few options to consider. I pondered what seemed like the only viable solution at the time. I was tired, and needed an exit.

I stood on the edge of a decision. I could continue to live the chaos, or choose an alternate route. What I wanted most was for malice to quit stalking my every move.

I'm not even sure I had a grasp of the notion yet—I had never spoken the word "suicide." I told myself that crossing over would be uncomplicated and surreal, like a slumber party for one. It's strange how once I chose the path, I acquired peace of mind. It was almost euphoric. No drug could seduce me like the promise of never again waking up to this bullshit. I needed peace, an end to the madness. And the lure of escape was intoxicating.

I welcomed the relief a break could provide. I was afloat on a cloud of calm. There was a space the shape of me that I longed to occupy. It lingered somewhere between nothingness and serenity, where stinging words were silenced, touch no longer scorched, and eyes ceased to judge.

I had found a path to somewhere quiet. I heard nothing but the sound of my breathing, and it wasn't strained anymore. My thoughts were fluid, like a movie running in slow motion, capturing every detail of the best frames. I was going to free myself, and the road to liberty was crystal clear.

I had never considered this type of solution before. I needed to formulate a plan. A scene from an old TV program came to mind. It portrayed someone self-destructing. I let the idea sink into my brain for a moment. Then I rummaged through the bathroom cabinets, searching for an accomplice.

I didn't immediately notice the little intruder at the doorway. The whispered flit of tiny feet caught my attention. I froze with my hand on the prize, like a thief caught holding the loot. I cocked my head to one side and caught sight of a spectator. A little blond boy wearing a faded onesie stood in the semidarkness. He had his thumb in his mouth and an index finger cradling his nose.

His look of perfect innocence hijacked my cause. His little boy-body rocked with easy calm, back and forth, from one foot to the other, and his gaze never faltered. I wanted to say, "Please stop looking at me. I can't do this if you're watching."

I didn't have the strength to make him go back to bed.

I was forced to absorb the sense of how a tragic loss would impact the life of a two-year-old boy. The only worthwhile thing I had ever accomplished was to have a beautiful son. I was his singular point of reference—everything he knew about life he had learned from me. What legacy was I planning to leave him?

I was almost convinced my death would have no consequence, but the truth was I couldn't destroy myself without destroying a part of him. I hated abandonment, and callous to consider handing it off to my own son. My almost-decision struck me with a sudden terror—I could be the un-doer of his life.

I knelt to the floor, strained and clumsy. I watched my little boy. As tears blurred my eyes, I held back from embracing him. I no longer felt worthy of the privilege.

Perhaps he would have been better off without me as his parent. It's an outcome I could never learn. I knew one thing for certain: no one else loved him as completely as I did. And I needed to believe that my love was enough to make up for past, present, and future mistakes. I might not have been able to provide him a plentiful life, but I could give him great love—even though I had none to offer myself.

My exit strategy was unacceptable. I needed to find another way to cope and stay alive. Contending with the hopelessness was brutal. The dark thoughts I had toyed with continued to occupy a secret place in my psyche. I kept them there for future reference, in case I required them again. I had discovered a dangerous new manner of reasoning—one that approved of solutions outside of rational thought.

Undoing the suicide decision was painful. Before me was the dirty, tattered garment of my life, which I had attempted to discard. I had to purposefully put the rag back on—yet it fit awkwardly, like a hijab on the pope.

I eased back to my dismal reality. With caution and purpose, I committed to work through the mire. My life was a mess. I needed to fix it, and I prayed that none of its grime and filth would contaminate my child.

CHAPTER FOUR — THE PROFESSOR

> But the stars are burnin' bright like some
> mystery uncovered
> I'll keep movin' through the dark with you in my heart
> My blood brother
> *Bruce Springsteen*
> *"Blood Brothers"*

Denis was three persons in one—a trinity. There was the Denis before the accident, the Denis after the accident, and the Denis after the onset of his illness. Each had his own distinct personality. About the only things the three had in common were his body, soul, and remarkable intelligence.

I don't have an accurate recollection of Denis, or what he was like before the accident. He was almost seven years older, and I was four when the accident happened. He was a free spirit, full of confidence, and not afraid to try new things. I doubt he had much interest in spending time with his younger siblings.

He had expressive eyebrows, a sweet smile, and remarkable eyes, framed by long lashes. He had the look of a choirboy—innocent and angelic. My older siblings revealed he was more like a character from the old sitcom *The Little Rascals*. His fiery spunk likely contributed to the injury that knocked him down. He was wrestling with some boys in the backyard, fell, struck his head on a rock, and nothing was ever the same.

Normally a fall or a scrape from messing around would call for a cold cloth, a hard rub, or a swipe of Mercurochrome. My brothers and I were always tending minor wounds due to gutsy exploits. We got goose-egg lumps from rock fights; we punctured our feet on rusty nails from running barefoot through junkyards. I had a tooth knocked out playing road hockey. These bumps and cuts warranted basic attention, without cause for concern—unlike the injury Denis acquired.

It didn't appear to be a severe fall. There was no visible gash. Blood didn't ooze into Denis's hair, making it sticky and wine-coloured. Mom checked his scalp but found only a small bump in the spot where his head had met the rock.

Kids cry when they get banged around, and Denis was no different. Mom tried to settle him down, but he kept right on crying. She rang up the doctor's office, and they advised her to watch for certain signs, like vomiting and losing consciousness. He did neither, so Mom waited until his upset played out. The doctor told her there was no point getting anxious over a minor ding to the head.

Denis occupied the sofa to work out his troubles. He looked fragile as he lolled in the couch's loose embrace, his boy-body slumped in a nest of shapeless cushions. I felt bad for him watching him cry the blues, with stringy snot snaking down his cheek.

By suppertime he was less rattled by his mishap. His bawling quieted to a snivel. He had no interest in eating, so he stayed on the couch in the living room, and we dined to his ditty of hiccups and whimpers.

Mom became concerned by his prolonged distress. Denis's demeanour wasn't moving any closer to normal. After supper, Dad tried listening to the news on TV. He sat at the end of the couch, and kept a gentle hold on Denis's foot to offer him comfort.

After a while, Mom noticed Denis growing quiet. She tried rousing him, but he wasn't responding to the nudges. His eyes were open, but he wasn't recognizing her.

Mom called out: "Something's wrong!"

Mom's tone chilled me like a sudden drench of icy rain. Dad was stunned, until the message sunk in. He jumped up from the couch and flew into motion. He gathered Denis in his arms and carried him to the truck. Mom grabbed a blanket and followed close behind. This time they didn't hesitate. Mom and Dad were taking Denis to the hospital.

Mom climbed into the passenger seat, and Dad set Denis on her lap. He fumbled in his pocket for truck keys and got behind the wheel. The engine fired up, and he jerked the truck forward onto the street.

There were no goodbyes, no *see-ya-laters*—only the roar of the motor racing the pickup westward down the highway. I watched as the truck carted them off toward an unknown fate.

A bulky silence descended after they left. The commotion dazed me and my siblings, and toppled our calm. We couldn't fully grasp what had just transpired. For the longest time, we stared out the window, as though expecting them to turn around and come back. Perhaps there was a huge misunderstanding or it was terribly inappropriate joke, and they would soon realize the mistake. But they didn't return, so our worry remained closed to hope.

The nearest hospital was ten miles away. It was no more than a clinic with beds. I learned that when Dad and Mom arrived at the hospital with Denis, the doctor made it plain that treating a serious head injury was beyond his skill. He could only direct them to take Denis to another hospital for emergency surgery. It was a five-hour drive to get there. There was no ambulance to transport them or medical staffer to assist them. My parents were on their own delivering him to Saskatoon.

"You need to leave now." The doctor was adamant. In their haste, they hadn't planned for an extended drive. They needed gas money, and it was inconveniently stashed at home. The doctor pulled out his wallet and handed some bills to Dad. "This should be more than enough to get you there and back. Now go."

As they prepared to leave, the doc called after them: "I'll make arrangements with the surgeon. Someone will meet you at the emergency entrance. Just get there safe."

Dad locked away his worry and focused on controlling the vehicle as they travelled. All he could do to help Denis was drive and hope to make it there in time. Mom held Denis in her lap, his boy-body dormant and his breathing shallow. The possibility of him slipping away was too painful to consider, so she prayed instead.

When they arrived at the hospital entrance, medical staff collected Denis and laid him on a stretcher. They rushed him to the operating room. A surgeon worked to relieve the pressure on his brain caused by a massive haemorrhage. He survived the surgery. The doctors waited with guarded optimism for him to emerge from the coma.

My sister, Pauly, took charge of our care after Dad, Mom, and Denis left for the hospital. At thirteen years of age, she had plenty of experience helping Mom raise kids. Mom depended on her that way, which was often tough on my sister.

Pauly made us go to bed, even though it took us a long time to settle down. In the morning, we woke to silence. Normally we could hear Mom busy in the kitchen, but this time no one was making noise. Mom was still missing, along with Dad and Denis.

The silence sparked our worry. The quiet was unnatural, and we manoeuvred through it nervously. Rod brought out the toaster and fed it a couple of bread slices. Pauly grabbed milk from the fridge and filled our glasses. She pulled dishes and peanut butter from the cupboard and placed them on the table. John helped our baby brother Mitch climb into the high chair. I sat down to eat breakfast, troubled and deflated.

"Is Denis died?" I wanted to know.

Pauly set a plate in front of me. "No, he's not *dead*. Just eat your toast."

Mealtime was usually chatty and rushed, but I could hardly find the motivation to feed myself. I poked at my food, chewing and swallowing with an unprecedented lack of enthusiasm. The three empty spots at the table didn't help diminish my worry.

Rod and Pauly kept me somewhat focused on the odds of a positive outcome. Their hands were full looking after three young siblings. Little Mitch was the only one unruffled by the turmoil—his only concerns were playing and being fed.

Pauly divided her attention between us and the switchboard, which, despite the turmoil, still needed manning. A call came through the long-distance line from Mom.

"We're in Saskatoon, at the hospital," she said. "They operated on Denis last night. So far, he's doing OK. We're waiting. He's still not awake."

We crowded around Pauly to hear the news.

"You're going to have to look after things until we come home. Go to Grandma's and Auntie's for help with the kids."

After she hung up, we peppered Pauly with questions. The best she could tell us was, "So far, so good. Denis had surgery, and he's resting. We need to wait and see now."

Our family doubled down on worry as we tried to get through the next few days. Denis didn't venture far from my thoughts.

Denis woke, and he spoke. He did all the things to indicate he was on the mend. Recovery was a slow process, but he improved a little more each day. His stay in the hospital lasted several weeks, until he was finally well enough to be discharged.

On the day Mom and Dad brought him home, my siblings and I waited with Grandma and Grandpa as they sat with us at the kitchen table. John and I jockeyed for their attention. We showed off every treasured toy and handmade work of art to gain the spotlight. They rewarded us with tenderness. We invented as many distractions as we could to pass the time.

It was nearing suppertime, so Grandma and Pauly rummaged through the cupboards for foodstuff. They prepared a simple meal, but delayed serving it until the rest of our family arrived. My belly was begging for sustenance when, at long last, the sound of tires crunching on gravel announced the approach of travellers.

We crowded at the entrance to greet them. Denis advanced timidly to the centre of our attention. We were so happy to see him that we converged on him with too much enthusiasm. Denis flinched, and took a step back.

Mom coached us, "You need to give him space. Be gentle."

We hadn't intended to upset him, and none of us had anticipated his reaction.

He was sensitive to fuss, and Mom and Dad said we should give him time to adapt. We celebrated Denis's return with gusto, while he quietly sat and observed. My family didn't know how to manage around people with traumatic head injuries, but we would need to learn.

Denis needed time to adjust from the quiet of hospital life to the fizzy energy of the family. He didn't look damaged, other than the surgical scar chiselled on his scalp. His motor skills, speech, and memory were intact. According to Grandma, though, he wasn't the same kid as he had been prior to the accident. "He's not the same as before. It's like someone else is taking over his body."

Grandma didn't imply the new Denis was bad—just different. If anything, he was much easier to appreciate—so unlike his former plucky self. He was meeker and less animated—almost angelic.

Denis had survived a severe crack to the head, surgical tools had cut into his brain, he had slipped into a coma and re-emerged—he couldn't have come any closer to the afterlife. Sometime during his ordeal, he experienced a religious conversion of sorts. He talked of it—the near-death experience. He revealed a stunning encounter.

"I saw Jesus, and he spoke to me." He said it as if it were the most natural thing to share.

I took his words at face value, because I was a little kid, and believed in things like that. Others were baffled. Our family accepted his revelations, though perhaps with a smidge of hesitation. Denis wasn't known to make up fairy tales, so there was no reason to doubt his message. His story sparked our curiosity. He made us want to believe, and most tried for his sake. But the story was too mystifying for many to grasp.

Denis didn't allow doubt to alter his perception. His kid-like faith was unshakeable, and he carried it everywhere. At home, we didn't hamper his enthusiasm, but kids at school weren't so tolerant. They couldn't pass up an opportunity to heap meanness on him. No one wanted to listen to his Jesus story. They poked nasty fun at Denis's expense. Even the nuns, garbed in their black habits under the guise of piety, didn't take his claims seriously, other than to exploit his new-found sense of service to God. They were more than happy to direct him spiritually *with chores*. They conned him into thinking his labour would be pleasing to the Lord. My parents tried not to dissuade his fervour, but the nuns' expectations got out of hand.

Denis came home from the convent one day after doing charity chores. It was late afternoon in mid-winter, the sky was darkening, and the temperature had dropped to cooler than cold. He arrived home through the back entrance, barely able to grip the doorknob with hands numb from chill. Tears and snot were frozen to his face, and frostbite lick-tested his fingers.

His trek home had nearly done him in. Denis entered the house looking as though he had been extracted from an ice cube. Mom helped take off his parka and wrapped him in a blanket. The sight of Denis in such a state upended Dad. He went into a tirade at nuns who weren't within hearing range.

I could tell from the pitch of Dad's voice that he was having a big upset. He was using his lay-down-the-law tone. The only two words that I heard with any clarity were "black" and "bitches." I'll wager the full content of his rant sounded something like, "Those black bitches can do their own damn grunt work from now on!"

Denis needed quiet time to recover from the accident, so Mom and Dad gave him a bedroom all to himself. If he needed to escape the din of the rest of us, he could find solace there.

He fixed his room to suit his personality. He organized his stuff with precision and kept his space neat and orderly. There was a Meccano set with all its parts, a stamp and pad collection with no missing stamps, and an assortment of Elgo building bricks. A chess set occupied a prime location next to his bed. He kept his books on a shelf, arranged in precise order. His organizational system intrigued me and drew the attention of all his younger siblings. We were attracted to his room like magnets to metal. Knowing his space was off limits only made us keener to trespass.

"Denis, kin I watch you?" I stretched to see above the tabletop.

"OK, but don't touch anything." He resumed his task, and then added, "Who was in my stuff yesterday? You guys need to stay out of my room."

To keep us out, Dad installed a hook-and-eye lock on the door of Denis's bedroom. We couldn't reach the lock unless we used something to stand on, so Dad gave us a stern warning for added effect.

Denis remained sharp and curious, despite his brain injury. He was in his element while learning something new. He kept his nose buried in books, which prompted Dad to invest in a costly set of encyclopaedias—the complete 1966 editions of *Encyclopaedia Britannica* (twenty-four volumes) and *Encyclopaedia Britannica Junior* (fifteen volumes). We had the best home library in town, though we didn't yet have an indoor porcelain toilet to set our backsides down onto.

Strict reading conditions were imposed to protect the pricey textbooks from damage. Dad laid down a new law: no reading on the bécosse. We had to consider the possibility of losing a volume down the hole in the outhouse.

Dad's aim was to inject some class and culture into our days. It was an attempt to counter the backwards of our life in the boonies. The books fed a hunger we didn't know we had. We made new discoveries on every page, and our minds filled with more than trifle.

Dad didn't stop there. He wanted to give us music, too. He used to go on and on about how much he would have appreciated learning to play an instrument. He said, "In my family, my baby sister was the only one who got that privilege. You kids should learn to be grateful, and take advantage of that kind of opportunity."

Denis was more apt than the rest of us at taking up music. When a music teacher came to town, Dad paid for Denis to take piano lessons. We didn't own a piano, so Denis practised at the convent. At home he played scales on a make shift keyboard he constructed out of cardboard. Eventually Dad purchased a second-hand upright piano, and music became a sweet distraction from the typical household racket.

Denis was left-handed, like Dad. At the time, being left-handed was considered a defect. It became a contention between Denis and the teacher nuns. The nuns expected him to use his right hand to record his schoolwork, against his natural tendency.

In his youth, Dad was pressured to conform—he learned to print with his right hand instead of his left. He had no intention of imposing the same stress on Denis. When Denis came home from school, Dad allowed him to complete his homework in whatever cast he wanted. The nuns weren't fooled by the backward-slanted scrawl of Denis's script. Eventually their attempts to force him to use his right hand petered out. I like to imagine Denis scored a victory by opposing their groundless demands.

Denis worked on projects with keen focus. His hobbies took on a magical quality. Once, he designed a mechanical sorting system from a deck of playing cards. Using a hole-punch, a pair of scissors, and pencils, he marred them. His goal was to create an alternative method for shuffling cards, by applying binary logic.

I watched as he perforated a row of holes along the edge of each card. He notched some of the holes, until every card had a unique combination of holes and notches. He placed the deck on its edge, threaded a pencil through the holes, and lifted the pencil. Some cards caught where the pencil hooked the holes. Some cards didn't catch, because the pencil slipped through the notches. He used this method with more pencils to sift the cards in a specific order. The system may have had its merits, but we wouldn't let him use it for playing poker with us.

Denis didn't have many friends, and I don't recall him hanging out with other kids. None of his classmates came home with him to play or study. There was no chess club at school, which might have attracted likeminded kids. Denis didn't seem bothered by solitude, so he occupied his time with things other than pursuing friendships. Having six siblings was perhaps more than enough social exposure for him.

The one social priority he valued was visiting Grandma. Her house was like our second home. She lived next door, which was some kind of handy for us. The sound of kids' feet shuffling at her threshold got her up from crocheting. The door was never locked, so we let ourselves in. She perked up at the sight of us, unless we happened to interrupt her favourite pastime, which was watching soaps.

Every day she and my sister, Pauly, followed *The Edge of Night* on TV. If we showed up during the show, our job was to keep quiet. That half hour dragged by like an undeserved jail sentence. We bided our time watching the screen, seated in ancient armchairs.

Grandma's armchairs each had a big-ass depression in the centre of the seat cushion. Two of us could fit into one chair. The indentation was prominent. We tried sitting level, but our skinny bodies kept leaning into each other. We looked like a people-mold of an upside-down V.

For Uncle Emil, *The Edge of Night* bordered on racy. He took offense if there was display of steamy romance between a couple onscreen. Disgusted, he would leave the room, muttering in French, "*Cochons, cochons.*" We laughed at his reaction, which was the best form of entertainment for us during the show.

Normal resumed when the program ended. Grandma lifted restrictions on noise, and we rekindled our gusto. She liked having us around to play board games with. Maybe Grandma thought we would stay longer if we were having fun.

One game in particular suited us best. It was called Sorry.

Grandma fetched it from the cupboard. "Pull out the table and get more chairs," she instructed while we organized ourselves to play.

One kid claimed his tokens. "I want the red *bonhomme*."

"Hey, it's my turn to get red. You had them last time," another kid argued.

Grandma settled the rift so we could get on with play. We crowded around her kitchen table, elbowing one another for more space.

The room was small, and the furniture was old. Frilly doilies and Jesus pictures gave the space a grandma feel. The kitchen smelled of pipe smoke and roast chicken. A statue of Mary sat atop a wooden shelf, high up on the wall. From her lofty perch, Mary kept us honest. We dared not cheat while those benevolent blue eyes bore down on us.

Afternoons at Grandma's passed like the space between schooldays—never slowly enough. At Grandma's house, Denis could give his busy mind a break. There were no theories to prove, no mysteries to unravel, and no tasks to finish. Instead, he spent time playing games with us. Winning or losing was immaterial—cookies and juice were guaranteed.

My family hosted Christmas every year. Mom began preparations weeks ahead of time. She always had a baking project on the go, and she put me and my sister to work washing an endless supply of dirty dishes. By the time Christmas Day came, there was more than enough food to feed the entire extended family, plus a few extra guests. Sometimes Mom invited old bachelors from town who would otherwise spend Christmas alone.

Dad was in charge of getting the tree, which he always put off until the last minute. He took up the axe and, with Rod's help, headed for the bush to make a selection. Dad had a knack for picking out the ugly tree. Perhaps he was showing mercy by bringing an end to a sapling's sorry condition.

Dad and Rod brought the scrappy fir into the living room and propped it up in a pail filled with rocks and sand. They had a long-winded discussion about which side to face forward.

"Turn it this way . . . no, the other way."

We waited with tree ornaments in hand for them to figure out which was the least-worst bare side of the tree. When they were finally satisfied, we started decorating, though no amount of popcorn garland or tinsel could effectively fill the gaps between tree limbs.

As Catholics, we were obligated to attend Midnight Mass on Christmas Eve. My family occupied an entire pew near the front of the church. My brothers served as altar boys as each became old enough to do the job. They had to wear altar boy gowns and learn altar boy moves. At least one of them would be up front helping the priest, who was garbed in the finer Christmas threads.

While the priest waved his hands and gave God lectures, the altar boys sat quietly along the wall. Within minutes, their heads bobbed as they tried but failed to keep from nodding off. When the priest delivered the final blessing, the boys quickly perked up, as if doused with cool water.

The first course of action after Mass was to go home and open presents. We held no delusional notions that Santa Claus had brought them. First off, we had no fireplace with a chimney for him to slide down. Second, why would he keep presents stashed in Mom's closet? Third, how could wrapped presents turn up under the tree *before* we left for Midnight Mass? Unless a white-bearded baby swaddled in a red parka became part of the Christmas crèche, we weren't giving the Santa story any merit.

Mom was especially adept at picking out great presents on a limited budget. I think she was good at it because she had the heart of a child. I got a knitting kit for making Barbie clothes, Mitch got a toboggan, and John got a pellet gun.

After opening gifts, we went to my aunt's house to celebrate and have a traditional midnight supper. We arrived at her door, sometimes gripping our treasures, ready to fill up on food. My aunt prepared roast turkey, tourtière, and other hot dishes. We feasted like royalty.

Kids flaunted Christmas booty while adults poured and downed libations. Typically we celebrated until almost four in the morning. Then we hauled our tired selves home to catch a few hours of sleep and resume festivities at sun-up.

We speculated whether Mom caught any sleep at all. She was up and at it long before we dragged ourselves out of bed. The raucous sound of pots banging and cupboard doors closing announced she was hard at work. Cooking smells wafted up our nostrils, coaxing us down the stairs.

Mom delegated tasks for us before we had a chance to shake the circulation back into our tired extremities. Helping with preparations felt like the fuss of fall suppers at the parish hall—expeditious, with military precision. People started arriving at noon, filling up the house. The kitchen was soon crammed with helpers working out details of the meal plan.

We stuffed ourselves with ample portions of fine food. Everyone was satiated, and not without a proper measure of gratitude. Then, we anticipated the next event on the holiday agenda. The whole day was predictable—a banquet, followed by fun and games. The plan was to eat, clean up, and get ready for sport.

Most of the action occurred in the kitchen. The dinner table was soon rimmed with coin stacks, ashtrays, and brown bottles. We were revved-up for the other main event—poker. Players called out various instructions.

"Dealer's choice."

"Ante up."

"Hide your cards."

"Call the game."

"Take your pick."

"Chicago. Roll your own. Baseball. No peeky. Five card stud."

"Deal 'em."

One curious player stared another down, perhaps trying to mask a bluff. His smirk didn't give anything away.

"What you hiding?"

"You want to know, then pay."

An epic cat-and-mouse standoff developed between the two. The cloud of cigarette smoke thickened overhead. The pot became richer with the wagers of bold gamblers. Coin stacks were shrinking, pressure was building, and nobody was backing down. One player flipped his winning hand over, and everyone at the table busted into cackles. The cocky winner reached for the loot, while the loser shrugged off his loss.

The kids were as much part of the riotous scene as the adults. We lingered at the periphery of the poker game. Someone would give up a knee so a kid could sit close to the action and perhaps sneak a sip from a brown bottle. But our loyalty wavered loosely between things that hooked our attention. Some watched until they got bored and then wandered off toward the next big intrigue.

Denis was more of an observer than a player. Since the accident, he slowly grew accustomed to loudness—the din didn't disturb him as much. He enjoyed and participated in the festivities, though he preferred to linger on the fringe. He never pushed to be first in line, or demanded attention. He was part of the celebration and, at the same time, insulated from the rush.

He found a quiet nook away from the poker game to explore the gift he had gotten for Christmas. Denis unlatched a wooden box that opened like a book. It contained bottles, skinny tubes, corks, a scoop, a bottle brush, an instruction booklet, and other kitchen-like tools.

I asked him, "What you got Denis?"

"It's a chemistry set."

I reached for a bottle, but he stopped me. "Don't touch that, it's not for kids," he said.

John and I stared at him, dazed. I inquired some more: "What's it for?"

"You make things with it."

"What kind of things?"

He explained, "It says here you can make a rocket or a miniature volcano. Even invisible ink."

"Can you make me a rocket?"

He ignored me and went back to reading the instructions. John wanted Denis to teach him how to make a stink bomb, but Denis told him, "Maybe later."

We fidgeted, while Denis focused his attention on the book. Waiting on him was beginning to lose its appeal. I became impatient and pestered him: "When are you going to make something?"

"Dad said I have to wait until everyone's gone home. Too many kids around to be messing with potions and stuff. And you guys can't help."

"Why?"

"'Cause Dad said so."

Through our victories and challenges, my family kept living, tolerating, respecting, and often disagreeing with one another. There was a good balance, and it accommodated all our personalities, including Denis's. For the most part, we were a solid unit, and Denis fit right in.

Like all good things, Christmas Day came to an end. By late evening, the revellers had toned down their excitement and were preparing to leave for home. They suited up in heavy coats and scarves to protect themselves from the cold. Some kids had played themselves tired and were crashed out on the couch or the floor. Parents gathered them up, dressed them, and hauled them out into waiting vehicles. Family members exchanged goodbyes, and one boastful poker player flaunted his winnings on the way out the door.

At age fifteen, Denis attended a boys' college, a Catholic boarding school located about two hundred miles east of our home. Educators at the school ran the curriculum as an introduction to seminary for potential priests. I'm not certain whether the idea to send Denis originated from my parents' persuasion, our religious community's influence, or Denis's own ambition.

My parents thought the environment at the new school might fit his personality—that maybe the place would draw him out of his solitude, help him make friends and connect with peers. They were concerned with Denis's lack of social involvement. But the separation wouldn't be easy on them.

Denis packed his belongings and prepared for the four-hour road trip. I don't recall whether he was motivated by enthusiasm or obedience. He didn't share his feelings openly, and I wonder if he interpreted the move as an extraordinary adventure or a banishment from home.

I followed Denis as he hauled his suitcase from his room to the car. Dad was checking the oil and tires to make sure all was in good working condition for the trip. He opened the trunk, and Denis put his luggage inside. Mom brought out a box packed with sandwiches and drinks for the road.

"Did you remember to pack a toque and mitts for when it turns cold?"

"Yes, Mom, I got them. And I brought a scarf, too."

Denis climbed into the passenger seat, closed the door, and waited for Dad to finish inspections. Mom and I stood next to the car, watching. I don't think Denis realized we were waiting to tell him goodbye.

Mom tapped on the window to get his attention, and he rolled it down. She touched his cheek and said, "Be good, learn lots, and before you know it, you'll be home again."

"These are for you." I handed him a bookmark made from popsicle sticks, along with a matching pencil I had crafted at school. They were stick trolls, with blue fun-fur hair and googly eyes. I thought he might like to use them at his new school.

"Thanks, Céc." He grinned as he examined them.

Dad walked to the driver's side, got in, and started the engine. Mom and I backed away from the car when he put it into gear. We waved and called after them: "Goodbye."

"Bye, Denis."

They turned the corner and disappeared from sight.

Denis attended Grade 10 at the college, returning home for short visits on holidays when my parents could afford the travel costs. We were excited to see him and he seemed genuinely happy to be back, even if only temporarily. He provided little information about his school life. I wanted to hear inspiring details of his experiences, but the most he said was, "There's more homework, and a lot of competition to get the best marks."

He never divulged anything regarding friendships or social involvement. Instead, he preferred to reacquaint himself with the luxury of personal space by holing up in his bedroom. For Denis, it was a pleasant change from dormitory living.

Denis did not resume studies at the college the following year. Maybe there weren't sufficient funds, or the school wasn't benefitting him enough to justify the expense. Or perhaps Denis chose not to return. He came home and fell back into his old habit of quiet detachment. Mom and Dad were troubled that his social outlook hadn't been positively influenced by the academy. If anything, he was even more withdrawn.

Denis finished high school in relative obscurity. He didn't make a significant mark or set himself apart in any way. He completed his schoolwork, passed all subjects comfortably, and didn't earn glowing recognition for his achievements. He maintained a low profile, and wasn't particularly concerned with the future. He attended his graduation ceremony, though it seemed he would have preferred to avoid it.

Dad suggested he consider enrolling in business college. Denis offered no resistance to the notion. He thought it was as good a plan as any other. He inspected the curriculum and determined it was a possible fit.

"Are you ready to fill this out?" Dad handed Denis a college application form.

"Sure. I'll do it now." Denis pulled a pen from his breast pocket and completed the form.

The business college approved his application, so he packed his things and once again relocated to a larger, distant community.

The campus was small and served its students well. An administrator helped Denis find a nearby place to board. He settled into his new surroundings and made himself ready for the first day of class.

The school's dress code required business attire, so Denis wore his graduation suit. The suit was typical sixties style, conservative brown with a necktie. Leisure suits were popular, but Denis bypassed that trend. Someone had given him an old leather briefcase for his textbooks. It opened from the top like the yawn of a wide mouth bass. Dressed in his suit with his bag in hand, he looked like the poster boy for young executives. He walked to campus, crossing city streets alive with traffic.

According to Denis, the classes were interesting and practical. Instructors drew relevant content from their experiences. The course was a good match for his temperament.

Denis was casual with classmates, while remaining somewhat aloof. He didn't exactly snub his peers—he was friendly with them—but he didn't get the point of attending after-class socials.

A student said, "We're going to the Alberta for a beer. Would you like to join us?"

"Thanks, but I made plans already."

After he turned down several invites, they stopped asking him.

He preferred to focus on his studies. He absorbed the lessons and sailed through semesters. Within a year, he acquired marketable skills and a business diploma to frame. It stated that in 1972, Denis had successfully completed the business program at Reeves College.

Prospective employers arrived at the campus hoping to recruit from the pool of recent graduates. Denis's clean-cut good looks, decent grades, and smart apparel gave him an edge. He was offered a junior managerial position at a bank. He accepted.

Another move, another town, another rooming house. . . the new community was small and quiet. It moved at a slower pace and had fewer amenities than the city. Outside the town limits, there was wide-open prairie—grassy plains that merged with the sky somewhere beyond the horizon.

Denis explored his new surroundings and determined they were all right. The only drawback was the increased distance from home. Communication with family was sporadic due to the high cost of long-distance calls.

Whenever he phoned, Denis gave us brief renditions of his daily activities. I anticipated details of a refined life, dripping with prestige. Instead, he gave a rundown in the tone of a waiter listing menu options—wake up at dawn, eat breakfast, brush teeth, comb hair, dress, walk to work, file papers, type notes, calculate sums, balance accounts, go for lunch, do more papers, notes, sums, accounts, go home, have supper, watch TV, go to bed.

I felt shorted after hearing details of Denis's routine, like the feeling I got from being late for supper and finding all that was left of the roast chicken was the neck.

Denis regarded his job training as an extension of business school. He was comfortable with the logic and repetition. He learned common office procedures, further honing his skills. His competence and confidence grew. His supervisor gave him added authority by putting him in a managerial role.

Initially, Denis welcomed the challenge. The new position was a step toward potential advancement. His workload expanded. The tasks were complex. Managing staff became a new responsibility. It was essential he learn to manage his time better, as the adjustment affected his routine.

Increasing demands began to overwhelm him. Denis began to doubt his ability. He realized he preferred to remain in a clerk's position, though he didn't share that information with anyone other than Mom.

His transformation didn't happen all at once. It eased into being, and slowly altered his behaviour. Denis began showing signs of struggle. Clues cropped up almost daily. He divulged some of his troubles to Mom, but she learned only fragments of what was really going on. The minor details painted a broader picture of how Denis's work life was progressing. Knowing Denis, I imagined a scenario that didn't venture far from what could have transpired and contributed to his downfall.

Making decisions at work caused Denis anxiety. He adopted avoidance and delay as coping strategies. He didn't complete tasks, ignored customers and co-workers, and his physical appearance showed signs of escalating neglect. Mr. Dufresne, his supervisor, became increasingly concerned. Attempts to discuss the matter with Denis were met with vague responses and strained silence.

"Denis, can you step into my office for a minute?"

The request caught Denis off guard. It spooked him, and he stammered a reply: "Sure. I just need a washroom break first."

"Of course. Just come in when you're ready."

Denis gave himself a few moments to settle his racing thoughts before stepping out of the washroom and approaching the door to his boss's office. He stood facing it, nervously inspecting the doorknob, shifting his weight from one foot to the other. He hesitated, and didn't enter.

Mr. Dufresne was a small man, with delicate features. His smile accentuated the grey in his eyes, which matched the color of his hair. He wore a tailored suit and carried himself with dignity. Honesty was his best quality, and he managed operations at the bank with integrity. The staff respected him, and regarded him as the symbolic grandfather of the office.

Mr. Dufresne sat at his desk, perusing a document while waiting for Denis. He looked at his watch and noted that more than fifteen minutes had passed since requesting the meeting. He became concerned, so he rose from his desk and went to investigate. He approached the door, opened it, and nearly collided with Denis, who stood in the doorway, blocking the exit. A startled Mr. Dufresne greeted him: "Come in, come in."

Mr. Dufresne held the door open as Denis walked awkwardly inside. Denis cocked his head and took a sideways glance at the interior of Mr. Dufresne's office.

A large executive desk made of teak was situated prominently in the centre of the room. Several folders and stacks of papers were neatly arranged to one side of the desktop. A phone, an adding machine, and a framed portrait of Mr. Dufresne's family occupied the opposite corner. There was a high-backed leather chair with armrests where he sat and made daily decisions. Denis observed a cushioned chair that was situated at the front of Mr. Dufresne's desk. He pondered sitting in it, but remained standing instead.

Mr. Dufresne encouraged him: "Please, sit down."

Denis did as he was told while Mr. Dufresne took the seat behind his desk.

Denis noticed a plaque that hung on the wall directly above Mr. Dufresne's head. He stared at it, wide-eyed, with his mouth slightly agape, avoiding eye contact with his boss. He wrung his hands nervously in his lap, hoping the meeting would end quickly.

Mr. Dufresne leaned forward and propped his elbows on top of the desk. He cupped his hands together and rested his chin on top. He recognized Denis's discomfort, so he spoke in a tone that was reassuring.

"Denis, since you've arrived you've been a great asset to our group. Your work is flawless, and you complete tasks well ahead of time. This is not a criticism of your work. I simply wonder if things are well with you. In the last few weeks, you've seemed distracted. Is anything going on that you'd like to talk about?"

Denis quickly looked at his shoe as if it held the answer. He squinted his eyes, puckered his lips, and tilted his head while slowly shaking it. He gave what sounded like a thoughtful reply: "I don't think so."

"What I mean is . . . is something or someone bothering you? Lately, you seem agitated. If there's some way I can help mend a situation, please let me know. I'm concerned about you, and I want to ensure that your needs are looked after."

Denis paused, contemplating a response. "Well, I don't get much sleep. The phone keeps ringing."

"The phone keeps ringing?"

"Yeah. It always rings at two o'clock."

Mr. Dufresne hinted concern for Denis's lack of rest: "Why two o'clock?"

"Because I'm trying to sleep. It doesn't seem to bother anyone else."

"Who answers it, then?"

"I have to get up, go upstairs, and answer it, because nobody else will, and it'll just keep ringing. Then, all I hear is someone on the other end crying, and they won't talk, so I hang up. And then, I can't go back to sleep, because I'm worried they'll call back."

"Well, I don't know how to fix that. It's too bad your sleep gets disturbed. Can you talk to your landlord about it?"

"It's the government's fault. They keep sticking their nose in my business."

Unsure of how to respond to the odd comment, Mr. Dufresne leaned back in his chair and quietly observed Denis for a moment. After a long pause, he suggested, "Perhaps you should take the rest of the day off and see if you can get some rest then. We'll look after things here. Try and get some sleep, and I'll see you tomorrow."

One day, Denis simply failed to show up for work.

The details of his breakdown were never made clear to me. At first, my parents didn't divulge anything. It was humiliating and disturbing to learn about Denis's trouble from Dad's loud-mouth cousin, who was more interested in our affairs than her own. At school, stories circulated. Rumours spread that Denis had sniffed aerosols and gone off his rocker. Another story alluded to violent criminal behaviour and an aggressive takedown by police. Both accounts fuelled the minds of fools, who exaggerated particulars with each repetition.

Perhaps Mom and Dad thought they were protecting us kids by hiding the details, and that it was their duty to shoulder the responsibility themselves. It wasn't the kind of conversation my parents were willing to have with me, so I imagined the worst. Perhaps they didn't realize how much not knowing would affect the rest of us. They couldn't keep the truth hidden forever. Eventually, I learned more details— which I couldn't entirely comprehend.

In February 1973, Denis was admitted to a psychiatric hospital, assessed, diagnosed, and medicated. The verdict: he had scored front-row seating to a shit show called schizophrenia.

He'd had his first psychotic episode, and the disease promised to deliver more of the same.

Schizophrenia didn't apologize for stealing his future. It held his mind captive, imprisoned in a grey-matter cellblock. He was given a life sentence of chemical restraints without parole. The medications the doctors prescribed him were as frightening as the disease itself. A mixed dose of anti-psychotics, mood stabilizers, and anti-depressants became part of his daily regimen.

In retrospect, the onset of his symptoms likely began years earlier, but Denis kept silent concerning any strange notions penetrating his mind. He might have been afraid to admit things he couldn't explain. Friends and family assumed his sometimes-odd behaviour was nothing more than a quirk. The depth of his suffering had gone unnoticed. No one had had the intuition to identify the malignant invader taking over his person.

He spent months in the hospital. Doctors and therapists examined him, and gave him talk therapy. They prescribed drug mixtures that tripped him out. They tested and observed him, like a mad science experiment. They altered his dosages and scrutinized the effects.

The experts eventually settled on a drug cocktail. They justified the prescription based on a loosely shared view of Denis's "improved behaviour"—which translated to the radical altering of his personality. They might have stepped back to observe the results of their work as though inspecting a finished product on a factory floor. Perhaps they said, "Well, this one's ready to go," and discharged him into my parents' care.

A pattern was forming. Every ten years, Denis came home to recoup from some life-altering calamity. First, he recovered from serious head trauma at age ten. We were glad he had foiled that disaster's attempt. Then, at age twenty, he returned home from another hospital stay. Only this time, genuine recovery seemed doubtful.

His homecoming was unremarkable. One day there were six of us living at home, and the next there were seven. We arrived home from school and he was sitting quietly at the kitchen table. He showed no hint of joy to be home. It was his blank stare that greeted us, like he was lost right where we found him. It caused my parents dismal sorrow. The robust future they had envisioned for him was nothing now but a lofty wish gone bad.

For the second time in his short life, we became reacquainted with Denis. He was a peculiar newcomer with residual qualities of his former self. The change was obvious, and it perplexed us. The heavy dosage of meds flat-lined his spirit and gave him a look that lacked alertness. It took more effort for him to interact with us. He was slower with returns, and we had to be patient. We adapted to the new Denis. My family learned to manage the unfamiliar and re-establish a meaningful relationship with him. It could never be exactly the same as it was before, so we created new bonds.

Our perception of ordinary family life was already somewhat skewed. We didn't watch TV shows like *Leave it to Beaver* and *Father Knows Best* to learn of typical American-style harmony in the household. Up until 1972, CBC television was our basic reference, and it offered few traditional examples of family interaction for us to relate to. We watched Mr. Dressup, who cross-dressed and talked to hand puppets as if they were real people. He hoarded stuff in a trunk he named Tickle.

How much further from normal could things get? Denis's odd behaviour didn't severely alter our view of ordinary. In fact, his contributions made our days more interesting.

Denis didn't cause trouble—there wasn't much of it to find in our remote little village. He managed to add a bit of weirdness and humour to our days. His reaction to situations was often inappropriate. It's not that he was intentionally disruptive, but his timing could have used refinement. He would laugh out loud when it was time to be sombre, which made me laugh. Sometimes, he performed a piano recital in the middle of the night. The interruption didn't particularly bother Dad, because Denis always played Dad's favourite tune—Lara's theme from *Dr. Zhivago*, "Somewhere, My Love."

Denis zoned out often, like he was focused on things other than what was directly in front of him. He chain-smoked, and paced obsessively. He navigated an imaginary line on the floor. Walls gave him pause, so he spun on his heel and back-tracked as if inside a hamster ball. We often had to swerve out of his way to give him room.

Sometimes, he prattled, and identified himself as the devil, which had the effect of a sock monkey imitating King Kong. His social life was non-existent—not that he cared, one way or the other. His world became quite limited, though it some-times managed to include a portion of ours in its periphery.

A typical conversation between Denis and I could go something like this:

"I am the Antichrist."

"Uh-huh?" *Long pause, sideways eyes, raised eyebrows.* "Think we could go see a movie?"

"Sure."

The medication caused crazy side effects. Denis's whole manner changed. The drugs triggered in him a dependency on tobacco, coffee, and pacing. Denis's gait became awkward and jerky, like a palsy had taken over his body. His tongue was in constant motion, as though chasing a spicy morsel on the lam. He gained weight, and he lost his ability to be curious and focused. The meds stole the brightness from his eyes and numbed his brain. It seemed the colour in his world had turned murky grey.

I don't recall being particularly affected by the changes in Denis. As a kid, I adapted—which didn't stop his illness from altering our relationship. The disease and the meds chipped away at his character. Some days, he was childlike and vulnerable to abuse. He couldn't be as much of a big brother anymore. In a way, we swapped roles—which should have prompted me to be more protective of him.

Some of Denis's interests remained constant—like music, television, and movies. The disease couldn't take those away from him. When he wasn't playing piano, he was listening to rock and roll. His playlist included songs by The Beatles and CCR. Tunes blared from our tired old record player. He'd be rocking to "Hey Jude" and "Born on the Bayou," driving everybody "Up Around the Bend"—another CCR number he often played. He'd bob his head to the rhythm of music while sucking steady drags off a smoke. He held the cigarette at face level, between two fingers. The grip and slant of his hand made it look like he was giving himself a horizontal peace sign.

When the music stopped, the TV was switched on. He and I shared a common taste in programming. Side by side, we watched favourite sitcoms, like *M*A*S*H* and *All in the Family*. Listening to music and watching television weren't exactly productive ways for Denis to pass time, but few other options were open to him. His goals of living independently and being self-sufficient were growing dim, like the TV screen fading to black at the end of a program. Fate was the heartless bitch making him unemployable.

Denis spent most of his days close to home, avoiding people. I don't believe fear held him back. It was purely a lack of interest in socializing. He could, on occasion, be persuaded to risk a break from his routine, though convincing him to leave the house was a challenge.

An outing with Denis could be either somewhat normal or freaking embarrassing, depending on the occasion. Trips to the lake fell under the freaking embarrassing category.

Jumbo Beach drew a lot of visitors during the short summer. Its popularity peaked in July. Sun-deprived locals gathered at the beach *en masse* to reap the heat and snuff out the residue of winter.

The beach had all the right stuff—a wide stretch of sandy shoreline, enough trees providing shade for the sun-shy, unspoiled landscapes across the pond, and a playground in the water. Boats were tethered to the dock, occupying one end of the beachfront. Beneath the dock were rocks, and beneath the rocks were leeches. The swimming area extended from the dock to the opposite end of the shore, where a large change house was located. Preferred sunbathing spots were hard to snag on a good beach day. We tended to arrive late by beachgoer standards, so our choices were generally confined to a patch of sand near the dock.

I remember one particularly fine day, it was perfect for a lake outing. The sun was hot, and the shoreline was crowded with sunbathers. The best spots were taken, so we spread our blanket on the sand far from the change house.

The lake was calling, and I wanted to get my feet wet.

"I'm going to change into my swimsuit," I announced.

Denis echoed, "Me too."

The change house was as busy as a weathercock in a wind storm. Everyone seemed to be suiting up for the beach. Denis and I exited the change house at about the same time. We started walking along the shore back to our spot. We passed through the crowd of sunbathers, and it felt like their eyes were boring holes through my skin. I was fourteen, self-conscious, and didn't like the feel of being on display. But I shouldn't have been concerned, because they weren't paying any attention to me.

I wasn't bothered that Denis wore a slick, Mark Spitz-style bathing suit. The design was popular with young men. It fit him well and looked suitable enough—until I noticed the tenting at the front. The dread really hit me when I realized that almost everyone else was noticing it, too. I'm not sure if Denis wasn't aware, or didn't care what he was flaunting down that sandy runway. I was flustered, but the sunbathers gaped and seemed amused.

I should have disappeared back into the change house and waited for Denis to leave on his own. But everything seemed to be moving in slow motion. I was dazed, and couldn't think quick enough. I wanted to rush to the far end of the shore and be done with the embarrassment, but my legs refused to move fast. I tried pretending I wasn't associated with the strange man-boy with the boner, though it was obvious I was escorting him down the beachfront.

I burned with humiliation the rest of the day. I should have taken a cue from Denis and not let such a trivial thing exasperate me.

Going to the movies was a somewhat normal outing with Denis. It was something he and I could do together without drama. My other siblings had either moved away or forged their own social life. Sadly, there were no plans or invites on my social calendar, which freed me up on most weekends. Hanging out at the movies with Denis became a welcome diversion from boredom.

At the movies, we'd lose ourselves in stories that were more exciting than our own. I scarcely allowed myself to blink for fear of missing an important scene. I shrank in my seat during *Walking Tall*, held my breath on *The Poseidon Adventure*, and burned with righteous rage through *Scarecrow*. I fell in fan-love with Gene Hackman and Al Pacino, even though my heart belonged to Alan Alda.

Ours proved to be a symbiotic relationship. I loved movies, and Denis had a driver's license. I loved pizza, and Denis was of age to buy beer. We always followed up a movie with a visit to the pizza place, where, by coincidence, liquor was served. To make sure Denis didn't overindulge, I would take a pull off his beer through a straw while the waiter's attention was focused elsewhere. It was a beautiful arrangement.

I would have gladly shared the movie experience with my quasi-best friend, but she was slightly freaked out by Denis's behaviour. Our friendship veered into the stall lane once she became a boy-magnet. I was a little slow out of the puberty gate, whereas she was busting out in all the right places.

Before discovering boys, we hung out regularly. At that time, we cared squat what boys thought. We glutted on raw potatoes and cabbage to spark fart contests. Then, it started to matter what we did with our nether regions. Things changed, and her priorities shifted. The attention she received from the boys went to her head, and she began to think she was irresistible to all men. She propped herself up on her own little pedestal. When I tried to invite her to the movies with Denis and me, she answered matter-of-factly, "He might rape me."

I responded with stunned silence.

I wished I'd had a comeback, like, "And what drugs do you take to medicate *your* delusions?" But the quip bypassed me.

Perhaps it was wrong of me to assume she would want to fill her free time with a movie, instead of using it to cheat on her boyfriend.

Saskatchewan Government Telephones dismantled the switchboard in our home, along with the monthly income our family depended on. Installers equipped every household with rotary dial phones. It was a sign of the times, and we did our part in the name of progress, whether we liked it or not.

Soon after, Dad's health temporarily failed him. One day, a sudden, severe pain dropped him to the ground. Doctors removed his gallbladder and sent him home, good as new. Dad considered that since he had *almost bought the farm*, or in other words: *almost died*, it would be a good time to sell the farm. A neighbour made him an offer on the land, and Dad accepted. He placed the proceeds in the bank and managed it with a tight fist, like flow control through an eyedropper.

Dad joined the time-card punchers at the sawmill in Meadow Lake. The work was good, but there was little job security. Operations at the sawmill sometimes shut down temporarily. If the closures worried Dad, he didn't show it. The money was good while there was work. He planned ahead and put some finances aside to carry us through the downtime.

Our home situation wasn't spared from bouts of the jitters. Financial concerns and Denis's mental instability only added to the strain. My siblings and I conformed, and became accustomed to Denis's odd habits, but the adjustment wasn't easy for my parents. The brunt of the stress fell on Mom's shoulders.

While we were at school, things could get tense at home. Denis needed to pace. He chain-smoked and drank coffee by the pot-full. His obsessions disrupted Mom's routine. The kitchen became too small a space to share. Mom found herself constantly sidestepping Denis, who couldn't be bothered to watch where he was going. He criss-crossed her path, frustrating Mom as she tried to get housework done.

The illness made Denis self-centered. He couldn't read another person's intentions or consider anyone else's needs. He understood logic, but that wasn't very useful for connecting with other people. The one thing he could do was absorb bad vibes.

Over time, the illness's progression—along with the potent effects of the medication—muted the person Denis used to be. It wasn't simply the loss of his former identity that was alarming, but the nothingness that crept into its place. His lack of response and motivation was a constant obstacle. Mom urged him to be more attentive and look after himself, but her efforts to encourage him were met with empty stares. Denis became more remote, and his wall of isolation thickened.

He embarked on a downward spiral. His outlook grew murky from lack of purpose. He was unable to make authentic connections, and he imagined perils. He couldn't trust or be trusted. So many doors had closed to him—people didn't understand, and they used their prejudices to protect themselves from him.

Hopelessness advanced on his mental state, and he internalized it. It seemed he was an island unto himself. As far as he could reason, we were beings on a distant shore, dispatching the occasional smoke column in a lame attempt to communicate. No one had the tools to pull him out of the mire.

I don't recall whether a caseworker helped with Denis, or if any professionals followed up on his progress. Someone, perhaps a doctor, determined Denis needed to be where he could access professional treatment. A plan was put in place, and a new home was found for him. It was located near the psychiatric facility in North Battleford, where he was first hospitalized. The move came as a relief to my parents, who were feeling overwhelmed, and powerless to provide the support Denis desperately needed.

Like in the children's game KerPlunk, Denis was a marble dropped into strange new surroundings. The system promised appropriate help, so we kept our fingers crossed.

He settled into a group home, and for the first time in a long while, he seemed to benefit emotionally, mentally, and physically. His routine was regulated. He was expected to take on certain responsibilities, and he lived among peers he could relate to. The schedule grounded him, and his mental health improved.

Denis spent a few good years in his new living arrangement in North Battleford. He was near enough to make the occasional bus trip home. We enjoyed his company during these visits. It was easier to appreciate his quirkiness in small doses.

We waited for him at the bus stop. Sometimes he brought a package along, and he carried it under one arm, protected. The package usually contained a board game.

He was tester for a company that marketed new products. He volunteered to test their goods, and they provided him board games to evaluate. He never arrived with games for little kids—only ones that were more complex. I don't think the company paid him other than with free merchandise.

He'd barely have settled in at home before we'd be pestering him to set up the board. We were a good test market for the game. Denis gave us a spiel about the object of play, which we listened to with feigned attention. Some games didn't yet have written instructions. We weren't too concerned with that, because we preferred making up our own rules anyway.

It didn't take much coaxing to bring out the challenger in us. Dad built things for us and taught us how to construct things for ourselves—things like slingshots. We engineered them from tree branches, and our designs kept improving. We put our finished handiwork to the test and spent hours target practising, knocking off numerous tin cans, vying to outdo one another.

The bigger the dare, the more determined we were to meet the challenge—with certain exceptions, one of which was hockey against bruiser chicks built like brick-houses—something I was not particularly into. But if the same bruiser chicks challenged my team to a game of softball—which meant they had to rely on skill and hard work instead of roughing me up—I was good with it.

Sports, board games, and card games were irresistible. We played them all with an intensity that rivalled Canada Cup hockey. The kitchen table became one of our playing fields. We were focused, and intent on applying bold strategy to the new game Denis had brought. Each player sought the upper hand, and adjusted his game plan accordingly. We tweaked rules for the sake of good competition.

"That doesn't make sense. You should lose a turn when you get to that square—otherwise, what's the point of it being there?"

"That's for sure. And not only that—you should have to give up a card."

Play stalled when opinions differed on how and when a rule should apply. We discussed each issue at length, and somehow the time spent playing always came up short of the time spent deciding on what was fair. We were OK with that, and Denis went back to North Battleford with plenty of feedback for the game planners.

On these rare occasions, Denis kicked his illness to the curb for a while and was finally able to join the party. The silliness and punchlines weren't lost on him. He'd catch onto a joke and rock back in his chair, turning his face skyward like a wolf pup howling laughter at the moon. His thick, tangled mane added to the werewolf quality of his mirth. It felt good to exist with him. We could have stayed with Denis in this uncomplicated realm for as long as his illness allowed. But these periods of mental stability, we learned, were sporadic.

With the help Denis was receiving, he seemed to be making good progress. Support workers taught him skills to manage his mental illness. One of their suggestions was for him to keep a daily journal of his activities. In line with his work ethic, he kept on top of it, filling pages with details of daily matters. He described his mind exercises and relaxation techniques. Sometimes he couldn't get past the relaxation part without falling asleep, which delayed the rest of his morning routine.

Whenever there was an interruption in his living arrangements, he would come home for a while. He moved back in with us for a few months during the winter of 1975-76. We noticed a change in him. He was more involved and cooperative with family and community—a side of him that had been dormant in the recent past. Denis's optimism was a new experience for us. He was more inclined to get out of the house and socialize, which motivated my brothers to include him in their activities.

The relationship between John and Denis had been testy for years. Generally they avoided each other's space. Perhaps it was maturity that helped put an end to their acrimony. Denis discussed it with Ernie, my sister Pauly's husband, and then noted it in his journal—along with other challenges he had to face.

January 31, 1976

I should also use willpower to make friends instead of sleeping all day, like today. Sure, I went to the bar. Had a good talk with Ernie. He told me that I've improved considerably in the past few months as far as perceptiveness goes. I'm getting along with Johnny a lot better.

February 1, 1976

I don't know, I feel very restless nowadays. I'm excited with living, but the trouble is, I haven't got too many friends—I should try harder.

Fifteen-year-old Mitch arranged a business partnership with Denis. They became co-caretakers of the ice rink. It provided them both some spending money. Snowfall was frequent that winter, and the boys stayed busy clearing blankets of it from the rink.

The job gave Denis purpose, and the opportunity to manage his finances. He accounted for every penny coming in and going out. He set up ledgers and kept tabs on loans he provided to his brothers and their friends. John became a regular borrower. Denis even went so far as to look after an

NSF cheque John wrote to the local pub owner. Denis never pushed for payment, though—he wasn't cut out to be a loan shark. Most times the debtors never repaid him.

Dad bought a used Ski-Doo primarily for recreation, but the boys used it to commute to and from the rink. When Denis and Mitch weren't using it, John monopolized the sled for his own personal use, which meant the rest of us didn't get many turns riding it.

The snowmobile's engine roared like thunder when we gunned it. A smelly haze of gas fumes wafted from the under the hood. The machine couldn't garner much speed, but its big sound gave it authority. The ride was rough, and my knees smarted long after a run was over. Driving it was exciting, though the ride was seldom pleasant.

Following another snowfall, John and Denis rode the Ski-Doo to the rink.

February 12, 1976
Johnny and I went to the skating rink and cleared the snow to the boards. Mitchy was supposed to blow it out with the snowblower. After clearing the ice, Johnny and I went to the bar and had one drink (of beer) and a couple of games of pool—I lost the first one and won the second one—I paid for both. I guess Johnny didn't have any money.

Other than caretaking at the rink, Denis picked up a couple of bookkeeping jobs and landed odd chores around town for pay. He pushed to be normal, but the stigma of mental illness stuck to him like a skin he couldn't shed. In his journal, he considered the effects on his future.

February 15, 1976

Got up at 9:30 and shaved to go to church at 10:30. At church, I went to Holy Communion. I hope God answers my prayer. I prayed to get a steady job in bookkeeping.

February 28, 1976
I've got this business inferiority complex. It's because I've been in the mental hospital, and that is a flaw in my career. It has helped me a great deal, but it is also a label that businessmen will place me in [sic] and I doubt that I'll be promoted because of it. So my only answer is university. I plan to have a little business of my own in the future (after university). Well, if I try hard enough, I'll get what I want, even if it kills me.

We went to church every Sunday. Denis didn't have to be prodded to go—he was spiritual, in spite of his mental illness. He embraced religion as long as his illness allowed him. He didn't pretend to be flawless. He accepted his humanity with candour.

One day, he went back to North Battleford.

March 16, 1976
Got up at 9 a.m. Had some coffee and cigarettes. Dad told me to get ready because we were leaving at 10 a.m. So I searched everywhere for my stuff. I even brought my porno books. We left at around 10 a.m. We got stopped for speeding, and dad got pinched for $25. When we got to NB, we had a hard time to get served [sic] at the Capri. It took at least 20 min. to get a menu. We ordered two hot hamburgers and two beers. The beer alone cost us $1 apiece. Went to the mental hospital and Nurse Wally showed me the workshop and my board and room house.

Denis settled into his new room, and Dad drove home to Makwa.

March 17, 1976

Got up at 12 a.m. Couldn't go to sleep. I suppose I was anxious for the big day ahead of me. I tried to read *Psycho Cybernetics*, then a few other books. Then, I read an article in one of Gregg's books called *Psychologie* today. After that (it was about 3 a.m.), I went to bed, only to be awakened by my clock, which read 5:30 a.m. Tried to go back to sleep, but couldn't, so I got up and shaved. Ate breakfast and then smoked a bit. Gregg and I walked to the workshop (we had our lunches with us). I drew up a picture, then I worked on stencils. After workshop, we went downtown to cash my cheque. I did. Then we went home. I took a shower but I forgot my shampoo. Went to a workshop dance. Had a ball there, but became quite tired by the end of it. Took the bus home.

Denis described a routine in his journal, recording daily events that followed much the same pattern, "... At work, I did one stencil, then I went into the sewing room, where I cut threads that were loose on aprons. Then, I stamped, which read, [sic] 'Battleford Sheltered Workshop' ..."

Other than filling his day constructing work aprons, stencils, and plastic flowers for weddings, Denis developed friendships. He mentioned three co-workers—Alphonse, Gene, and Gregg—and their shared activities: "... When work was over, I went to Alphonse's place and made a phone call to the bus depot. Boy, was that lady of the house mad at me for calling without asking. She almost threw me out of the house .... Walked back from the workshop with Gene and Alphonse. Gene immediately went home, but Alphonse, the bastard, followed me to the co-op. Fortunately, I just had one cigarette left in my pack, so he couldn't bum one off me. However, he tried to bum some money off me. I said I'd give it to him tomorrow. But I've decided not to give it to him . . . . We had our evaluation. I was low, according to them, as far as expressing myself. Then, Greg was interviewed— he told me later that he couldn't stop crying and laughing at the same time . . . . During the second period, Greg had a fainting spell. Then he came back up, unloading the clothesline of aprons. Then he fell on his head down the balcony. He's in the hospital now. He'll probably stay there for the rest of the week . . . . Allan was quite serious about some of my remarks. He told us not to make jokes about Greg's accident (or suicide attempt) . . . . Then, after supper, I went to Alphonse's boarding house. We went together to see Greg at the Union Hospital. He gave me his Mad Magazine. Also, I had brought him his safety razor. Learned that Greg is going to the Sk. Hos . . . ."

Sometimes, Denis wrote about getting into trouble at work: " . . .Went to work via the shortcut. Read dirty magazines (some of Ed's) . . . Made a phone call to dial a time. Ed didn't like that too much. Later, at noon, [Ed] got mad at me for bringing an ashtray into the office. Then I asked him if he wanted a fight. He said, 'Sure, but after work, I'll meet you downtown.' This bugged me—especially because of his size. We put papers into a big van, all day long. Then, at the last break, I went to see Jane. She told me I had nothing to worry about . . . Lorraine didn't mean mouth me today. I think she's a bitch. I worked, drawing aprons, but they weren't satisfied. So I went to the flower room and did flowers . . . disappointed about having so little money and frustrated at having to quit smoking. Didn't buy coffee nor smoke any cigarettes for the first break. I told Patty off in a gruff sarcasm [sic]. After dinner, I smoked cigarettes—unable to minimize my smoking...."

Denis described a female co-worker who wouldn't leave him alone. "...Helga was after me all day long. She even moved into the sewing room with me. Really, she's just there for looks. She hardly did any work. Today, I learned who was her Lawrence. He's supposed to have screwed her once or twice or so. She even said so.... Got to the workshop and sure enough, Helga was there to 'greet' me. She's starting to get on my nerves...I don't know, maybe she still feels that I'm her boyfriend. She might be right. But she ain't my girlfriend, and that's a fact.... After the first break, we were still silk-screening. Helga was after me, just pestering me. I told her I didn't want her, but she kept bugging me.... Got to work at 8:05 a.m. Had a few cigarettes, and Helga again was bugging me [sic]. Frankly, one of these days, I'll tell her off, but good...."

Going to church remained important to him. "... Went to the 10:30 a.m. Mass at Notre Dame church. But since the church is under reconstruction (renovation), we went into the gym. It sure was crowded in there. It was Palm Sunday, so I bought myself a palm leaf. The Mass was long and a bit boring... Got up at 9:30 a.m. Shaved, got dressed in my formal clothes, had coffee, and went to church—St. Joseph's. I don't know what's wrong with me, but I feel depressed. It's because of Helga and the character analysis by the workshop. I had poor readings, but that was because I was a newcomer. I felt tired—or was it 'depressed'—all Sunday afternoon...."

The script in his journal began declining in form and content as winter approached—a clue that his struggle was escalating again.

October16, 1976

My name—Annette and I [sic] are sitting in my room and we're talking about how we write. We are also bugging Greg, or at least trying to, because I'm mad at myself for getting grounded, and I'm talking [sic] it out on everybody around me (except for Dennis) the only thing good that ...

November 17, 1976

I dreamt of holding up a pair of silvery white shoes which were stuck together.
I feel like I have no ambition.
Yesterday, I took inventory of the Canteen, and it took me over 1 hour to do so. Helen was very angry at me because it took me so long. I went to deliver flyers after coffee and must have lost my ticket booklet. I went, after a boring dinner hour, to deliver flyers, and fell asleep while waiting to get more flyers. Jane came by and balled [sic] us out because of that. After work, I bought a new tape for my typewriter and recked [sic] my typewriter.

The next and final entry in his journal was on November 26, 1976:

I was in a war against some kind of mob. We drove our van ...

... and that was all he wrote that day.

I graduated from high school in 1977. My first real job was at Saskatchewan Government Telephones in North Battleford, where Denis was living. Neither of us owned a vehicle, and our residences were a fair distance apart. Coordinating visits was a challenge. Denis frequented the downtown Native Friendship Centre, which provided Indigenous people a safe place to meet. I learned its doors were open to anyone, and the location was easy for me to access, so Denis and I arranged to meet there.

The Friendship Centre was housed in a structure that looked like an old warehouse. The inside was dimly lit, with areas sectioned off for lounging, recreation, and dining. A counter occupying more than half the width of the room separated the front area from the kitchen, with storage space in the back. The furniture was in rough condition. The air was heavy with cigarette smoke, and country music whined from an ancient radio behind the counter.

About a half-dozen people meandered between sections, debating on where to settle themselves, I suppose. I scanned faces in search of a familiar one, but Denis wasn't there. The patrons observed me with curiosity. I wasn't bold enough to assume I would be welcomed, so I decided to wait for Denis street-side instead of inside the building.

I spotted Denis coming up the street, his head down as though looking for loose change on the sidewalk. His steps were clumsy and jerky. People assumed he was drunk and gave him a wide berth. It was obvious to me that the medication was causing more assaults on his senses.

His clothes made him look scruffy—they didn't fit him right, and the colour and cut didn't conform to the look he'd once preferred. The only garment he wore that fit his signature look was someone's cast-off suit jacket. If he had the funds, he would have shopped for better than what was offered at Goodwill. In another time and place, his style might have been considered unique and expressive, but the world wasn't yet ready to accept *different*.

It was hard to make sense of the changes happening to him—I wanted to be able to turn them around. He was losing more and more of himself over time—a slow drowning of sorts. He never let on that it bothered him. But if he wasn't troubled over it, I would do that for him. I buried the worry in order to deal with it later. For now, I wanted to have a decent visit with him.

I followed Denis through the entrance to the Friendship Centre. The guys inside welcomed him with relaxed recognition. Denis nodded in their direction. We ordered a Coke and coffee at the counter and sat across from each other at a table in the eating area.

"So, what's new?" I asked.

"Oh, nothing much." He took a drag of his smoke and sipped his coffee. "A new guy moved in. He likes to steal things."

"Is he taking your stuff?"

"Sometimes. I caught him once and made him put it back." He puffed and sipped some more.

I took in the details of his condition. His black-rimmed glasses were held together with hockey tape, which made him look like one of the Hanson brothers. I wondered how he had broken them in the first place. The tremors in his hands were worsening, and despite the good care he was getting, the effects of the meds were adding years to his vanishing youth.

"Do the people who run the place know about it?" I lit up an Export A to contribute to the smoke haze.

"Yeah, they know."

"Are they going to do something about it?"

Denis shrugged, then turned his head to inspect a poster on the wall. The matter didn't warrant much of his attention, so we dropped the subject. We attempted more conversation, but it was hard to find common ground. Even so, I appreciated our quiet companionship.

A ping-pong table was situated in the recreation section. No one was using it, so we played a game to pass the time. We practised a few lobs for Denis to get the feel of the racket. Our progress was slow, but we eventually managed to get a game going.

A group of teenage girls arrived and sat near the ping pong table. At the end of our game, one of the girls walked over and challenged me to a match. I accepted. I hoped it would spark a new friendship, as the locale's namesake implied.

Sometime during the second round, I surmised that no cordial exchanges were likely to take place. Actually, I sensed mounting tension and that perhaps I was invading someone's territory. Nervous jitters ran through me as I recollected hockey chicks body-slamming me against the boards at the ice rink. The encounter had me second-guessing our decision to meet here. It wasn't as though the girls looked like they were planning to beat me up, but I didn't want to take the chance.

I blew the last game—maybe on purpose, maybe because I was feeling skittish from the tension. Whatever the manner, I was planning my exit.

A clearer picture emerged of how different our worlds had become. Denis was casual in these surroundings, but I was far too green. I was too young to decipher all this new shit, and it scared me sometimes. The Friendship Centre was a portal separating two domains. One realm was safe for him and hostile toward me. The other, outside the centre's walls, regarded him as a freak not worthy of consideration. This place gave him refuge, and for once, he wasn't alone. Seeing his situation opened my eyes to the reality of his isolation. I was glad he was able to occasionally step outside the boundaries of his solitary life.

I set the ping-pong paddle down on the table and made up some lame excuse about getting to work on time. I hadn't meant to abandon Denis so abruptly, but I saw he was safe there. And then I left.

I considered whether Denis was born into the wrong era and culture. I imagine Denis's mental illness might have been accepted and esteemed by ancient civilizations. What if his condition was considered a gift and sought after by shamans and medicine men? A senior spirit guide could have mentored him. He would have been revered. His journey between the physical and spiritual worlds would have been normalized.

Perhaps doctors used the daily drug cocktail to stifle intangible abilities in their patients. What if there was an alternative solution to their ineffective panacea meant to treat highly misunderstood symptoms? Mainstream medicine was far too closed to the spiritual.

The Indigenous culture held deep-seated beliefs regarding sacred connections. The root of those beliefs was evident in the elders. Some may have frequented the Friendship Centre. Perhaps this was why Denis felt so comfortable there. What if he was born into the world too white and too late?

I met with Denis once more at the Friendship Centre. We sat at the same table and talked about the humdrum of our daily activities. Our exchange went relatively well, though I might have appeared nervous, as I kept checking over my shoulder for signs of trouble. Our routines progressively diverged, and we saw each other less and less. A few months later, I moved away, and then only saw Denis occasionally, when our visits to Makwa coincided.

Everything about Denis at the time, centered on his illness. The anti-psychotics kept his mind in check promising to keep his behaviour on an even keel. The drugs gave his outlook a certain amount of optimism . . .until they didn't. The illusion failed, and the carpet was ripped out from under him.

The meds didn't prevent the ebb and flow of symptoms, and there seemed to be no escape from the disease's pattern. Finding the right prescription mix and dosage was about as effective as betting at crapshoot. Doctors gambled with the future of their human lab rats.

They decide on drug cocktails to help patients function within hypothetical standards. The doctors rigged up Denis like a windup toy. They cranked his key with meds and pointed his head in the right direction—voilà, problem solved.

Every time Denis's meds were altered, he adapted. He described the transitions that clouded his thoughts and left him with brain fog. He adjusted and attained a loosely stencilled normal life. He'd reach a plateau, and the disease wouldn't seem to hijack his thoughts as much. Regardless of the struggle, he strived to maintain a routine that included work, recreation, and socializing with peers.

One day, a shift occurred. Something changed in him. Whatever the cause, it generated concern. Someone sounded an alarm.

True to the illness's nature, dark symptoms resurfaced. Agitation, paranoia, delusions, and withdrawal regained control of his psyche. His mind performed circus acts inside his skull. He was readmitted to the psychiatric hospital.

This stretch of hospitalization was brutal for Denis. It happened in February 1979. Few details were forthcoming, but I imagined a disastrous scenario.

He felt betrayed and victimized by his friends, his family, and the system. He railed against the injustice of his incarceration, and hospital staff subdued him in ways an outsider would consider unnecessarily cruel. Eventually, he submitted, and donned a cloak of self-control. Then, in a state of bitter calm, during a mealtime gathering, unobserved, he plucked a butter knife off the table and drove it into his chest with the fury of a cornered animal.

The dining room erupted. Some patients panicked, like a cage of primates thrown into turmoil. Others sat paralyzed and watched the event unfold. Two attendants raced toward Denis and forced him to the floor before he attempted a third thrust of the knife into his body. They wrestled him down. Blood coursed from wounds hidden beneath his hospital garb. They seized the weapon and fought to restrain him. Denis resisted with Herculean strength.

"Could use some help here!" one hollered, avoiding Denis's flailing limbs. "Get the injection . . . now! Hurry up. I can't hold him forever!"

Staffers rushed to follow commands as Denis continued to struggle. One of the helpers drove a syringe of a taming cocktail into his exposed skin. Denis arched his body in one last attempt to break free, and then he began a slow, drunken descent into drug-induced submission. The sedative relaxed his tortured mind and offered him merciful oblivion. His body calmed, and a lone tear snaked from his vacant stare.

The attendants released their hold and fell back on tired haunches to catch a breath. A medic examined the wounds, applied first aid, and prepared Denis for transport to the hospital. Nervous calm descended on the other patients as they slowly recovered from the disturbance. Most resumed their places at the table, but others were too distraught to eat. Orderlies wheeled Denis out of the dining room on a gurney. His departure from the institution was broadcast by the fading wail of an ambulance's siren.

I wasn't aware Denis had been readmitted to the psychiatric hospital. No one shared that information until after his suicide attempt. The news of it hit me like a hammer's blow. I soon realized how severely and quickly Denis's situation could change. My initial reaction was disbelief.

Denis was alive, sedated, and recuperating. The knife's blunt edge hadn't ripped into his vital organs. For his own protection, doctors were keeping him restrained to a hospital bed. The sedatives helped mellow his anxiety, though nothing could make him look less vulnerable.

Denis convalesced in a different hospital, in a different city. The failed suicide attempt would hang over him like a dark cloud. As if he needed more challenges to manage. My parents and I stood at his bedside, helpless and bewildered. We didn't know what to say, how to say it, or when to remain silent. Our nervous presence, which he interpreted as unified disappointment in him, only added to his discomfort. We were clueless as to the depth of his despair. None of us had ever been on a journey such as his, and we had no idea how to react to it. We were chickens under hypnosis, pecking out of sequence, ridiculous to observe. Fortunately for Denis, we weren't the guides designated to steer him toward recovery and stability.

Professionals treated his body and medicated his mind. The process was slow and complicated. After his physical wounds healed, he was brought from the hospital to another group home, where he was observed and cared for.

His progress was evident in the way he responded to us. He became easy with his surroundings and relaxed enough to appreciate a good joke. Knowing he was improving calmed our fears. We didn't get so uptight around him, which helped settle his anxiety even more.

"How do you like living here? Is it better than your last place?"

"I miss my friends in North Battleford. But I don't miss the workshop. They had me doing stuff a six-year-old could do. I want something better."

"You don't need to worry about that. You can make your home here instead. Maybe look at taking some courses at the university. That should give you a better way to use your head."

"Yeah, I'd like to try that."

Denis became more confident and less agitated and isolated. He religiously consumed the drug cocktail prescribed to him. He explored the city and made friends. He met a girl and embarked on a new relationship. He adopted a different perspective, which helped heal his wounds.

Saskatoon is known as the Paris of the Prairies, Stoon, and Bridge City. If the province could grow body parts, Saskatoon would be the heart. On a map, road lines radiate from the centre of a large dot resembling a starburst in the centre of Saskatchewan. They lead to and from the city in all directions like arteries—which explains how it got its other name, Hub City.

If there is a contest, Saskatoon wins the award for being the pretty city. It has class, with natural and historic features.

It is a city of progressive thinkers who promote the arts and education.

Denis's appreciation of academics fit it well, so he adopted Saskatoon as his new home. He settled into a respectable routine. He relaxed and felt more secure about his future. Every so often, he was shuffled between group homes, which meant more adjusting and adapting. He resolved to make the transitions, and for the most part, things worked out for him.

One of his new homes, however, was less than suitable. The group home was managed by some rather exuberant evangelical Christians. They provided all the necessities, but their focus extended beyond serving the basic needs of the unfortunate. Their mission was to win souls to the Lord.

Perhaps Denis proclaiming to be the Antichrist didn't go over so well, or maybe his standard of reverence didn't meet their satisfaction. Whatever the cause, one wintery day in November 1980, they abruptly evicted Denis, turning him out on the street.

He wasn't alarmed he'd been kicked out. Denis took the abuse as if it were a regular occurrence. The street was no stranger to him, though he preferred not sleeping on park benches or taking up residence in cardboard condos. He used his cunning to work out a survival plan.

Saskatoon was a college town, home to many intellectuals and scholars. On the day he was evicted, Denis was dressed in a decent suit that fit relatively well. A pair of new, dark-framed eyeglasses and a not-too-scruffy beard gave him the look of an eccentric professor. He took his almost distinguished look to an upscale restaurant, where they seated him appropriately by himself, at a table for two.

He perused the menu and ordered according to his extravagant taste. All evening, he sipped and nibbled, and dabbed his lips with an elegant linen napkin. He made the occasional trek to the washroom, but mostly he sat quietly, enjoying the pleasant atmosphere of the dining room.

"How was everything?" a genteel waiter inquired.

Denis looked up from the table and answered, "It was good."

"Will there be anything else?"

"Yes, more coffee."

The waiter had lost count of refills several cups ago and was wearing a trail on the carpet between Denis's table and the kitchen. The restaurant management had become suspicious of their curious patron, who remained comfortably seated at his table long after other customers had left for the night. With closing time fast approaching, the waiter attempted to extract payment from the wacky professor. He placed the bill on Denis's table and asked, "How would you like to pay—cash or credit card?"

"May I have a moment to decide?"

"Certainly." The server took a step back and held his position.

His proximity had no effect on Denis's composure. Denis resumed smoking his cigarette and consuming coffee with an indifference not uncommon to the traits of his condition. If any discomfort resulted, it belonged to the waiter.

Denis eventually responded, "I may have misplaced my wallet."

The waiter raised his eyebrows, nodded his head a couple times, spun stiffly on his heel, and returned to the kitchen. He informed the restaurant manager. The manager advised him, "Call the police."

Officers arrived on the scene. Without resistance or drama, Denis allowed himself to be escorted outside to the waiting police cruiser. They arrived at the jailhouse and brought Denis into the station. The policemen scratched their heads, trying to fathom the easy composure of their newest criminal. They filed the paperwork, gave him a blanket, and led him to a private cell. Denis laid on the cot, removed his glasses, and retired for the night.

Denis read the manner in which the officers treated him, as proper etiquette for a bellhop accommodating an important guest. He appreciated the gesture. All in all, he scored a rewarding outcome consisting of adequate sustenance and shelter. Denis had fared as well as or better than most in similar predicaments.

Between 1981 and 1987, Denis's situation began moving in a positive direction. Within a couple of years he gained autonomy. Being able to live independently marked a huge milestone for him.

He moved into a one-room apartment and furnished it with items collected from Goodwill. Some pieces he bought at a bargain, if the cost fit his budget. He salvaged treasures from the trash people discarded. He acquired two old TV sets that had technical problems. One he used for video and the other for audio. Between the two, he had the benefit of a fully functioning television set. The apartment represented the freedom so long beyond his reach. The space wasn't a castle, but it was at least his.

During this favourable stretch, Denis and his girlfriend became husband and wife. They solidified their commitment with a quiet ceremony. It had been a long and arduous road for them, and no two people were more deserving of authentic joy. They each battled their own psychological demons, and their loyalty to each other, in spite of the struggles, remained solid. Their devotion showed in the caring way they constantly held hands.

Then, Denis found a new place that offered him dignity and security.

Crocus Co-op was a member-run organization that provided a safe and welcoming environment for persons facing psychological challenges. In 1983, the organization opened its doors in downtown Saskatoon. It gave clients a place to drop by and hang out. The centre offered a haven for social interaction to persons suffering mental illness, without fear of intimidation.

It became a daily ritual for Denis and his wife to drop in at Crocus Co-op to offer their services, meet with friends over a meal or coffee, or simply hang out. Denis attended workshops and learned skills to help with the centre's day-to-day operations. He used his training in accounting and office management to assist with administration. His ambition was put to good use, and his outlook on life continued to improve.

Denis gained the sense of purpose that had long eluded him. The ability to say, *This is where I belong*, and believe it, held deeper meaning for someone in his position. To Denis, Crocus Co-op was the home where his other family resided.

Each morning, as soon as the centre opened its doors, people converged in the open area. They brought their hope and loneliness. The place was a safe alternative to the streets, and for many, it was the only escape from the elements. At the same time, it attracted worrisome characters.

The nature of the centre's function drew all kinds of individuals. Caseworkers had to be flexible and experienced, and they needed a high level of tolerance to ensure harmony was maintained. They had to be skilled in conflict resolution and, in some circumstances, defuse sudden severe clashes.

Generally they settled situations before they could escalate, but there was the occasional exception.

On a cool spring night in 1987, an embittered client was planning to cause trouble. He had a grudge against someone or about something that had happened inside the walls of Crocus Co-op. He couldn't overlook the slight, so he had plotted to get even.

A blaze lit up the city centre that night. It glowed as bright as the sun, and it fed on the remnants of an important structure. Firefighters worked to douse its appetite, but the fiery tongues licked at them, too. The flames pushed them back, and soon there was nothing left of the building worth salvaging.

By morning, the fire had totally destroyed Crocus Co-op. People hoping to visit their favourite hangout gazed upon its ruins. Denis, along with the others, stood by, stunned by the loss of their shelter.

TV crews were on site to report the devastation. Reporters described a rundown of events leading up to the fire. The publicity and exposure helped shed light on the plight of persons suffering from mental illness.

The report instigated a human-interest story. It was filmed by a local TV station, and depicted the dismal state of living with the stigma of mental illness. At the centre of the piece was a comprehensive interview with an active client. His name was Denis. They filmed him in his home. He sat at a decrepit kitchen table, nursing a cup of coffee. Across the table, a reporter scrawled notes as Denis gave a candid narrative of a day in the life.

The segment ended with a film shot of a stocky, bearded man wearing a timeworn suit and taking a pull off a cigarette while inspecting the charred remains of a once-influential structure.

CHAPTER FIVE — THE SECOND TIME

And I've been down on Earth and in this town
And I swear there's got to be something better
Headstones
"Three Angels"

The second time I contemplated suicide was during a bout of depression—only I didn't know I was depressed. I had no knowledge of the term for the condition. I was thirty years old, considering dying might be the way to fix my despair.

I hadn't put myself into another abusive situation. I was actually doing fine and making a life for myself. I had gone back to school and gotten a good job in agricultural research. I spent summer days working outdoors, tending field plots and using electronics for data collection. I maintained automated weather stations and installed sensors for measuring soil temperatures and moisture content. In the winter, I was in charge of bringing labs and offices up to date with new technology. I learned to program and interface scientific equipment with computers and other devices. My work life was interesting and challenging.

I bought a car and a house and managed to save some money—everything was working out well financially. My son was growing into a fine, decent young man. He excelled in academics. I gave him extra push to participate in sports because I knew the benefits of recreation and team play. I burst with pride watching him compete, amazed by his confidence and success.

Life was moving along the right track, but I couldn't reconcile with the darkness that often overwhelmed me. I considered that surviving was easy, and thriving was not. From the outside, my life seemed to be proceeding smoothly, at a comfortable pace. So why were my inner workings veering off onto a side road?

I knew I couldn't follow through with a plan to kill myself. I had my boy to look after. I needed to believe in the possibility of positive change, and I felt the only way to accomplish that was to move closer to losing everything and hopefully emerge with a brand-new outlook on life.

I decided to avoid the finality of suicide by making a compromise—I thought it necessary to reach the brink. I contemplated downing a bottle of aspirin, but settled on half a bottle. I knew it wouldn't kill me. I didn't need to die—only to see the edge.

The detour was surreal and emotionless—kind of blank, actually. I poured tablets, four or five at a time, into my hand and chased them down my throat with a glass of rum and coke. The flavour and texture were just as I remembered—bland grit with a chalky aftertaste. I didn't gag. There was no drama. Then, I simply waited.

I was alone and free of distraction. The house was quiet, and I didn't have to think about anything—especially consequences.

It took a while for the dope to take effect. My head started to feel thick, like I was wearing a too-tight headband. The effect of the medication worsened, and my thoughts blurred. Water molecules crashed against my eardrums, and all I could hear was the dull roar of sloshing liquid, which was both loud and muffled, with a pulsating echo. I felt pressure against the back of my eyes, so I closed them tight. I lay down to rest, trying to calm the ruckus inside my skull. Eventually, I succumbed to a sleep that was busy with drunken dreams.

I awoke to a new kind of morning-after. I felt hungover, without the stink of stale liquor. For the next few days, I functioned as close to ordinary as I could manage. The thick inside my head gradually eased. The brain fog diminished and clarity came back. No one suspected my little escapade, and I was glad they hadn't recognized the sham. I think I would have been more embarrassed than ashamed had anyone learned the truth.

I'm not sure what I expected, but I received no epiphany. I heard no voice through the clouds telling me everything would be OK. I didn't gain anything other than more of the same. Basically, I got zilch. If anything, my mock suicide should have scared me, but nothing about it caused me concern. However, the experience ensured that next time, I wouldn't be making compromises.

I didn't totally abandon the idea of suicide, but I decided to store it away until a more appropriate time. I would only revisit the decision under certain conditions; that I was no longer needed or useful, that I was unable to rise out of my despair, or that my pain had escalated to more than I could bear.

Suicide became my plan B—an exit strategy on the back-burner until required.

CHAPTER SIX — IMPLOSIONS

Through these fields of destruction, baptisms of fire
I've witnessed your suffering, as the battle raged higher
Dire Straits
"Brothers in Arms"

February1976

Denis walked in through the door of the pub. It was midafternoon, and he'd just arrived from working his part-time job at the rink in Makwa. He needed a refreshment to reward himself for shovelling snow off the ice for the second time that day. Mitch was still in school, and couldn't uphold his share of the caretaking deal. It would be another half hour before he'd be free to lend a hand.

Denis stomped the snow off his boots before approaching John, who sat alone at a table by the jukebox. The silly smile on John's face revealed that he'd had a head start on drinks.

"Sit down," he said. "I'll buy you a beer." He signalled to the bartender for a pair of Pilsners.

Denis raised his eyebrows. "OK. With whose money?"

"Funny you should ask. Can you lend me some? I'm a little short this week."

Denis fished in his pocket for cash to pay the waitress for the drinks John had ordered. She dropped the change on the table, and Denis grabbed a couple quarters to feed the jukebox. He selected tunes by the Rolling Stones and BTO. Denis sat down and took a sip from a brown bottle—but not before John raised his in salutation.

"To long life and short skirts."

John got up from his chair and ambled over to a pool table situated at the far end of the barroom. He racked the balls and grabbed a couple of cues. He brought one to Denis and challenged him to a game: "Wanna play?"

"Sure."

"You break."

Denis lit himself a smoke before chalking the stick. He studied the table to determine where to place the cue ball. He aimed head on and sent coloured balls flying in all directions across the green felt, sinking none.

John asked him, "So, what you do at that workshop in Battleford?"

"I help make work aprons and wedding decorations, mostly."

"Is it good pay?"

"No."

John rubbed his chin and pondered his first shot. "So, why don't you find something else, then?"

"Like what? Do brain surgery?"

The boys put their heads in the game, with John sinking several balls. More green space opened up as the competition progressed. Soon, they landed most of the balls in the pockets, with few left on top.

"I'm going to work on the rigs. Rod thinks he can get me on his crew," John shared while taking aim.

"Good. Then you can pay back the money I keep loaning you."

John smiled and sunk the eight ball, winning the game.

"Want another game?" John asked.

"Yeah."

"And we need another beer," John added.

John missed a couple of shots on the second game, and Denis lucked out with good positioning of his stripes. He didn't leave John many decent shots, and soon Denis won the game.

A couple guys John recognized entered the bar. They sat down and ordered drinks. John picked up his beer and joined them at their table, leaving Denis on his own.

It wasn't unusual for the two to part ways when better options crossed their paths. Denis didn't take it as a snub. He would do it himself in a hot second, but it didn't mean one wished the other ill fortune.

I don't recall any specific moments of excessive or thoughtful brotherly interaction between John and Denis. They never seemed to find enough common ground to have that type of relationship. Each had his own conflicts to contend with, and their paths to coping seldom crossed.

It was as though they were magnets with similar polarities, often resisting each other's space. They had no interests in common, and few shared concerns to relate to one another. Neither could empathize with the other. There was a measure of animosity between them for a while, so they steered clear of each other as a general rule.

I inherited a black-and-white photo of them together. The image was captured one summer, probably just before my family moved to town. Denis was about five years old, which means John would have been around a year and a half. A scar like a blister belt ringed the side of John's little potbelly, a remnant from the surgery he'd had the year before.

They looked playful in the photo, grinning, with twinkle eyes. Behind them a clothesline was laden with wet laundry. It hung like a curtain between them and the bush line surrounding the farmyard. They were carefree and shirtless, and the sun was shining bright. They looked to be having an outdoor bath and it didn't matter if water splashed over the side of the washtub.

The camera lens focused on their fun. The shutter blinked and captured two lively youngsters at play. The snapshot held them inside a quiver of time, and if I fix hard enough on Denis's stare-back eyes, I can bring the moment back to life.

Emil

Saskatchewan amazes with big sky. The expanse dominates, and on a clear, still night, it provides remarkable serenity. Summer warmth permits late-night callers to linger beneath it. During the worst of winter's dark, nights aren't so accommodating, and that's when cold delivers a bite through to the bone. Spring and autumn give everything between the two extremes, but few nights make a body want to stay and keep its companionship—unless one has fortitude to endure it or nowhere else to go.

Emil's evenings were quiet, possibly quieter than he preferred, so he watched for John to arrive home from the hotel bar. He waited for a sign that John might spend some time in the backyard, maybe even fire up the barbecue. It was a good night if Emil didn't have to spend it alone.

During summer, the sun's glow didn't sink completely below the skyline. A band of teal and turquoise glimmered on the horizon, and the sky featured a picture show of perpetual sunset or sunrise. Most times, John was game for extending the night. Perhaps he ran out of beer money or was kicked out of the bar after getting on bad terms with another patron. As long as the weather held out, adequate warm clothes were available, and appetites were worked up, John and Emil took advantage of pleasant surroundings and broke bread together.

Their association was simple—two guys with nothing better to do and no better place to be. They kept the grill warm so it cooked the food and radiated heat. They each gleaned comfort from the arrangement—John could speak his piece without interruptions, and Emil didn't have to be alone.

Uncle Emil was the audience to John's nonsensical ramblings, which were commonly fuelled by spirits. John's deep, gravelly laughter cut the night's calm with the occasional snort at the telling of his own joke. He kept Uncle amused and alert. Emil wasn't a passive listener—he hung on every word. Uncle's chuckles were punctual, but he could never fully grasp the punchline.

As autumn 1989 approached, the weather became too unpleasant for John and Emil to hang outdoors. John put away the barbecue and lawn chairs for the winter. It bothered Uncle to watch John dismantle their meeting spot, but it was something he would need to accept. Tarrying outdoors lost its appeal, and it forced them to take a temporary break from their comfortable habit.

By late March 1990, the sun was rising earlier and bedding later, like a candle burning brighter at both ends. The boost of extra daylight was unmistakable, promising the return of warmer weather. Evenings still had a bite to them, though.

Stargazing wasn't tolerable for extended periods. It was best to stay inside, guarded against the cold, and safe, until winter's sting lost its punch.

Emil wandered still. Nights were too quiet and too long to spend alone. Better to find a home where he was welcome to sit for a while. Uncle wasn't a bother. He was a straight-up kind of guy who didn't impose himself on others. He was happy to be in the midst of friends or family. A hot cup of coffee was all Emil asked of his host, but most were quick to offer him a slice of pie, a cookie, or even a meal. Emil was happy to accept.

One night, he opted to trek a little further up the highway. He ventured west about a quarter of a mile out of town to visit his sister at her home. It was on an acreage, surrounded by a small forest of tall evergreens.

There was always risk walking along highway in the dark, but if Emil kept to the shoulder, essentially in the ditch, he was safe enough. Headlights from oncoming vehicles blinded him momentarily, but traffic was rarely heavy. Most times, he could plug along, enjoying the view of the night sky by himself, unless a stray dog decided to keep him company.

It was an easy hike up the hill. The night air was crisp but pleasant. Emil slogged onward, hoofing it up the highway, turning onto the driveway and making his way to the door. There was no need to knock or wait to be invited in—it was normal for him to simply enter.

He sat and drank his coffee, watched TV along with the family, and simply observed as they went about their routine. A couple lazy hours passed, with scant words exchanged, and then it was time to go. He went through the rigmarole of putting all his winter garb back on, and out the door he went, into the night.

Emil didn't make it back home that night. Morning came, and his bed hadn't been slept in. It wasn't like him to be away for so long. An eerie calm settled in the empty space at the table, where he should have been downing his first cup of morning coffee. His absence prompted a search around town. Calls on neighbours amounted to naught. Emil had left no clues to indicate his whereabouts. Concerns mounted. Uncle Dan called the Mounties, requesting assistance.

"Who was the last person to see him?" they asked.

"Can you describe what he was wearing?"

"Could he have gone somewhere else instead?"

His disappearance was as much a mystery as a shock.

The search began at the last known place where Emil was seen. Officers questioned my aunt, who informed them of what time he had left her home: "It was around ten-thirty last night. He went out the back door, and it looked like he was heading home."

"Was anyone else in the yard? Did you hear anything?"

"There was nothing. The dog didn't even bark."

The police walked the stretch of highway looking for clues, but found none. They returned to the yard and widened their search. It was as though Emil had never left the acreage.

They found a lone set of footprints in the snow, leading off the driveway onto the rough, past the machine shop and into the forest. One of the officers remarked, "Looks like he might have gone into the woods from here."

The trek through forest wasn't an uncommon route for Emil to consider for any season other than winter. The path to town was shorter and more direct cutting through bush. There were trails in the woods, and Emil was familiar with them. But that year, there were obstacles making the hike especially difficult. Construction crews had felled trees the previous summer to widen ditch and roadway. The crew had dragged razed timber into the forest and dropped the logs clumsily onto and across trails. Snow accumulation on the forest floor would have made it hard for Emil to locate the path.

Officers retraced Emil's footsteps, which spilled an account of the night before. Tracks snaked to the edge of forest and paused, as though considering direction. The footpath would have been hidden to him, concealed somewhere beneath the white blanket. There were no markers tipping off the trail's location.

Emil's footsteps entered the forest. Large boot prints had broken through the crunchy surface of thin ice and sunken into dry, beady snow. Deer tracks crisscrossed them, poking more holes through the snow's upper crust. They led in and out of the woods, and didn't favour any particular route.

Maybe a gamble, maybe on instinct or recall—boot tracks pushed eastward toward home. The clearing gave way to woodland and horizon vanished. On that night, a ceiling of clouds veiled a crescent moon, casting a darkish gloom. Ice crystals draped the forest in a misty fog, softening edges and reducing visibility. It could have been, for Emil, like stepping into a dream.

Emil's tracks revealed grim details. Signs indicated he fell trying to step over an obstacle. Instead of turning back, he had circled around it and continued further into the belly of the forest. A second hurdle in his path had caused him to hesitate and scope out a new direction. Uncle chanced a few steps to one side and retraced them. He ventured down a different line and then another until he chose what looked like a passable route.

It would have been a struggle, trudging through deep snow—especially for a sizeable man like Emil. At sixty years old, he didn't have a sedentary lifestyle. If he needed to get somewhere, he walked the distance. Even so, this particular hike would have been difficult.

He'd snagged his foot on a distended tree root buried beneath the white carpet. He landed hard on the ground. His flailing arms and legs carved a snow bowl in the powder, a hint of his growing exhaustion. On hands and knees, Emil crawled for a bit—and then he paused and thrashed another hollow in the snow. The effort flushed him—sweat glistened on his skin. Hot breath escaped his lungs, vapour haloed his face. He furrowed a third snow crater and rested. Uncle gathered himself and continued on foot. He dropped a lone mitten and left behind a spectacle of failed snow angels.

He had strayed off course, aiming deeper into the bush instead of toward the edge. The exertion took its toll, and Emil's progress stalled. Officers followed the trail made by his faltering gait to where the track stopped cold. He had fallen, with finality, landing facedown into the icy embrace of a snowdrift.

Rescue attempts no longer mattered. He had reached the end alone in the wild. Sometime during the night, beneath a murky canopy, a ruthless forest reclaimed peace and tranquility. It had denied thoroughfare to a gentle soul, depriving him of light and direction, and abruptly stilled his once beating heart.

The autopsy would reveal he'd had a massive heart attack. The one thing the autopsy couldn't explain was why Emil had opted to take such a difficult route. Perhaps a person's end is predetermined, and fate leads like a seeing-eye angel of death. Maybe he felt something primal—a fundamental drive to reach home—so he passed through a portal to the next life.

That night, beyond logic and reason, he passed, and a small community went into mourning.

John

The first step to planning a funeral in the Catholic tradition is to secure the services of a priest. There weren't many left in Northern Saskatchewan. One priest came to the parish about once a month. But for the purpose of burial rites, he made himself available. A date was set, and the priest accommodated it.

A few family members visited the funeral home, where they picked out a casket, chose the flowers, penned the obit, and left clothes for Emil to be buried in. They paid the director a fat wad of cash for his services. As the group was leaving the funeral home, one of them made a remark: "Maybe we should remind him to fuel up the hearse."

The family bought a burial plot and had the grave dug. Auntie booked the church and selected hymns and scripture readings. Another auntie planned the prayer vigil and arranged for an organist, a leader of song, someone to give the eulogy, and two people to do the readings. Mom arranged for six pallbearers, and lined up a caterer for the funeral lunch. The costs added up, and they paid with more cash.

Neighbours and friends delivered food to the house. Mom and I organized the limited fridge space to store it all. People also brought heartfelt condolences. It was comforting to learn how much Emil had impacted the community.

An influx of relatives came from out of town to attend Uncle's funeral. Family opened their homes to them and made spare beds available, though they spent more time sharing memories and sitting up late than sleeping. Drinks and food were standard elements of family socials, whether the occasion was sombre or not. That's the way gatherings went. Stories were rehashed, and relatives brought up details of past encounters. We forgot about sadness and embraced jocularity instead.

Rod recalled a time we were at Grandpa's and our car couldn't make it to the road. "Do you remember when we got stuck in deep snow leaving Grandpa's farm, and we thought we needed the horses to help pull us out?"

Dad joined the conversation: "That was in January 1966, when it snowed like hell. But we didn't use the horses ... Emil pushed us out—practically by himself."

"Man, that boy was strong."

"As strong as a horse, for sure."

Pauly reminded us, "He didn't want anyone using the horses to do hard work. Those were his pets, you know."

Uncle Dan pulled a beer from a twelve-pack, popped off its cap with an opener, and handed it to Dad. Dan wanted to make sure everyone had a drink to toast his big brother. "This one's for Emil. I hope he finds a ranch up there, so he can keep looking after the horses."

Another uncle called Armand, who owned the general store in the village, told us about Emil's shopping practices. Grandma used to send Emil to the store to pick up groceries. Uncle Armand explained, "He'd come in the store and wander around, checking things out. I knew Mémé sent him to pick up food."

He took a swig of beer, leaned forward, and continued: "You know, that sneaky bugger, he never had more than a two-dollar bill in his wallet. He figured he didn't need to spend it."

Armand looked around to make sure everyone was paying attention.

"So, he'd ask for things like bread, bologna, and butter . . . the usual stuff. Then, he'd add cigarettes and candy to the order. I didn't think that was strange, since Mémé smoked and kept a stash of treats for the kids. I put them on Mémé's tab. She always paid at the end of the month when she got her old age cheque."

A few chuckled, sensing where the story was going.

"All hell broke loose when she came to pay the tab. She thought I was padding the bill. After that, she phoned in her grocery list, and Emil had to pay for his own damn smokes and candy."

My cousin initiated another group toast: "To Uncle Emil . . . the best damn bologna sandwich-maker, ever."

Each took a turn coming up with more tributes to Emil. A few deferred to toasting with water, others didn't.

Uncle Emil's prayer vigil ran on the eve of the funeral. Some of us tore ourselves away from socializing to attend it. Stragglers procrastinated and never made an appearance—for some, other spirits ranked higher than those of the religious kind. A few kept busy all night indulging in the liquid variety.

St. Thomas Roman Catholic Church stands at the junction of Highway 304 and Church Avenue at the heart of Makwa, Saskatchewan. The structure is sturdy enough for an old building. It looks as if it could have been a dance hall, except it has a steeple. It holds as many as one hundred church goers for Mass. Inside is mostly wood finish. Floorboards creak under the weight of footsteps. The climb up squawking stairs to the choir loft is reminiscent of a scene from the movie *The Hunchback of Notre Dame.*

Besides darkish woodwork, the church has religious-themed art on its walls. Gospel chronicles, set in colourful mosaic tile, help brighten the dusky nave. In stark contrast, the front area is radiant, with ornate mouldings, beams, and walls painted white. The rich mouldings frame the altar, amplifying a space considered holy. A vaulted ceiling gives the impression of a heavenly realm, even as heating costs hit the roof every winter.

The entrance occupies the back of the church. People coming into the church face the altar. A centre aisle extends toward the altar between two rows of pews. A hard right, just inside the vestibule, puts visitors at the doorway to the cubbyhole confessional. The little cubicle is wedged into the underside of the choir-loft stairs.

As if first in line for confession, the casket holding Emil's body was situated in front of the confessional. People passed it as they entered the church. Some paused before the casket, possibly to whisper a final goodbye to a gentle friend. Others filed by, teary-eyed at the sight of their sleeping giant.

The church pews filled—friends on the right side, family on the left, and one bench reserved at the front for pallbearers. As people filed into the church, organ music played, keeping the mood solemn. The smell of melting wax wafted from candles lit in remembrance of loved ones already gone.

The priest, pallbearers, and family lingered in the vestibule. There was a delay, so the start of the funeral stalled. One pallbearer was noticeably absent. The others checked their watches and requested a few moments to accommodate John's late arrival.

Earlier on, we hadn't been able to rouse John—but not for lack of trying. He was numb to our goading, and completely passed out at home in bed. We couldn't get a mumble out of him. We left for church hoping he would come to on his own. The best we could do was to buy him some time.

Eventually we had to concede he was a no-show. Rod was recruited to stand in for John as pallbearer. By the time the casket was lowered into the frozen hollow and covered and people had dispersed from the funeral lunch, John was beginning to climb out of his inebriation. He'd made it as far as the bathroom. Afterward, he returned to the bedroom, locking himself inside.

It was shame that kept John closed to the world—it was part of the addiction package. He'd wanted to follow through with being pallbearer for Uncle Emil. I knew what it meant to him. But the liquor was too readily available, company was too accommodating, limits weren't imposed, and morning came too soon.

My brothers and I tried to draw him out, but he kept himself hidden. We pressed him, hoping he would open up and let us in. I wanted to reassure him we weren't upset with him, that we simply wanted him to be with us.

"John? Could you open the door, please?"

"Come downstairs and get some food."

"There's no point beating yourself up. It won't change things."

Perhaps I should have said, "Uncle's OK now. He's earned his rest."

There was no consoling John. His mind was made up, and his stubbornness had more stamina than we had time.

For most of us, the days went back to normal. We returned home to work, play, or study. We accepted our loss and found closure. We'd never forget, but we would move forward. For John, the rebound wasn't so simple. The stinger remained lodged, the potency of its venom undiminished. Grief would prove to be one hard bitch for him to get past.

It was easy to see that John was disgusted with himself for not getting his drunk ass out of bed that day. He realized with contempt that he was late—too late for the funeral and too late to save Uncle. Knowing Emil had nowhere else to be on the night he disappeared likely added to John's despair.

Perhaps the reality of missing Emil's funeral played in his mind like a constant rerun of a bad scene. His thirst escalated, as if he could score redemption at the bottom of a whiskey jar. He seemed to have one goal: drink Emil's death out of his memory.

Spring arrived, and ditches filled with runoff. Water seeped from the underside of shrinking snowdrifts and found the easy path to creeks and rivers. The sun intensified its potential to provide heat.

John might have dreaded the return of spring. It meant there would be no easy companionship at the barbeque after a night at the bar. Was it the pain of spending evenings alone in the backyard that caused him to revisit old habits?

Late-night binge drinking ended on a different note now that Emil was gone. No more firing up the barbecue and placating his hunger. Instead, John got behind the wheel of his four-door beater.

The old Plymouth had its mechanical challenges—a broken shifter jimmy-rigged with vise grips and a tall screwdriver to bypass the whacked starter solenoid. But the body and motor were in relatively good shape. He gunned the engine to make big noise and cover ample distance.

He cruised empty streets, claiming a semblance of control by being the lone traveller. He tackled the road with vengeance, burning U-turns, pitching gravel bullets, and carving tire troughs across lanes. He caused disturbances that drew attention and soon resulted in serious alcohol-related charges. He pushed the patience of the law and received a summons to appear in court.

The outlook wasn't good. A stay at what John called the crowbar hotel was the likely outcome. He had a couple of months to think about it before facing the judge.

We came home for Easter, Mitch and I with our families. The house was full. Mom busied herself making sure we settled in, and Dad doled out fivers to the grandkids. Our visit provided John a break from hanging out at the pub.

I always felt good returning home. Stresses vanished the moment I crossed the threshold. The easy, slow pace of home soothed me like balm. I revisited the best parts of childhood and reinvented time, as though the pages of a calendar could reattach themselves, or a clock's hands could spin backwards.

Once again, we made elbow room for ourselves at the crowded supper table. We passed food platters between us and heaped our plates with good home cooking. We shared news and stories between bites, our gab in constant competition with chewing.

"Did I tell you about the time Grandpa made me a wooden bicycle?" Mitch was stringing together a new tall tale for his girls. Their brows furrowed with skepticism.

"Sure Dad."

Some were doubtful of most of his chronicles. Yarning was a skill he had perfected, laying out his tales straight-faced, with a playful squint. "It was the same time he made us wooden shoes to wear," he added.

"Did they give you splinters on your blisters walking home from school?" Someone just had to ask.

"No, because I rode my bike. You know, the wooden one?"

"So you got splinters on your ass, then."

"Don't say 'ass' in front of the kids."

A kid echoed with a snicker, "Ass."

The confabulations continued even as we cleared away dishes and cleaned up the kitchen. With all the reminiscing, our hunger for nostalgia moved us to search out old haunts. After supper, we embarked on a group stroll through town—everyone except Dad, who wasn't into walks. He nursed a tepid cup of coffee in front of the TV instead.

The kids led the way, traipsing figure-eights up and down streets and avenues. We managed to cover the entire town with ease. Points of interest caught the kids' attention from time to time, and we dallied at bridges that spanned creeks running through town. We paused while the kids exhausted themselves throwing rocks into the rushing water.

We reached the school at the same time the janitor arrived. She gave us permission to roam the hallways.

It was an old habit to remove outer footwear at the entrance—a rule we followed during our schooldays. The boot rack jarred a memory from when I was seven. I was leaving for home after class when I discovered that my boots had marched out the door without me. Losing them made me upset. I was so proud to get new winter boots, which were a huge upgrade from my beat-up galoshes. The only boots left on the rack were of a similar style to my new ones, except they looked old as dirt. I vaguely remember thinking, "Who took my new boots and left these crappy ones?"

I didn't know how I would explain the sudden aging of my new boots to Mom and Dad. The loss didn't go unnoticed, and no one blamed me. Even so, it was one anxious night for me. At school the next day, I went on a hunt for them, and found them on the boot rack. Somehow they reappeared, but

I wasn't comfortable leaving them out of my sight even for a moment, so I kept them in my book bag.

Mitch and John recalled some of their own school memories. They shared stories about times they had spent in the principal's office, and their lame attempts to hide from the principal in the boys' bathroom. Mitch showed us where he used to climb into the ventilation duct of his homeroom. He hid in the empty space between the walls, screened by the grilles that separated two rooms. He surveyed the lesson in the adjacent classroom without being noticed. Meanwhile, the teacher fussed over the unexplained disappearance of a student.

John pointed out the spot where his nose may have left a permanent imprint on the wall in the hallway. I remember having to press my nose against the wall once or twice for misbehaving in class. The worst was when other kids walked past and laughed at me. John's worst part was the nun coming out of class and catching him out of pose. He was either sitting down or wandering the corridor, and he got a yardstick across the backside for it.

We left the school, and spent the rest of the evening in the backyard. Mitch brought sparklers for the kids. There was a trick to igniting them that required persistence. The kids patiently waited for us to light their sparklers, and then they ran around the yard, waving them in the dark. Tiny shards of light shot off the end of their wands, looking like fairies dancing low to the ground.

Mitch tied a string to the end of a sparkler, lit it, twirled it above his head, and let it fly. It gained altitude and wrapped itself around unseen power lines. The lines sparked from a power surge. For a moment, we thought we had caused an outage, but then the power held and settled.

The sparkler dangled from its lofty perch, firing tiny, flaming arrows, lighting up the night. It looked like a lone star had chosen to visit us up close and share its brightness with us for a while. A dog ran past, barking up a fuss at the light show. John called it over: "Here, boy."

The dog kept barking, so John went to it, knelt beside it, and rubbed the back of its neck. The dog leaned into him, welcoming the affection.

It's surreal to remember John from that time. He always wore a baseball cap, its beak-like visor set low to shade his eyes, as though to mask dark, sad features. The glitter raining off the sparkler looked like a veil of tiny embers above his head.

We watched as the mini torch burned itself out. The night grew silent, and we went inside to get ready for bed.

Quiet might have descended like thick fog blanketing the house after Mitch and I left with our families. Perhaps it deepened John's anxiety, and the memory of past struggles returned to haunt him. Pressures that he was able to stave off for a while might have resurfaced.

It had been three years since the accident on the rigs when John lost his four front teeth. The pipe that struck him on the mouth had left more than a physical wound. His body had healed, but he had lost his nerve working on the rig floor. He hesitated in his duties and caused minor mishaps. Drillers didn't see slipups as minor. They ran him off a couple of times, and he was banned from working certain rigs.

He was rarely employed anymore, and his savings had quickly dwindled. At thirty-three years old, he no longer had the strength and stamina for hard work. Drinking to excess was taking a toll on his body. With too much time reflecting on his situation, his mental state had declined.

I imagined he felt the world closing in on him as he fought to hide from it. The upcoming trial for too many DUI offenses tormented him. His back was up against a wall facing potential incarceration. Alcohol helped him cope with the loneliness and the fear, but it couldn't change his situation. And when the alcohol failed to provide an escape, he selected a different course.

It made sense that he chose a location that reminded him of summer evenings and good companionship. Perhaps there was no other place more suitable for his goodbye than the one where he spent so much time sharing meals with a friend.

It was by some kind of amazing grace that no one heard the gunshot, that it was my aunt and not my parents who found him slumped half in and half out of the driver's side of his car, that Auntie kept my parents from discovering his body, and that his death was instantaneous and had left him no time to suffer the wound. Even so, this all was little consolation.

For the second time in less than two months, we arranged a funeral. Despite the stun factor, we managed to work through the details. It was as if Emil's funeral was a trial run to make the process simpler for us.

The church didn't have a cry room to accommodate my family's privacy. The vestibule had limited space—hardly room enough for a small crowd to linger. It was spring, and the day was warm and sunny, so my family waited outside for the funeral to start. A steady stream of friends and neighbours arrived and conveyed care and concern.

I watched the flow of people pass by as if they were riding a slow-moving carousel. I couldn't focus properly, and the motion made their faces blur into one another. People approached and cupped my hand in theirs. They cradled it as if it might break. A few offered kind words, but I couldn't hear them. Many had no words at all. Perhaps there is no language that fits to sort out this odd kind of sorrow.

I wasn't the only one wounded. I could see my parents and siblings were, like me, lost and defeated, stone-faced in their anguish. Words were scarce between us. Our attempts to comfort each other were weak—I suppose we were too overwhelmed to consider each other's pain.

One of the ushers approached us and said, "It's time to go inside."

I watched my brothers help Mom and Dad, as they guided them into the church. It took a moment for me to realize that I was supposed to follow them.

There was a long, low thrum that filled my skull and robbed me of logic. My head felt thick and numb. I worked hard to achieve normal. I concentrated on putting one foot in front of the other to move myself forward, to gauge the church steps without tripping, to open the door and cross the threshold. These things required special effort and attention, and I struggled with their new complexity.

The funeral went according to script, and we complied with wooden composure. The priest looked to be voicing something, but all I saw was the fish-like gape of his mouth sucking and blowing, with no sound escaping. He wasn't speaking to me, so I shut him out. It was easy to do that.

Something like essence or will drained out of me. I could feel emptiness taking residence in the space that used to house my soul. I was dying inside, and I didn't want to be saved.

I couldn't cry . . . I didn't cry . . .

And then I couldn't stop.

Denis

A partial wall stood, blackened and charred, as Denis poked around in the ashes trying to dig up a remnant, a keepsake, a reminder of what Crocus Co-op had once meant to him. City workers barricaded the site to keep looters out, so Denis stood near the edge and reached over the barrier with a stick to stir up debris. Perhaps he was pondering on how to manage his days without a drop-in centre to visit.

In late 1987, the organization found another home. Clients resumed a semblance of familiar within new walls, under a new roof, in a different location. They were able to meet up with old friends again. Some may have been a little nervous at first, fearing the prospect of another blaze.

Denis visited the new venue and re-established a routine. The place provided him stability and helped keep the symptoms of his illness in balance. The fire had rattled the clients, including Denis, but they managed to get past it together.

He might have had a bit of celebrity status for a while after the television interview, but he never played it up. He was very practical in recounting the experience.

"Somebody had to do it" was his no-nonsense comment about the interview. He was modest, recognizing its temporary appeal. Reporters weren't banging on his door to give him more airtime. The hype faded, and Denis went back to just being non-celebrity Denis.

Marriage added joy to Denis's life, but it also brought stress. Both he and his wife struggled with the details of blending their lives. They each brought unique psychological conflicts to the mix, and there was no guide to help them work through the hurdles.

They faced challenges combining their households. Neither had many possessions, and the sharing of their meagre resources sometimes caused friction. Denis was too generous—he gave things away or loaned money to friends who didn't always feel obligated to repay him. It put strain on his household. To his detriment, he kept the Bank of Denis open.

His support cheque barely covered food, rent, and smokes. Saskatchewan Healthcare subsidized his medications, which were expensive. Without the subsidy, he wouldn't have had enough money to meet living expenses.

Mom and Dad were concerned he'd be short on basic necessities. They tried slipping him cash to pay for extras. They urged him, "Take this money and buy yourself a winter coat."

His coat was old and worn. He was thoughtful before he turned down the offer: "Thanks, but I don't think so. The one I have will do me fine."

Denis was honest to a fault. The money was a gift, but he kept reporting it as income to his case worker. Subsequently, the amount of his support cheque was reduced by the same amount of cash given him, and Denis was no better off than before. There seemed to be no getting past that conundrum.

I spent time with Mom and Dad on holidays when I could. On Victoria Day weekend 1988, they decided to visit me instead. Denis came with them, which was kind of sweet, since Denis had never been to my home before. His wife had decided to spend the holiday with her family in Saskatchewan. No one mentioned anything about problems in their marriage, though clues indicated there was.

The first priority for Dad and Denis when they arrived at my house was to light up cigarettes. They were considerate and took their habit outside. I appreciated that they didn't smoke in my house. I set out lawn chairs so they could have a puff in comfort. Mom still indulged, but she didn't light up as often anymore.

It was spring. The snow was gone, the sun was out, and the temperature was very warm. I pulled out the barbeque and fired it up. I grilled some burgers and we feasted. I watched as Denis chowed down a few good portions.

"I don't get to have this very often," he informed us.

I was glad to see him enjoy his meal. I told him, "If the weather holds out, I'll cook steak tomorrow."

"I'll take meat over vegetables any day," he said, as he stacked another bun with cheese, a burger, and condiments. "Did anyone follow the Winter Olympics?"

"Why didn't you try going to Calgary to see them in person?" Mom asked me.

"Too far, too expensive, too little time off, too chicken to drive in a strange city . . . guess it'll never be that close again in my lifetime."

I remembered a long-ago school trip to the Meadow Lake Stampede parade. I was in Grade 1, and the teacher nun said that if she were a parent, she wouldn't have allowed her kid to attend. "A loving parent should keep their child at home" were her exact words.

At the time, I considered what she said, and I determined to prove my mom loved me, so I refused to go. Mom just wanted me to go have fun, and I didn't gain a damn thing by missing the parade.

Mom was still trying to persuade me to live a little: "You could have stayed with Rod. Maybe he could have driven you in to watch."

"Maybe . . . too late now. But the coverage on TV was good."

"We watched Eddie the Eagle. He was the best." Denis described the watch party he had had with his friends. "We even made a poster of an eagle wearing skis, and we hung it on the wall beside the TV."

"That crazy meathead," Dad added. "He could have killed himself coming off that steep jump."

"What about the bobsled team from Jamaica?" I asked.

"We watched them, too," Denis replied. "We cheered for all the underdogs."

I told them about the snow roller race in my yard that happened at the same time as the Games. Curvy trails in the snow revealed a contest of sorts, ending in a scatter of snowballs in the backyard. No one had been throwing snowballs around. It was simply nature's way of playing a trick on us—a weather phenomenon that occurs on rare occasions.

Conditions need to be ideal for snow rollers—temperature, wind, and snowfall work together to trigger self-rolling snowballs. The wind picks up a small hunk of sticky snow, pushes it across the white surface, growing it into a mass of icy fluff. The spectacle is eerie, like watching a dozen invisible children build snowman body parts.

After supper, Alex pulled out the chess board. He challenged Denis to a game. He said to Denis, "You can have white."

"I haven't played in a while. I hope you take it easy on me."

"Don't worry. I can beat Mom, but she's old."

"Not as old as me."

"How old are you?"

"I'm thirty-six."

"Wow, that's old."

The game kept them busy while Mom and I cleaned up the dishes. I brought out a deck of cards and announced, "Time for cards, boys. Come join us when you finish your game . . . unless you're scared of losing to us old people."

We sat around the kitchen table for the rest of the evening playing rummy and thirty-one. It was Dad's night for winning, and he showed us how it was done.

At ten-thirty, I said to Alex, "It's time to go to bed now."

"Aw, Mom. Can we have one more game, please?"

"Only one. It's way past your bedtime."

The final game of thirty-one was a slam-dunk for Alex. He won a fist full of quarters, which made him happy to call it a night.

I assigned sleeping arrangements. "Mom and Dad, you take my room. Denis can sleep in Alex's bed. We're going to rough it on the couch and living room floor."

I was lucky that Alex could sleep basically anywhere and through anything. His easy sleep habit came in handy once, during my college days. I couldn't afford a sitter for a party I was invited to, and the girls putting it on wouldn't take no for an answer. They said to just bring my five-year-old kid along with me to the bash. They said it would be OK.

At this particular gathering, Alex wouldn't let me out of his sight. He absolutely had to be at the centre of the party with me. When Alex was tired, there was no stopping him from getting sleep. There were bedrooms available, but he wasn't interested in occupying one. Eventually, he fell asleep right where he was, directly in front of the biggest damn stereo speaker I had ever seen—and it was blasting rowdy tunes beyond measurable decibels.

A college mate of mine, who was halfway inebriated and feeling no pain, was amazed at Alex's ability to sleep through it all. My friend was Asian and wearing a half-face Einstein mask. He slurred in broken English: "I *rish* I had a mom *rike* you, who teach me how to *pawty*."

With Denis occupying his room, Alex would have no problem sleeping on a makeshift bed on the floor. I took the couch—but not before I made sure our guests were well settled in.

The next morning, I took them out for breakfast. Pancakes were on Alex's mind, and Smitty's had the right kind of menu for all of us. A hungry man omelette suited Denis just fine. Eggs benedict satiated Mom, Dad, and me.

The waitress kept our coffee cups filled—except for Alex, who had chocolate milk. Talk around the table was stifled as we devoured our food. We ate to the sound of tick-ticking cutlery against plates, like finger-tapping dots and dashes in Morse code. Diners bowed their heads and worshipped together at the altar of nourishment.

We filled our bellies, slouched in our seats, remarked on the food, and sipped refills. I asked them, "Was that good?"

They smiled and nodded assent. Denis added, "Hope we come back here gain."

Alex quietly slipped a couple of orange rinds onto Denis's plate. Denis flipped them back into Alex's plate, which triggered more horseplay. Mom grabbed the rinds to temper their zeal and circumvent a food fight. The guys feigned disappointment.

We watched as a commotion developed outside the window at our table. An elderly lady was backing her car out of a parking spot, blocking lanes in the lot. She kept hesitating, and it looked like other drivers were becoming increasingly impatient. A young man offered to assist, and she was glad to accept the help.

"Looks like the traffic jam is over. Want to go for a cruise?"

We left the restaurant, and I gave them a tour of the town, including a walkthrough of my workplace. At the research station, I directed them through labs, offices, a greenhouse, and work bays. I showed them my office, which was filled with electronics, spools of cable, and assorted tools, including a solder gun. They followed me outside and I led them across a footbridge to a park located on the other side of a waterway from the station grounds. We relaxed at a picnic table beneath shade trees before heading home. The outing took up a good portion of the afternoon.

Alex shadowed his grandma, keeping her close. He wasted no opportunity to hoard her attention. He also managed to get a few more chess games in with his grandpa and Denis back at the house.

I had a chat with Denis. I learned what items he might need to help settle into his new digs. I knew the stress monetary gifts caused him, so I avoided the topic of money. I packed him a box of household items from the extras I had on hand.

"I sure could use a toaster," he added. I didn't have time to go buy one, so I gave him my used toaster. He mentioned he was returning home by bus and couldn't transport anything too heavy. The box of goods worked out well for him, and I didn't want the caseworker nazi to come down on him for accepting cash gifts.

The weekend passed quickly, and soon it came time for our visitors to hit the road. Denis hauled the box of goods out to the car. Dad climbed into the driver's seat, Mom rode shotgun, and Denis relaxed in the back seat. Alex and I waved as our guests drove away.

It was hard to read Denis's reaction to the news of John's suicide. We were too wrapped up in sorrow. Mostly I remember Denis at the periphery, minding his own. It was easy to get lost in your own thoughts, even in a crowd.

During the days leading up to John's funeral, a steady stream of friends and neighbours came and went, leaving behind heaps of food we couldn't scare up an appetite for. The house was full of people, yet I had never ached with such emptiness. I felt we were pieces on a game board, moving from square to square according to some kind of gameplay instructions. I wanted to land on the Free Parking square and just stay there until the game was over. I didn't want to engage anymore.

Denis sat at the old piano, repeatedly playing Dad's favourite tune. I suppose he had discovered his own way of coping. The melody was about the only thing that soothed us. For a guy so emotionally challenged, he hit the exact notes to carry us a little easier down this difficult path of sorrow.

My four brothers—Rod, Denis, Mitch, and Gus—were pallbearers for the funeral. They wanted to honour John by being among the six to carry him home. It was an awkward job for Denis, so the others gently guided him.

The edge of the grave was rimmed with green outdoor carpeting. A couple of straps hung taut across the opening like skinny suspension bridges. The pallbearers brought the casket and set it on top of the straps, so that the box with John inside seemed to hover over the hole.

The priest waved his hands in the air and muttered some prayers. He sprinkled some holy water and closed his book. The funeral director worked a hand crank to loosen the straps and lower the casket into the hole. At some point the gear ran out of strap and the box dropped to the bottom like a hammer—the impact boomed, almost like a gunshot.

Mom, Dad, my siblings and I took turns dropping plastic tiger lilies into the hole and then we walked away leaving

John alone in his new digs. The goodbye felt rather crass, and it didn't seem like we'd given him much of a housewarming.

About a year and a half after John died, Denis veered off on another dark descent. Relations became tense between him and my parents. He reacted with anger at their attempts to help him. Denis thought they were conspiring to cause trouble for him, to make it easy for the caseworker to find fault with him. He believed his support would be cut off and he'd be left to survive on his own, out in the street. Mom and Dad urged Denis to apply logic and reasoning to the matter, but their attempts were lost to his delusions.

He avoided communication with Dad, Mom, and all other family members. For a long time, he remained withdrawn. We learned the struggles in his marriage had escalated. He and his wife eventually separated. His isolation was near complete.

Word came to us one day in May 1992 that he had put himself in the path of an oncoming train.

I read once that people who step into traffic to commit suicide will deliberately turn to face the oncoming vehicle. The theory is that they attempt to make eye contact with the driver at the last possible second, perhaps to establish a bridge between themselves and one other soul before passing.

In one sense, I hoped Denis had been able to break through his isolation and make a connection with someone before he died. But I was also in conflict, because I felt bad for the train engineer. I wondered if he dreaded going to sleep at night. Was his rest interrupted by recurring dreams of a man blocking the path of his fast-moving train?

Denis's wife and friends arranged a memorial to celebrate his life at the Crocus Co-op Drop-in Centre. The remembrance fit well with how he lived. It gave us a glimpse into his ways, which we weren't always privy to. His family at Crocus knew him best, as a man whose challenges they understood and shared.

They provided dialogue that focused on his life instead of on how he died. The atmosphere was relaxed and welcoming. We shared in the loss of our brother with them. They didn't tiptoe around the subject of suicide, but accepted it openly, with a thoughtful measure of consideration. They didn't look upon suicide as an unnatural way to die but as the unfortunate end to a terminal illness. Perhaps it was a common way for this community to lose friends. I remember wondering how the hell anyone could ever get used to it.

As part of the tribute, they presented a slideshow played to Denis's favourite tune, "Superman's Song" by Crash Test Dummies. The lyrics pointed out so many of the honourable traits he'd possessed. Like the hero of the song, Denis's life journey wasn't sophisticated or easy, but he lived it with purpose. I play the song often to experience him again.

We were nourished and supported in ways that could only be understood by people acquainted with this type of loss. The compassion extended by our hosts was genuine. Sadly, these same people would be ignored, devalued, and overlooked outside the walls of Crocus Co-op—though it was vividly apparent to me that they were the other superheroes in the story.

Crocus Co-op was Denis's other home, the place that kept his heart. We reminisced on his life within its walls. Remembering him there made it a sacred space, a harbour where he had lived his life as completely as possible. The Superman lyrics affirmed an undeniable truth: *the world will never see another man like him.*

It was easier this time.

PART TWO

CHAPTER SEVEN — REMEMBER

When the dark wood fell before me, and all the paths
were overgrown
When the priests of pride say there is no other way, I
tilled the sorrows of stone
Loreena McKennitt
"'Dante's Prayer"

Here are some things people say to you after a brother dies.

"So sorry for your loss."

"You and your family are in my thoughts and prayers."

"If I can help in any way . . ."

Here are some stupid things people say to you after a brother dies from suicide.

"That was really cowardly and selfish of him to do that."

"What was he thinking?"

"Why would he do such a dumb thing?"

Here are stupid things born-again Christians say to you after a brother dies from suicide.

"You know, he should've invited the Lord Jesus Christ into his heart."

"He'll go to hell if he wasn't saved."

"Did he used to play with a Ouija board?"

Here are things you wish someone would say to you after a brother dies from suicide.

"What was he like?"

"May I see a picture of him?"

"Tell me about him."

The things people say make me want to be left alone. It's better for me to maintain distance from their stupidity and awkwardness. Many won't get the point. They have good intentions, but most times they miss the mark. Maybe the problem is that I don't know how to express my feelings. Perhaps I shouldn't expect anyone to understand.

I tried attending a support group for grief, but it didn't help. It seems there are too many reality shows coaching us to grandstand and hold the limelight. Everybody wants to one-up each other's stories. Well, maybe not everyone ... just the loud, pompous folk. You know the kind. Instead of listening, their focus is on working out a case for their next line. I can tell by the dullness in their eyes that they care jack shit what anyone else is saying.

I should have given them a song and dance for kicks. "It was a tragic death by chainsaw ..." Long pause for added drama. "He was trying to shave his junk. It went horribly wrong."

Some people feign sympathy with a duck face. I long to drive a fist into those scrunched up lips, usually worn by the same individuals flying high on meds. They want to lead me by the hand, take me to their lollipop land. That's where the magic is, apparently. And it'll take my sorrow away.

I don't want my sorrow taken away, or my memories whitewashed. I never want to forget. Perhaps I'm wallowing and not able to move on. No shit! I don't think anyone has yet come up with a manual for this.

So I choose to stay shut. I won't let people place expectations on me. I won't let them criticize me, sass me, bully me, feel sorry for me, guilt me, or patronize me. There is not much they can do to me when I go into my I-don't-give-a-shit mode. Pushing people away has never made me more lonely—it merely satisfies my need for isolation.

When I was seven, Dad signed me up for piano lessons. A nun taught me to play. I was excited to learn about music. Once a week, I arrived at the main door of the convent. I rang the buzzer and the butler nun ushered me in. The first thing I noticed inside was convent smell. Everything within was hospital-like, sterile, and squeaky-clean, but the place always skunked a smelly brew of Pinesol and wet wool.

I removed my boots and placed them on a mat. The piano was situated in a small room at the back, so the nun led me through a series of hallways and rooms. A crucifix and a font of holy water hung on every door jamb. The waxed tile floor was slippery beneath my socked feet, and I glided along, as though on skates. The nun opened the door to the music room, showed me in, and left. I was given a few minutes before each lesson to practise on my own. Then, the music teacher nun joined me and gave me instructions.

Lessons were held in the evening, during fall and winter, and I was responsible for arriving at the convent on time. I had to hoof it there rain or shine—but mostly snow. It was a ten-minute walk for adult legs, but mine were short, so it took me longer to get there. And the sky was almost always dark, both coming and going.

I wasn't afraid of the dark. Contending with the cold was enough to keep me anxious. Night takes up seventy-five percent of the day during the winter in Northern Saskatchewan—I had no choice but to get used to it. There were no streetlights on the way to the convent, and there was seldom any traffic to help brighten the road. I had nothing practical like a flashlight to show me the path. I sensed I was walking through a tunnel and blackness was closing in on me. When clouds blocked the moon, making the street dark as dirt, I relied on other senses to navigate.

It didn't help that I was nearsighted and had astigmatism. It was almost impossible for me to extract light from any source, near or far. My eyes struggled to focus, and I couldn't distinguish objects—especially ones that were distant. I was prescribed eyeglasses at age eleven, and that's when I discovered the wonder of stars, lightning, and the shimmering Northern Lights.

On particularly bleak nights, the walk to and from the convent dished out challenges. I listened to the sound of my steps to discern whether I was crunching gravel or veering toward the ditch. Any sudden dip or snag gave me notice, and I would pause to adjust my course.

With nothing to focus my eyes on, I often lost balance. I extended my arms, mimicking a ballast, to keep myself vertical. I couldn't detect the horizon, and it was difficult to determine which way was up. Almost by reflex, I reached for something to grab whenever I stumbled, as though I could find a handrail to steady myself. Sometimes I fell, hitting the ground hard—but not so hard as to get hurt. I stood back up, checked my bearings, and kept going until I reached my destination.

I navigate grief the same way I used to manoeuvre the night walk. My journey follows a hardened path of gullies and crags. I travel with a particular loneliness that's not easy to describe, and an ache that can't be medicated.

I move forward, supported by memories—like how I used to rely upon the sound and feel of my footsteps to advance through the dark. The memories sustain me. I couldn't function without their reason and purpose.

I struggle to gain understanding and maintain balance. My head gets clouded with sorrow, and I lose stability. Falling is inevitable. Rising again is excruciating, but necessary . . . so I get back up.

A glimmer of light carries hope. Sometimes the light hovers beyond my reach, and other times it creeps closer, soothing the sting of sorrow.

The vast expanse of night is the guilt that consumes me. Instead of trying to dodge accountability, I allow remorse to crush me. I judge myself harshly with accusations of inaction. Mind games hijack my logic. My mental state suffers, as I continue to work the blame game.

Maybe there was something I could have said or done to change their decisions. My head spins as I consider the potential of alternate choices. If I had only . . .

If I had only what?

I am haunted by the unanswered question.

I was unaware how grief and guilt altered my thought processes. I remember having episodes of stress over little things, like where to place the stamp on an envelope. I was baffled. I needed a visual aid, like a picture of a stamped envelope, for me to get the placement right.

One day, I stopped at the post office to collect my mail and then walked home. I arrived at my empty driveway and panicked. Where the hell was my car?

After a long moment, I realized I had parked it at the post office, and it was still running, using up fuel.

I did a double-take at myself in the mirror one morning. I was applying underarm deodorant. My arm was extended skyward, and I was holding a tube of toothpaste to my armpit. *There's something wrong with this picture*, I thought, *but I just can't put my finger on it.*

I'm not above a little self-pity now and then. I have the capacity to wallow in my own misery without much encouragement. Sometimes, I drink in excess and scream at nobody, because no one is here to listen. I drink enough to *tro-up* on the kitchen floor, because I can't seem make it to the bathroom on time. Then I clean it up, because I hate leaving puke on the floor.

Thinking I could converse with ghosts in my drunkenness, I would implore my dead grandmother to tell me whether the loneliness she said she felt was anything like the loneliness I was feeling. She'd always had family near her, and no one had offed themselves while she was alive, so how the hell could she know this kind of loneliness?

And then I'd feel guilty for doubting the weight of my grandmother's heartache.

I suppose it's typical to want to find the cause behind someone's death—especially someone close. You ask questions and dig for answers to get to the root of it. Sometimes you find an explanation—perhaps it's a terminal disease, failing organs, old age, or a fatal accident. The end may be hastened by worsening symptoms, declining functions, or split-second miscalculations. All these things explain the reason for a death, and they help form a path toward closure. But suicide, like murder, is unnatural—and doesn't fit into any of the boxes. The motives and reasons aren't obvious at all. And even if you think you're getting close to figuring out the cause, questions keep spawning.

I'm always rehashing, re-examining, and reconstructing the events that led to my brothers' irreversible decisions. Remember what I said about endless questions? I examine our history to identify the ordeals causing their downward spirals. There were many—and I realize that I played a role in some of them.

I used to dream about my brothers and my parents occasionally, so vividly I could feel their physical presence. The dreams fed a missing part of me, and for a while, they filled a void. But then a dream would play itself out, and I'd awaken to realize that many of my family were gone, never to return. I willed with all my might for the dream to stay, but it was like trying to hold water in my hand.

I recall one particular morning when I awoke from a deep sleep feeling rather joyful for a change. I wondered how I managed to climb out of the heavy funk that had been weighing me down for days. I went to bed hating everything and woke up high on life. I felt I had the confidence to face any challenge. It was surreal—nothing could dampen my spirit. Then I remembered a dream from the night before. In the dream, John had paid me a most amazing visit. He was peaceful and content, and he didn't speak a word. He built a fire on the shore of a lake to cook us some fish. I recognized the beach. It was Jumbo.

But I haven't been able to dream like that in a long time now.

Letter from a sister:

Dear Bros,

You forgot something.

Me.

Are ya comin' back?

I hate it when you ignore me.

So, this is how it's gonna be, eh? Me missing you. Me unable to get my shit together, stuck here without you.

I've had a chance to think about what I could have done had I been with you near the end. If I had known your thoughts, I could have said, "Wait, this will pass. I promise." Then I would have waited with you for as long as it took.

I would have kept my mouth shut and my ears open, if that's what you wanted. I would have chased away stresses and made room for hope. I would have sucked my thumb and rocked on bare feet if the image could have made a difference to you, the way it once did for me.

But there ain't no such thing as time travel, and clocks don't spin themselves backwards.

You know how cool we used to play it, like we were *soooooo* independent and tough . . . like we didn't need anybody? Maybe that was just a load of crap. So I'm levelling with you. I can't seem to get this right. But old habits die hard, and I don't have the conviction to trust or lean on anyone else.

Anyway, you'd be proud of me. I got into a pissing contest with a millennial the other day. I don't think he likes me anymore. I blatantly commented on the size of his teeny tiny boy-berries, which, by the way, I didn't have to actually see to ascertain. It was in his eyes. I don't mean his balls were in his eyes, but the look that said, *I know more than you do, old lady*, which was an obvious attempt to draw attention away from the deficiency of his manhood. I held my ground and stared him down. Then he slithered back into his mother's basement.

I really have gotten rather nasty lately. I yelled at a guy walking his dog past the front of my house: "GET YOUR DOG OFF MY LAWN!!!"

He nearly crapped himself. I mean the guy, not the dog. But the dog did look like it was going to take a shit on my grass, and I know the guy doesn't pick up after it. It's happened before. Hasn't happened since, though.

189

So I managed to adopt a little bit of a *fuck you* attitude. Wish I had rallied this kind of nerve years ago. Could have gotten into people's faces and backed them off. Kicked some righteous ass. Turns out it's a lot more satisfying than getting my ass kicked. I would do it for you, now that I've got the hang of it. I suppose my newfound bravery and bold attitude are a little late.

So, this is what I will do:

I'll be your voice.

I'll bring you back to life.

And maybe I watch too many movies, but I'm gonna quote Emilio Estevez's line in *Young Guns II* . . . "Yoohoo. I'll make you famous."

Luv,

Your sister.

CHAPTER EIGHT — THE BIKER

Run away-ay with me
Lost souls in revelry
Running wild and running free
Two kids, you and me
X Ambassadors
"Renegades"

I had to relinquish my esteemed position as baby of the family to my little brother Mitch when I was one and a half years old. I have no recollection of it putting my nose out of joint. I was probably too distracted fitting in with the rest of my busy family to be bothered. Mitch's arrival transpired as notably as acquiring a new pet, which was good, because I liked cuddly little creatures, and he was a cute one.

Mitch became my fallback guy when my older brother John was off doing his thing without me. It's not that I preferred John's company over Mitch's, but the confines of home were too much of a drag for me. Mel Gibson's rebel yell for freedom in *Braveheart* resonated with my hunger for independence, and John's ways hinted at a good fit to satisfy my craving.

I was ill-prepared to take on the responsibility of big sister. I was conditioned to be a follower, not a leader. My skills at being the older sibling were generally acquired through trial and error. Fortunately for Mitch, he and Mom had an exceptional relationship, which he found more dependable than the one between him and myself. Still, I wasn't totally discouraged from trying to nurture him, since I had been given the official calling of a big sister.

Mud was a good medium for me to practise my craft at being the older sibling. It was easy to find and free to use, so I lured my two-year-old brother to a proper mudhole. It was shallow, so as to not pose a drowning risk, yet wide enough to provide adequate working space. It was also located in a spot not obvious to snooping eyes.

I sank my hands deep into the muck. I didn't need to prod Mitch to do the same. I told him, "We're makin' cakes."

I pulled out a handful of gunk and mixed in some dry dirt. I showed Mitch how to mould a cake and smooth it round to make it look like the buns Mom formed from bread dough. I busied myself with crafting a row of them.

Mitch used his own technique. I grew frustrated, antsy at his attempts. He wouldn't pay attention to my method. I couldn't seem to explain to him how to get the consistency right. He squeezed the muck through his little fingers, having fun instead of working at it. His creations looked more like lumpy dog turds than cakes. At least he was old enough to know not to eat them.

It didn't look as though Mitch planned to contribute to the stockpile, so I gave up the push. He tested the limit of my patience when he came after my stash, probably fixing to mash up the perfect sculptures I had formed.

We were too occupied with our task to notice Mom watching us. We had mud up to our armpits, and crud grimed into our clothes and hair. Mitch saw her first. He cracked a warm, toothy smile. She softened at his mirth. She motioned for him to come with her, so he scrambled to his feet and scudded after her like a fish caught on a hook. My words didn't come out fast enough. I wanted to say, "What the hey? Where you going? We're not done here! Come back!"

But it was too late to voice objections. He'd abandoned me. I'd lost him to her charm. Even so, I stood firm, refusing to be lured away from my task. It was bigger than the two of us. I was practising leadership. I did what any good leader would do—I resisted, and I expected him to follow my lead.

He didn't.

I watched him wander off, trailing his backside after Mom. The little traitor.

I knew one thing for sure, he wouldn't be following in my footsteps. He marched to his own damn drumbeat, and it rarely kept tempo with mine. My days of perceived influence were over before they had even begun.

It was hard to stay mad at Mitch. He had a killer smile like Mom's, and it could thaw an icicle at minus thirty degrees. To describe him as free-spirited is an understatement. He had smarts like Denis and independence like John, but he also had a vivid imagination that none of his siblings could match. Creativity flowed out of him and it swelled with each passing year.

If a new concept or innovation came about during our otherwise mundane routine, chances are Mitch was behind its creation. He didn't shy away from trying something different.

Even when others thought his ideas strange, he never let their negativity get in his way. He was bold and unique, which extended to his fashion sense—or maybe I had more effect on him than I realized.

Mom was a skilled seamstress. She particularly liked to sew dresses for me. There might not have been enough money to buy new material for her craft, but that didn't stop her. A large person's cast-off garb could supply enough fabric to stitch up a garment or two, and Mom had the skills to tailor a dinner jacket out of a burlap sack.

I had a good wardrobe selection as a result, and I didn't mind sharing clothes with my little bro. I'm not exactly sure how Mitch acquired a taste for dress-up. I may have coaxed him into trying on a frock or two—or maybe it was entirely his idea. Either way, he didn't mind getting glammed up.

The inclination to dress up wore off as he got older. Mitch didn't necessarily lose his fashion sense—he simply adjusted his attire to suit his character. Cravats were a popular British trend when Mitch was about ten years old. He cajoled Mom to sew him a paisley pink cravat from the same fabric as one of my favourite dresses. He wore his cravat all the time, day in and day out. He adopted the signature look of a dashing young trendsetter, and he cared squat what other people thought about his snazzy cravat. With his dark, wavy hair and black-rimmed glasses, Mitch could have been Mike Meyers's inspiration for the character of Austin Powers.

For Mitch, the rag room was an especially fun hangout. Halloween was his favourite opportunity to work his talent, though he didn't necessarily need a special occasion to get in character—any old day would do. He got inspiration digging through stuff that was on the verge of being thrown out. I tried, but I couldn't match his skill for assembling costumes. Good thing he shared ideas.

His best works paid off in armloads of Halloween treats. He was almost always decked out in old lady clothes—maybe because there were scads of grandma dresses stashed in the rag room. He slapped on makeup, donned a dress, and topped off the look with a hat and a handbag. The costumes transformed him completely. He emerged in grand style.

"Where'd you find that outfit? You look like you could fit right in at the old folks' home."

Mitch wore a large, flowered dress, filled out with padding for better fit. He pulled on a pair of long white gloves that had brown stains on the palm.

"Those look like you were milking cows in them."

A favourite of mine was his Mom of Ichabod Crane outfit. He accessorized his getup with a cohort he named Headless Barbie. For my sake, he could have reattached Barbie's head after he had finished with her. It would have saved me many anxious months of searching. I had lost interest playing with a doll who had little more than a stump for a head.

Mitch didn't need a particular reason to don a new look, but it helped. In 1973, my sister, Pauly, was living in Missouri with her husband, Ernie, and one-year old baby. They decided to relocate to Canada from the USA, and the moving van carrying their household items had to be returned stateside. Dad recruited Rod to deliver the U-Haul back to Havre, Montana. Mitch went along for the ride. For twelve-year-old Mitch, this called for a change of style. A road trip of this magnitude demanded a serious wardrobe review.

The contents of his closet didn't cut it, so he rifled through others' bureaus. He picked up a fedora hat and an old pair of Oxford shoes from Dad's collection, and he borrowed a suit coat from Uncle Emil's. He emerged looking like a midget hobo—all that was missing was the scruffy stubble on his face.

Rod looked at him with furrowed eyebrows and asked, "You're travelling in that?"

Mitch didn't let Rod's remark dissuade him. He was firm in his choice of attire. Rod surmised that there was no use arguing, so he gave Mitch a cigar to complete his new look.

The trip took a couple of days. The boys got their fill of adventure and scenery along the way, with Rod driving and Mitch riding shotgun. Their excursion was mostly uneventful—until they tried to cross the border into the USA.

Border guards posed the usual questions.

"What's the purpose of your trip?"

"How long are you staying?"

Then one said, "Could you please step out of the van?"

Maybe their strange association caught the notice of hard-nosed patrollers—a James-Dean-hot driver with a passenger looking like a young George Burns. The guards separated them and grilled them further.

The one quizzing Mitch stooped to look him in the eye and pointed to Rod. He asked Mitch, "Do you know that guy?"

The gears spun inside Mitch's busy mind. He couldn't pass up an opportunity to stir up fun shit. So Mitch gave him a red-hot retort. "Jah! Jah! Heece a Rooshun spy!"

The Cold War had everyone on edge—especially Americans. Mitch's comment spooked the guard, and they put Rod through the wringer, interrogating him for a couple anxious hours. After some ballsy backtracking, frantic explaining, and prolonged fact-checking, the guards released the boys and allowed them to enter the USA. The boys delivered the van and boarded a bus going north. Their bus trip home was much less remarkable.

Rod spilled details of their adventure to us. The story scored Mitch plenty of moxie points and bolstered his macho image. He took spunk to a whole other level. I could never stand up under that kind of pressure, so I made sure never to underestimate Mitch after that.

Before Mitch and I were old enough to attend school, we had our morning routine. Our siblings left the house at the same time every school day. We had the house almost to ourselves. Mom was busy with cleanup and switchboard calls—or perhaps taking a short break with a calming cup of coffee and a smoke. We headed upstairs to find Dad. Most times, he was still asleep. We waited bedside, like crows perched on a tree branch, waiting for him to wake up. We watched deep slumber breaths lift and sink his chest. We willed him awake with silent coaxing. His first image, most mornings, was the ogle of kids' eyes staring at him.

Then, it was like watching a rerun of a favourite episode— Dad shaking off sleep, climbing out of bed, gathering his clothes, and sitting on the edge of the mattress to start dressing. His method of putting on socks intrigued us. He caught the first wool sock in both hands, held the cuff open with his thumbs and rolled the tube into a fat doughnut all the way to the toe. He stuffed a foot into the opening and unrolled the sock up to his ankle. He kept the sock there while he folded the leg of his long underwear neatly to one side. Then he drew the rest of the sock up and over the fold, extending the wool tube almost to his knee. He repeated the process for the other foot. I aspired to the day when I could wear long underwear and do the same.

When Dad went to the bathroom, Mitch and I scouted for the best bed to use as a trampoline. None of the beds had firm mattresses. and the coils of the bedsprings had long ago stretched slack. There was a lumpy sinkhole in the centre, and gravity pulled tired, sleeping bodies into the sag. But for the sport of jumping, the beds served our purpose very well. Of course we weren't supposed to jump on the them, but we did anyway.

There were more boys than beds, so they shared—two boys per bed, and sometimes three. There was logic to sharing—body heat kept the boys from sleeping cold during the winter. It's not pleasant trying to sleep without enough heat. I shared a bedroom with Pauly. When I was eight years old, she left home. I didn't miss her as much as I missed her warmth. Her absence impacted my health in a negative way. I always seemed to have a cough due to a cold, which annoyed my family as they tried to watch *Bonanza* or *Wayne and Shuster* on TV. The usual comment, "Quit-chur barking. There are no cars going by," didn't strike me as being funny, though every-one else seemed to think it was. I kept a glass of apple juice at my bedside to help thwart coughing spasms. I had to break a film of ice off the surface before I could take a sip.

It didn't help that our parents were smokers. A thin smog haze generally hovered near the ceiling. Mom and Dad loved caffeine too, and it wasn't practical to have coffee without a cigarette. There may have been some value to their nasty habit—the build-up of smoke scum created extra layers of insulation on the walls. Maybe it was part of a plan to keep winter rightfully outside.

Dad's cure-all for chest colds was to hang a heat lamp, suspend it from a hook, and radiate heat toward a bare back. It was the kind of lamp farmers used to incubate chicks. It functioned like the underside of a mother hen providing warmth to her babies.

Basking beneath the lamp was some kind of bliss. Not only did it help suppress a cough, but indulging in its warmth relaxed winter's grip for a while. My eyes glazed over from the luxury while the dial on the electric metre spun a frantic twirl. Dad relaxed on utility costs when a kid's health was at stake.

Mitch and I managed the cold of winter by focusing on fun. We were good at building forts together. We constructed them outside in the snow when the weather was decent and built them indoors, out of blankets and chairs, when weather sucked.

We preferred building snow forts outside. Mitch could think like an architect, which helped with the planning phase. The snow texture had to be crusty and the right thickness to break off snow in chunks. We sculpted the chunks into squares. We levelled and cleared a small area, and stacked the snow blocks like bricks. A wall couldn't be erected more than three or four bricks high without it toppling. That was one of our struggles. The other was keeping snow from getting into our mitts and freezing our wrists. When that happened, it felt like something sharp cutting our skin, but we kept on building despite the irritation.

The other form of fort-building always seemed to coincide with sports on TV. My parents and older siblings watched *Hockey Night in Canada* more religiously than they attended church. They were fans of the *Montréal Canadiens*, and they worshipped their hockey gods, Jean Béliveau and Yvan Cournoyer. But I suspect my family's fidelity to the Habs might have taken a back seat to the Detroit Red Wings once Saskatchewan-born Gordie Howe joined the team.

Mitch and I didn't yet appreciate the sport—perhaps because we couldn't always follow the game. It didn't help that TV reception was often bad and we couldn't make out where the puck was going. Fans had to rely on the announcer to fill in the details. Foster Hewitt's voice couldn't hold my interest. Perhaps he sounded too much like Elmer Fudd, which detracted from the thrill of play.

Saturdays were packed with the usual order of events. It was bath day, and we took turns griming up the bathwater for the next kid in line. Mom washed and waxed floors, and we stayed out of the way until she was done. We watched Bugs Bunny while she cooked chop suey or baked beans for supper. Dad tended to his tasks early in order to free up his evening. The whole day felt like we were preparing for something important.

"Is that Mahovlich gonna give our team a hard run this year?" Talk around the supper table would naturally turn to hockey.

"They should sic the Pocket Rocket on 'em."

"To do what? Bite him on the kneecap?"

"He's tough for his size. Don't be surprised."

A kid would interrupt the discussion with a question: "Kin I have s'more beans?"

"Put some beans on Mitchy's plate there."

They opined about the new guy, Yvan Cournoyer. Perhaps he was the ticket to getting the team into the playoffs. The fans were somewhat divided on the topic. The season was only about halfway done.

"Think Montréal can take the Cup this year?"

"If they can slow down Keon and keep giving Bélliveau the puck . . . maybe. Leafs are pretty cocky with the last two Cups under their belt."

"I just like watching Eddie Shack play."

"Whose turn to help with dishes?"

"Not me!"

Once cleanup was done, all the sports fans moved to the living room to watch the game. Mitch and I got the run of the kitchen. We lined up chairs and draped blankets over top. We occupied inside the tent-fort while the hockey game on TV engaged the rest of our family. Sometimes, during a hockey game, we heard shrieks and cheers coming from the living room. The commotion tapped our curiosity and sometimes pulled us in. We watched as a scoring frenzy erupted or a particularly nasty fight broke out. We were careful not to get caught up in all the hype. Watching hockey was addictive, and we could easily get hooked.

It turned out that Mitch liked playing hockey more than watching it. He joined a team as soon as he was old enough. There were scarcely enough players to make a lineup, so Mitch was readily drafted. He was an energetic competitor, which suited the team well.

He didn't have decent equipment or proper skates, but he wasn't the only kid lacking hockey gear. Ill-fitting pads and jerseys passed through many hands, maximizing the wear life of shared property. As long as Mitch had a stick and electrical tape to wrap the blade, he was hitting the ice. He played defence because he was one of the few kids who could skate backwards.

Out-of-town games were rare, so most of the hockey action happened during practice or while playing shinny. Road hockey was common—especially when ice at the rink was junk.

Between siblings and cousins, we fired up a game of shinny on the street in front of our home. The road had gravel mixed in with packed snow, so the surface was coarse. We didn't have protective gear like pads, helmets, or gloves. Winter boots encased our feet instead of skates. The goalposts were gunny sacks partially filled with straw, and it didn't matter if a car drove over top of them. I was the only girl player, and they let me drop the puck at centre ice to start the game.

"You stand close to the goal and wait for me to pass you the puck." My teammate was lining me up to score goals. Nobody played goalie, because no one was worried about players whose long shots were mostly off target. I felt like the Rocket, waiting to earn a hat trick.

I stood near the goal watching the players pass the rubber disk between them and then lose it to the opposite team. Someone yelled, "Car!"

We scattered to one side of the street as a Buick approached and passed. The driver waved to us, and we showed him our hockey sticks.

Again I dropped the puck for the game to resume. The boys chased after it and converged like cats in a frenzied skirmish. The mob drifted to and fro across the playing field, moving as one to the rhythm of puck. With heads down and eyes on the ice, the boys waggled hockey blades and elbows, like duelling chopsticks.

The puck flew out of the din toward me and I froze in the excitement. I couldn't respond fast enough to score a goal before the players closed in on me. I was caught in the centre of the hockey storm without a hope of regaining control of the puck. The butt end of someone's stick met my face. I spit out a fragment that looked like a Chicklet. My tongue found the gap where my upper front tooth used to be. If I couldn't play like a hockey great, then I was surely going to look like one.

Shinny helped feed Mitch's appetite for action. He played with intensity, like he had something to prove. He charged at the puck with his head down, determined to knock anybody out of his way to get to it. Girl's hockey was becoming popular, so I played on a team for a while. I lost interest when the game got rough. I was outsized by most of my opponents. I wasn't gutsy like Mitch, who didn't let his smallness stop him.

Spunk was a trait Mitch shared with Mom. Sports seemed to bring out the grit in them. We witnessed Mom exercising her moxie once, when we were at the curling rink watching her compete.

My parents loved to curl—it was their favourite winter pastime. They put together a curling team every year. They recruited two additional players to complete the foursome and signed up to play in a league. We spent a lot of evenings at the curling rink, watching their games.

"Here it comes. Just enough ice to make it around the guard and . . ."

Someone shrieked, "Look at it curl! Like it's got eyes to find the shot rock! Great take out."

I learned the ropes of the sport observing their game strategy. Mom and Dad were competitive curlers, but their penchant for fun took precedence. For a few years, our village held an annual winter carnival, which included activities for adults and kids. Mom and Dad entered the curling bonspiel. Their games took a lot of time, so they missed watching most of our competitions.

Dad's team made it to the finals. He said to the skip of the other team, "If it's all right with you, we'd like to watch our boy play hockey. How about we play our game in a couple of hours?"

The other team agreed to postpone the deciding game, but the sponsor of the first-place trophy had other ideas. He was adamant the game go forward as scheduled. He became belligerent about it, so my good-natured, always-a-lady mom's reply to him was "Lester, why don't you take your trophy and stick it up your ass?"

Lester went home with his trophy, presumably to follow my mother's instructions, marking an end to the bonspiel.

Mitch should have learned from Mom how to pick his battles, but his temerity sometimes got in the way. He'd hold his ground and seldom back down from a fight. He brought his recklessness to school. One time, his teacher's point of view contradicted his, so he socked her one in the nose. The strange thing is, she really liked Mitch, and their little clash didn't change the way she felt about him.

Mitch had more outbursts at school, and the principal encouraged my parents to take him to see a psychologist. That suggestion went as far as a fart in a vacuum. No psychologist would venture this far north, and my parents couldn't afford to pay for travel and therapy.

Teachers documented the trouble Mitch got into at school. They saved the reports for parent-teacher interviews. The meetings with my parents ran long past the allotted time given for normal consultations.

"Your son could put more effort into his schoolwork," teachers always started conversations in the same tone, "if he could just apply himself. He's capable of so much better. He's more interested in goofing off than getting good grades."

My parents probably sat quietly, eyes downcast, mouths shut, hands jittery without cigarettes. They might have felt as though they were being reprimanded. Then, the teacher would bring up past incidents to make her point.

There was the time Mitch robbed the school bank. Well, it wasn't a real bank—the money was made of cardboard. The teacher used the fake money to motivate kids as a reward for exceptional schoolwork. Kids could use the currency to buy cheap trinkets and potato candy.

Since Mitch couldn't see a practical side to earning cardboard money, he convinced a couple of his cronies to help pull off a sting. No one ever went to jail for stealing fake currency, so the boys made a plan to rob the cash register.

It was during lunchtime, while classes were empty. The boys collected the loot box from the teacher's desk drawer. They filled their pockets with cardboard booty and walked away looking smug. They drew attention to themselves by flashing their swag in the schoolyard. The principal called them into her office and made them fess up.

Every spring, the same teacher who encouraged us with cardboard money oversaw a project having kids make and sell Easter baskets. She saw the opportunity to teach Mitch responsibility for his actions. She recruited him, along with others, such as myself, to build the baskets. We used a pattern to trim milk cartons to make them look like miniature crates with handles. We stuffed the hollow part with crinkled strips of paper to form a nest inside the basket. We topped the wadding with coloured eggs made from potato candy. The teacher arranged work parties at her house. She expected all the local kids to help out.

We raced around town selling the finished baskets. The proceeds went to a charity that fed rice to underprivileged kids in third-world countries. Perhaps those kids would have preferred potato candy. The charity should have worked on ways to ship candy overseas instead of disappointing kids with more damn rice. I could just hear them . . . "Rice! Again? What the hell! Why can't they send potato candy?"

The teacher's intent was noble, and she deserved recognition. In her youth, I think she aspired to become a nun—but for some unknown reason, she wasn't allowed to. My theory is that she was once assaulted by a man, so she set her sights on something other than romance.

She lived in a cute little house all by herself, across the street from the convent. She spent a lot of time with the nuns, maybe trying to fit in with them. Sometimes we weren't very considerate of her. One Halloween, I helped dump a nasty mixture of flour and water over the pink flamingos in her yard. I still feel bad about that.

Another time, she ran her little red K-car into the backend of a Massey Ferguson combine. The combine was moving slowly down the highway, perhaps toward the next field for harvest. The accident did little more than cause a small dent in her car, but the incident shook her up. After that, I became more mindful of her humanity.

Most teachers were nuns, but by the time Mitch and I had reached junior high, school administrators had started hiring more non-nuns. One of the first male teachers quickly became a favourite among students. I had a severe crush on him, and I wasn't the only one, which probably fed the nuns' anxieties about having men around young girls. But it was a wasted concern on him, because it turned out he was gay— though that didn't stop us from liking him. Nor did it keep the nuns from being scandalized.

Another of our teachers looked like a living shrink-wrapped doll. She was a life-sized walking, talking Barbie. She had style, and I don't think she was prepared for a classroom of adolescents. She freaked out too easily. That only made us kick things up a notch, and we plotted more pranks against her. First thing in the morning, she'd open a desk drawer to find a frog or a garter snake. She was squeamish about things like that.

Mitch jumped off the school roof once. I saw it happen. We were in the middle of a math lesson with teacher Barbie, and she saw it happen, too. I witnessed a momentary flash of arms and legs splayed out mid-fall, like the kid was plunging to his death. I freaked out a little, but not nearly as much as teacher Barbie. She gaped, squawked, and shuddered, and her face turned ashen. It was epic. A snowbank broke Mitch's fall, and he landed, as though dropping onto a bed of feathers. The stunt earned him even more notoriety.

Mitch needed distractions, so he came up with more pranks to keep from getting bored in school. During class, he'd disappear into the wall through a ventilation duct, Houdini style. His escapes fed his hunger for mischief. He always showed up again in another part of the school.

Mitch confounded teachers. They recognized his potential to excel, but he gave schoolwork little regard. He maintained a standoffish attitude toward book learning, unless there was a shot at earning rewards. Poster contests gave him cause to use his creativity. He bypassed essay competitions, which were too much like work. He preferred to craft with crayons and construction paper.

His creations received recognition. Mitch entered the Fight Against Cancer Poster Contest and won the top spot in the province, along with some cash. Then, he got an honourable mention in a national competition. Japanese videogame programmers might have seen the poster and taken their idea for Pac-Man from it—the fat C in the word *cancer* of Mitch's piece had spiky teeth, a feral eye, and attitude—characteristics that were effective for good animation in gaming.

Our family was the first in town to acquire a videogame. Dad bought us Pong, and it drew a lot of outside interest. It made our house a magnet for kids wanting to practise their gaming skills.

"What kind of game is this, anyway?" A neighbour drawn by the action on the screen squinted to try and fathom what all the fuss was about.

Mitch explained, "You can't let the other guy score on you."

"How does that happen?"

"See the little green bar? It's called a paddle. It moves up and down when I turn this button. The floating green dot in the middle is like a puck. You hit it with your paddle and knock into the other guy's goal to score."

Kids waited their turn, itching to get their hands on the game. Once they held control of a virtual paddle, they were hooked. They glared at the neon bullet floating across the screen as it ricocheted against digital borders. The kid's hand on the console spun the dial, sliding the neon paddle into the bullet's path, blocking a score. Excited players teetered and ducked in their seats, as though their body's motion could help deflect a shot.

Pong amused us for a long time, and then it got too easy. Winning didn't take much effort, so Mitch and Dad took the console apart and fiddled with the insides, trying to boost the speed. The result was smaller paddles, which upped the challenge again.

Mitch scored the label of wild child, but he also had a tender side. He wasn't a typical little brother—he was a take-charge kind of kid, which was more like older sibling material. Then, one day, he became a big brother—and he took on that role with big heart.

Mitch was the one our baby brother Gus tried to keep up with, look up to, and imitate. They were pals, and they shared and learned from each other. There were some serious lessons Mitch needed to hand down to our little bro—like how not to use your face to slow down your bike. It was a lesson he should have delivered in a more thought-out manner.

During a brief *Jackass* phase, Mitch accepted many dares trying to live up to a He-Man image. He never backed down from a challenge that held potential for good sport.

It was rare for families to move to Makwa unless they had a tie to the community. There weren't jobs to attract people or many available homes suitable for a family to occupy. Any new kids that arrived usually came through the foster care system. They were constantly being shuffled between homes. Government compensation was the only source of sure money, so people looking for a financial boost accommodated foster children.

Mitch was always the first to befriend the new kids. His natural magnetism attracted them. The kids brought their problems, their loneliness, and their crazy ideas. Mitch helped them forget their troubles and steered them toward fun.

Sometimes, fun came in the form of speed.

Racing bikes downhill didn't provide enough of a thrill anymore, so the boys put their heads together to figure out a better, faster way to travel. They waited on the side of the road, looking as though they were examining the finer features of a two-wheeler.

"Get ready. Here comes one now."

They watched as a car slowed down, coming into town from the west. It rolled past the gas station, the church, and the grocery store. It coasted clear of the bulk station, nearing the approach to the school yard. All eyes were fixed on the vehicle, measuring its progress to make sure it wasn't planning a stop before leaving town again.

Timing was key, and just as the car neared, a kid mounted the bike and his buddies launched him forward, parallel to the car. The kid pedalled hard and picked up speed, inching closer to the passing vehicle. The biker grabbed hold of the tailfin, stabilized the bike, and travelled with the car as it sped down the road, towing its hitchhiker.

He steadied the handlebar with his free hand, stood up on the pedals, and kept the bike upright, trailing the car. His shirt billowed, making him look like a wind-blown hunchback on wheels. The car accelerated on its way out of town, a kid still in tow. If the driver noticed the tag-along, he might honk the horn or slow down, then the kid would back off. Usually, the rider didn't let go of the car until excessive speed broke his grip.

One successful ride encouraged more of the same.

"Don't forget to let go. I want my turn, too."

Sometimes there weren't enough bikes to go around.

There was only so much speed a kid could achieve on gravel with a bike, and it was a matter of time before one took a nasty spill. That kid was Mitch, because he hung on until the last possible second. He wiped out in grand style, face first.

Out came the Mercurochrome and the Band-Aids. His wounds were superficial compared to the ass whoopin' he probably got from Dad.

Mitch didn't provide Gus any advice on how to avoid getting hurt from a fall of that nature. And then, one day, Gus fell off his bike and face planted on the sidewalk. To be fair, Gus wasn't trying to hotdog. The cuts, scrapes, and black eye would heal eventually. Thankfully neither of the boys acquired permanent scars on their nice faces.

They shared other things besides injuries—like how to make noise while Dad was trying to listen to news on TV. Dad was getting older, and had less tolerance for kid-folly. Mitch and Gus were minding their own, perhaps playing with too much gusto. They got lost in the mirth. Rather than reel in their enthusiasm with a curt warning, Dad threw a shoe. His aim was sure, and it got their attention. After that, the boys watched out for shoe-like flying objects when the news came on.

Mitch wasn't the least bit discouraged by a scolding, and I don't think he ever meant to intentionally mock Dad. Mitch was simply looking for the next gag. Like the time he found a pair of false teeth and wore them around the house. They belonged to Dad, but Dad wouldn't miss them—he kept them in a drawer. They weren't much use to Dad for brightening up his smile or chewing food by keeping them inside the drawer, so Mitch wore them for a while. He stretched his lips to hold the dentures in, but the teeth jutted out, lopsided and big. His distorted smile resembled a horse's sloppy grin. He mouthed old-man rants, and reminded us of Francis the Talking Mule.

When Mitch was six years old, he got us all into trouble with Dad. It happened at my grandparents' farm. A few of us were sitting on the trunk of the car, waiting to leave for home. Mitch ran a toy tractor down the surface of the rear windshield.

One moment, the windshield was in perfect condition and the next, it had morphed into a mosaic pattern of splintered glass. I watched, dumbstruck, as a star burst emerged from the centre of the windshield outward. It looked like a spider had webbed a silica net. Dad was pissed, but the windshield held.

As we ventured home that day, all of us in the back seat exhibited forward-focused, model behaviour for a change. We sat quietly so as to not bring attention to ourselves. We tried communicating with hand signals, but the messages were too cryptic to decipher.

Dad drove the car down the six-mile stretch of road going home. We rode in silence except for the sound of the motor and the crunch of tire against gravel. Fields and ditches rushed past our view. The ride was relatively smooth, until we hit a bump.

A sound like a gunshot went off behind us. The windshield imploded. Projectiles struck the backs of our heads. Glass shards rained down on us, dropping like ice chips into our shirt collars and onto our laps. I let out a shriek because I didn't know what was happening.

Dad stopped the car on the side of the road. It took a minute for me to realize we hadn't hit the rhubarb. No one was hurt, but my nerves were frayed by the close call.

We climbed out of the car, shaking off bits of glass. It took a while to clean the debris out of the back seat, and our trip home resumed with the added feature of rear hatch ventilation.

We remained sheepish for a time, until the memory of the incident faded. Dad had a new windshield installed, and life went back to normal.

"Want to go fishing?" Mitch needed only to ask once, and Gus was game to go.

Mitch played fishing guide and Gus trailed after him on their way to the creek. The water hole was within walking distance of home, and that's where they cast their fishing lines.

On opposite sides of town were part-time creeks. One branch of the brook gushed water through a culvert beneath the highway at the west end of town. The inlet was large enough to channel excessive outflow, keeping the road from washing out.

A bridge spanned the east-side creek. The stream beneath the bridge could swell to the point of causing floods, though that threat never daunted kids who were thrill-seekers.

There was a good vantage point atop the bridge and kids watched angry water rush past below, mesmerizing them with its power. The spinning and churning current pushed obstacles out of its path, as if it had a fixed destiny and an urgency to get there. Floaters littered the current—a moving picture-show of broken branches, a lost shoe, a dead muskrat, a pair of granny panties. Kids hatched wild stories of how these things wound up bobbing down the creek. The flow was ample after spring thaw, but it slowed to a trickle during dry summers.

The boys fished the creek on the east side of town. Mitch led Gus there, and they brought along crude fishing equipment—willow sticks tied with string, and twisted headpins as hooks attached to the end of the line. The chance of them catching a fish was remote. No one dared eat anything caught there anyway—too much risk of beaver fever. They were there for the thrill, following a primal instinct to hunt.

They passed lazy afternoons beside the creek. The boys waited on the bank with lines dangling in the water, their patience challenged. They brought a glass jar and corralled tadpoles into it. For Gus, the jar was like a fishbowl, and he kept it on a dresser beside his bed. The tadpoles intrigued him, and he waited for them to grow into frogs, but that never happened. The water became skunky, and had to be dumped.

So instead, he listened to the sound of frogs croaking while dangling his fishing pole.

The wait became tiresome, and caused a certain amount of restlessness in the boys. Perhaps fishing was too much like sitting through a church service. Gus needed to work out some energy, and his little legs became fidgety. Mitch couldn't keep him in one spot for too long a stretch. It was only a matter of time before Gus fell into the creek.

He went in headfirst, and only his legs were visible—and they were kicking up a frenzy. It probably took a second or two for the shock to let up and urgency to sink in. Mitch lunged in after him. He panicked, trying to get a hold of a flailing limb, but catching one was tougher than scoring a hit at whack-a-mole. Then Mitch caught a foot, pulled, and lifted out a nearly-drowned Gus.

They recovered on the creek bank, gasping and panting. They looked like a pair of near-drowned rats. Gus coughed up a stream and Mitch held him tight, keeping him close. He wasn't going to chance losing his little brother to the water again. He carried him home, making sure the kid was fully recovered. It was a close call, and the fright caused Mitch to double down on watching out for his baby bro.

Mitch was inherently a caregiver. He had a nasty temper, and he could hurt people when he lashed out. But deep down, he was a lover, not a fighter. Everyone was drawn to him, despite the risk of him turning on them. The attraction spilled over to animals. Strays followed him home, and we always had one or two pets underfoot. If stick-people decals had been the in-thing, the rear window of our vehicle would have had a collage of stick parents, a string of kids, a bunch of extra kids, and an endless line of dogs and cats . . . and maybe a frog.

"That dog looks like a goat."

The ugly ones always followed Mitch home.

"Are you going to name it?"

"Yeah, I'm gonna call it Horse."

I kind of liked the idea of having pets at first. But after watching a dog drag its butt across our newly-laid living room carpet, I reconsidered. Finding out it had tapeworms made me like them even less. I think it bothered Dad the most to have dogs as pets. Especially after Mitch sneaked one into the bathwater before Dad's turn at having a soak.

Strays sometimes came in the form of kids. Mitch once played host to a buddy who needed a place to crash for the night. Mom and Dad didn't mind, and Mitch told them the kid had permission to sleepover. The RCMP showed up at our door, searching for a runaway. Apparently, the kid favoured Mitch as a foster parent over his government-issued ones.

Mitch's easy way with his peers extended to townspeople of all ages. He fit in with any kind of company. In our small town, there were all sorts of people and no shortage of interesting ones.

Rosie Up the Hill was one of our town's special persons. She lived by herself in a rundown little house, on the top of a hill. She was about sixty years old, had a good nature with unique qualities.

Rosie was a bit frumpy, of French descent, and had a characteristic woman-stache, that kept her upper lip warm. She wore a heavy wool coat with a dirty sheepskin collar, and on her feet, a pair of rubber boots. In winter, she exchanged the boots for galoshes and kept her head warm with an orange toque that had a single white stripe and a pompom. On important days, like church days, she capped her lid with a satiny pillbox hat that had seen better days. For all other occasions, she covered her silver-white hair with a scarf knotted at the chin.

Rosie liked Mitch—everybody liked Mitch—and Mitch liked to kid with Rosie. His joking never lingered on the mean side or caused her discomfort. But he never passed up an opportunity for a little fun.

Rosie had a magnet she was particularly proud of. She kept the magnet in her purse, where it was handily available in case she ever needed one. She couldn't pronounce the word *magnet* very well. She worded it differently than the typical hasty way French people talk. She distinctly enunciated and spaced each syllable—"ma-ga-net," so the word came out of her sounding like the drawl coming off a turntable, playing a record at the slowest RPM.

One day, she decided to teach us kids about the magic of ma-ga-nets. She demonstrated how a ma-ga-net could pick up nails and needles and other metal objects. Mitch pulled a glass marble out of his pocket and asked her, "Can it pick up this marble?"

She shook her head and demonstrated again the magic of the ma-ga-net, how it could pick up nails and needles and metal objects. Mitch asked, "What about this shoelace? Can it pick up this shoelace?"

After the third demonstration, she decided the new generation was too dumb to grasp the concept of ma-ga-nets. She put it back in her purse and went home.

Mitch's dog Tutz had a litter of pups. I say Mitch's dog, but she was really the family dog. None of us wanted to admit we had such an ugly dog, so we let Mitch think she was all his. Anyway, Tutz had pups—obviously some male dog didn't mind her being ugly—and the pups grew quickly. Pretty soon, you couldn't step without catching one underfoot. Even when they were old enough to give away, Tutz remained very protective of her pups. Rosie found out how much a guard dog Tutz could be as defender of her babies.

Then, one day, Tutz disappeared without a trace. Mitch became obsessed with finding her. He reasoned that something sinister must have happened. He worked out the details of the case of his missing dog, *Columbo*-style. He deduced that, following an instinct to defend her pups, Tutz went after Rosie. Rosie freaked out and told her daughter about it. The daughter told her boyfriend. The boyfriend got his gun . . . and done finished off Tutz.

RIP Tutz.

As far as positioning in the family, Mitch, John and I were a unit of three, holding up the middle. Our three older siblings, Pauly, Rod and Denis, broke ground for us and sometimes kept us in line. Gus, our baby brother, got the benefit or disadvantage of all our care and consideration.

I received the same privileges, drawbacks, rules, and considerations as John and Mitch. Mom and Dad played no favouritism, treating the three of us equally and fairly. Instead of repeating a thing two times, they said it once for the three of us to absorb collectively. We seemed to be bound together, and when something happened to one of us, we all felt it, heard it, knew it. If Mom sewed a new pair of flannel pyjamas, it was twice replicated, so that we each got a new pair. We had one bike to share, and chores were assigned fairly and rotated for parity. What was good for one was good for the other two and there was never a doubt we were equally loved.

During the early years, if one of us wasn't included in a thing, it felt like a piece was missing. It was natural for me to belong inside a set of three, and I had to learn to cope when we didn't anymore. I suppose that's the challenge of growing up and apart.

I recall the first time my siblings, my dad, and I went to the Meadow Lake Stampede. Our neighbour from across the street, Mr. T, took us in his Mercury, which rode like a boat down a gentle river. Our car was temporarily out of commission with a busted out rear windshield, so Mr. T offered to drive us.

John and I, with Mitch between us, squeezed together to take up our tiny share of the back seat. Dad rode shotgun. Pauly sat in the front, between Mr. T and Dad. Rod and Denis crowded in with us in the back seat. Gus was too young to care about road trips. Someone had to stay home to man the switchboard, so Gus stayed home with Mom.

We were stoked. We watched with hungry eyes as the parade passed by. There were horses wearing fringe and tassels, chuckwagons and massive floats shimmering with glitter, clowns with balloons, dogs pulling tiny covered wagons, and a marching band with majorettes. It made me ache for a skimpy, shiny outfit with boots and a baton to twirl. What a rush.

When the parade ended, Dad took us to the Hub Café for lunch. We ordered cheeseburgers and Vi-Co. We feasted. Our booth had a tabletop jukebox. None of us knew how to operate it other than to turn the knob to flip the playlist. So we ate without dinner music. Besides, we didn't have supplementary cash to feed it.

"Dad? Can I have a nickel for the jukebox?"

"No." He reached into his pocket and handed over some coins. "Go to Madill's and buy smokes."

Madill's was a drugstore with a massive selection of goods to buy. It was a great place to get cigarettes while waiting in line to purchase cough medicine. At that time, you didn't have to be of age to buy cigarettes, and no one ever questioned why an eight-year-old needed smokes.

After lunch, we went to the Stampede Grounds and watched the rodeo action. It was wild. I particularly liked the barrel racing, because the riders were girls, like me. But after a while, we became bored. Dad took us to the midway, bought some ride tickets, and put us on the Ferris wheel. John, Mitch and I shared a ride. It was the freakiest thing we had experienced up to that time.

Mr. T bought us cotton candy, and we scarfed it down. After a ride on the Tilt-a-Whirl, we packed into Mr. T's car to go home. Between the Tilt-a-Whirl ride, the cotton candy, and riding in the back seat, I started to feel sick.

"I'm not feeling so good."

I might have spoiled the perfect day when I upchucked cotton candy in Mr. T's car. Good thing upchucking wasn't a collective undertaking for John, Mitch, and me. I was alone on that one. Mr. T never offered to take us anywhere after that.

Besides good rodeo, Saskatchewan had great football. When hockey season ended, sports fans watched football, and they were over-the-top devoted to the Saskatchewan Roughriders. Saskatchewan fans felt a strong kinship with the Roughriders. They remained loyal through losing streaks and never lost faith in the team. When the Roughriders won the Grey Cup, all of Saskatchewan cheered with absolute fervour.

I didn't catch football fever until I became a teenager. Being a fan was a symbol of prestige, though I didn't have any identifying merchandise to sport. I would have liked to flash some Rider-green garb, but I couldn't get my hands on any unless I attended a game—and that was not likely to happen.

I could have carved myself a melon helmet, but that craze hadn't yet hit the scene.

The Roughriders played home games in Regina, which was almost four hundred miles from us. It was insane to make that kind of trip just to attend a football game. Edmonton was somewhat closer, but catching a game there would be just wrong. It would be like selling contraband on some else's turf. Besides, we didn't have that kind of gas money.

The alternative was to watch games on TV. I picked my favourite player and cheered him on. And, of course, that was Ronnie Lancaster. The challenge was trying to keep track of him, or the ball, or any of the other players, through what looked like a blizzard on the field. Most games on TV looked like a storm happening—not because of weather but due to poor TV reception. The nearest TV station was a hundred miles away. Signals had to travel a long way before reaching our antenna. Good TV reception was sporadic. Usually, the best viewing happened during *Front Page Challenge* or *Question Period*—shows we were just *dying* to watch. The reception was rarely ideal for the better stuff, like movies: *Ma and Pa Kettle*, *Billy Jack*, or *Flap*.

Football provided distraction from my blank party calendar. Invitations to fun events weren't exactly pouring in. Mitch was way more advanced in the social department.

By the age of fourteen, Mitch had met the love of his life. He and his girl became almost inseparable—but she was from a different township. Mitch wasn't old enough to drive, so he put a lot of effort into making arrangements to see her. Most of his friends were older, and he'd buddy up with those who owned their own wheels.

Guys preferred girls from out of town. Not many wanted to go out with a local girl—it was too much like dating a sister.

Some thought pickings were better elsewhere, so it wasn't hard for Mitch to hitch a ride out to see his girlfriend.

One day Mitch found a good deal on a car. He and John pooled their cash and made the owner an offer. The guy accepted.

The little car was a Datsun that had seen better days. Japanese automakers built engines to last, and the little car's performance did not disappoint. It got the boys from point A to point B, which was better than walking. Its body was the colour of Pepto Bismol, which made the car stand out. The boys named it the *Pink Pig*. Mitch decided the Pink Pig needed an added touch to make its image really pop.

He had special talent painting shadow figures. He once painted a mermaid silhouette on the front of a hardhat, which brought Dad special attention at the sawmill. The Datsun needed something just like it, so he got busy designing another one. Before long, a luscious fish lady emerged atop the hood of the car. The painting gave the Pink Pig the uniqueness he was after.

The mermaid idea stuck with Mitch for years. Future Mitch must have been thinking about his Datsun when he carved mermaid tails in the sand, encasing his young daughters to the waist in beach grit. The girls posed on the lakeshore, water nymphs with flowers hooked behind their ears, looking Polynesian and pretty. Perhaps Mitch had envisioned this scene all along.

The Datsun, with its signature mermaid, was recognized everywhere. John drove because Mitch didn't yet have a driver's license. Sixteen was the age he anxiously longed to reach. Until then, John chauffeured—and that was OK by Mitch. It worked out well for John, too, giving him lots of opportunity to expand his social circle.

Car maintenance kept the boys busy. With Dad's help, Mitch and John learned a lot about mechanics. They picked up tips on taking apart a carburetor to clean it, changing spark plugs, patching tires, doing oil changes, and anything else a young car owner should know. And when Gus got tall enough to see into the hood, Mitch mentored him in the field of mechanics.

The boys did a lot of country driving, since Mitch's girl lived in the country. Many of their other friends lived on farms, too, and having farmer friends helped them stretch gas money. They racked up plenty of miles cruising in the Pink Pig, and a few bucks bought a lot of farm fuel—the purple kind. A driver had to be careful not to get caught by the RCMP. Sometimes cops used a siphon to extract a sample from the gas tank. They checked it with a gauge to detect a purple tinge.

"Looks a little mauve in there, lads. Want to tell me something about that?"

The boys couldn't look the officer in the eye. Without a word between them, they each hoped the next guy would come up with a good answer.

If the gas had a purple hue, the driver got a ticket. Only farmers were allowed to burn purple in their vehicles. They got a break on the cost of fuel, but only for the purpose of farm work. The purple dye was to keep everyone else honest.

Even though the boys got away with using cheap gas once in a while, keeping the tank fed was a hassle. Mitch was starting to feel the squeeze of keeping a girl happy. He was hellbent on giving his sweetheart the fine stuff, so he decided he needed a job.

Local employment prospects were scant. One of the few viable options was working as a farmhand. There were bachelor farmers looking for help, unlike the married farmers who had a wife and a string of kids to help out with farm work. The job was the kind most wouldn't wish on a dog or their worst enemy—picking rocks, cleaning barn stalls, and spreading manure.

John and Mitch put themselves out there, and it didn't take long for them to find employment. A bachelor farmer hired them to pick rocks.

The purpose of rock-picking is to clear a field of rocks and lessen the risk of damage to farm machinery. There was rock-picking equipment engineered for the task, but few farmers were blessed with adequate funds to purchase one. Hiring cheap labour was way more economical.

One alternative to costly equipment was a rig called a stone-boat, which looked like a barn door and was dragged on the ground behind a tractor. Pickers walked alongside the stone-boat and dropped rocks onto it. The boss farmer always drove the tractor, because he was the boss.

One particular farmer who hired the boys was a different sort. He resembled a guy named Relic, a character from a Canadian TV series called *The Beachcombers*. Relic was a beachcomber who drove a speedboat, salvaging stray logs along the Pacific Coast of British Columbia.

The farmer wore a toque that matched TV Relic's knitted beanie. Both had scruffy facial hair and a gruff persona. We envisioned *Farmer Relic* speeding his stone-boat across the field on a burning mission to salvage rocks, beachcomber style.

The boys worked through summer vacation. They left home for the week, and farmer-boss provided them accommodation. The living quarters were grungy, lacking comfort and cheerfulness. The farmer served up meals, and the boys slept on cots. They worked long days, performing jobs that gave them little satisfaction. By week's end, the boys were grimy, tired, and undernourished, but they had amassed a small wad of cash for their efforts.

Friday nights, they came home. Mitch walked into the house and headed straight for the bathroom to get cleaned up. John waited his turn, nursing a smoke outside the back door.

Running water had been installed in the house the year before. Both were relieved to not have to fill the bathtub from the town pump across the street. It was a welcome luxury, though supply was limited by the low-producing water well.

Mom prepared a meal while the boys cleaned up. Each emerged smelling clean and fresh. They sat down at the table, and she served up plates heaping with meat and vegetables. John dug in with fervour and remarked, "This is way better than we were getting at the farm. Old Jim only knows how to cook with a can opener."

The boys didn't notice Mom watching them with eyes clouded over with tears. She held back the waterworks, as any good mother of boys always does. They were growing up and away—too fast, in her opinion. She wanted them to remain boys a little longer. But her hanging-on would only stifle their ambition, so she smiled as they trooped out the door, anticipating a fun weekend for themselves.

Their farm careers slowed when school started in the fall. John and Mitch worked weekends during harvest. When work came to an end, their skimpy cash flow stalled. Mitch secured the caretaker role at the rink once winter set in. He partnered with Denis on the job.

Denis and Mitch made a good team—both were conscientious workers. They made sure the ice at the rink was in good shape by flooding, scraping, and cleaning it. Snow removal was the toughest job, and there always seemed to be snowfall in the forecast. That winter, the sky dumped huge amounts of the white stuff, keeping the boys gainfully employed.

The caretaker had the added responsibility of keeping the skating shack warm, stoking a fire in the woodstove and maintaining a woodpile. The rink lights had to be turned on by sunset and turned off every night at 9 p.m. Mitch arranged a schedule around his social obligations, so Denis acquired a generous share of the burden. Denis tended to the rink while Mitch was in school, out on weekends, and every other time the work conflicted with Mitch's plans. Each seemed happy with the arrangement. John sometimes lent a hand in exchange for payment toward his beer tab at the pub.

The boys managed to keep their money challenges to a minimum by adopting careful spending practices because their earnings were often too skimpy to cover the cost of their wants. Mitch's ego hungered for something better. It was only a matter of time before scraping by wasn't good enough.

Completing high school wasn't important to John or Mitch. They were in too much of a rush to move on and away from book learning. Pay was good working oil rigs, and the boys couldn't resist the lure of big money. Staff recruiters for drilling companies knew their best hires were boys skilled at farm work.

John got a job in the oilfield first. Rod was already working in the industry, so he helped John get started. Within a couple of years, Mitch had left home and found a job as a carpet layer. The pay couldn't match working rigs, so he ditched the carpet business, followed John, and went to work as a roughneck. Wherever Mitch went, his sweetheart followed. They were a team and had the common goal to build a life together.

Mitch and his girl were barely eighteen when they got married. Mitch was the first of my siblings to be wedded in the Catholic tradition, complete with reception and dance. Most other family nuptials had limited attendance, consisting of the bride, the groom, a couple witnesses, and a minister or judge.

But Mitch's was going to be a proper celebration. He and his bride would have a church wedding with all the pomp.

My siblings and their families crammed into Mom and Dad's house to primp for the occasion. We adjusted to limited space and privacy for dressing. Bathroom lineups and few mirrors were among the challenges testing our civility. The bustle and fuss were reminiscent of an ant hill in turmoil, and we learned the art of taking turns again.

I hadn't attended many weddings, and Mitch's was preparing to be a grand one. John and Gus were part of the bridal party. John was Mitch's best man, and Gus was a junior groomsman. They brimmed with pride in their roles. Both brothers were determined to do it right for Mitch.

The day was golden and warm, dawning on the heels of a summer solstice. I watched my brothers standing together at the church altar as they waited for the celebration to begin. They were handsome in their polished suits. The bride paraded up the aisle, followed by her entourage of bridesmaids. They took their places at the altar next to the groom and groomsmen. The priest took charge and initiated the marriage rites.

"Welcome, family, friends, and loved ones. We are gathered here today, surrounded by the love of God and the beauty of creation to witness the marriage of this young couple . . ."

The church was packed with family and friends. I rubbernecked, searching the crowd for familiar faces. Most eyes were focused forward, paying attention to the ceremony.

The priest performed the wedding ritual, gave a spiel about the seriousness of the marriage pact, and even dropped a joke. He gave a blessing and introduced, for the first time, the new husband-and-wife team. The couple exchanged rings and kissed. They walked down the aisle hand in hand, out the door and into the sunshine.

We peppered them with confetti. Our family was growing, and it was cause for celebration. The festivities got underway, with heaps of food, libations, laughter, and dancing to music played too loud. There didn't seem to be any problems or complications—only joy and fun. My mate Buck and I partied with family and friends until we were asked to leave.

My siblings and I had dealt with speedbumps as we aged into our twenties. We were adults, but we lacked experience and wisdom. We made mistakes and bad choices. We brought home significant others with personalities that didn't always mesh well. Buck had a strong temperament and a loud presence, and my family indulged him for harmony's sake. He wasn't so tolerated by my siblings' partners, though. There were occasional clashes, but nothing ever went beyond words. The arguments put me in a difficult position, failing miserably to keep everyone happy. Sometimes, I think they favoured squabbling over reasoning. They didn't know I ended up paying the real price for the conflicts.

Buck and I were having a good time at the wedding, dancing, socializing, and cracking jokes. Perhaps our laughter was too lively and spontaneous to not invite suspicion. Someone had the opinion that we were making fun of the bride with our mirth. I didn't understand how our enjoyment could be interpreted that way, but I suppose someone needed grounds to have us removed, even if the reason had to be invented.

Mitch approached us with a harsh request: "I'm going to have to ask you to leave." He said it more to Buck than to me, but still he meant the both of us.

"What?" I wasn't sure that had I heard him right.

"You need to leave. You can't be making fun of my wife like that."

"Like what?"

"You know what I mean."

Buck responded, "No, we don't know what you mean."

"How exactly are we making fun of your bride?" I asked, perplexed.

Mitch wouldn't look me in the eye, which made me wonder whether he actually wanted me to go. He might not have had a choice. He said, "Don't make this any more difficult than it is."

I pressed him: "What's really going on here?"

I stared at him, my mouth agape for a few awkward moments. There was no added drama, no bad scene. The message slowly sunk in.

"Oh, I get it. We don't fit here . . . . Fine."

I turned and walked away from him. We collected my son and our belongings, and drove the four-hour trip home.

I don't think anyone else realized what had transpired. Mom and Dad didn't learn of our absence until much later, and I'm sure they weren't made aware of the real reason for us leaving. They couldn't understand why we would up and take off without saying goodbye.

The knowledge I had brought this trouble on my family hung on me. I hadn't meant to hurt them. I felt powerless to change the story, and they never held the incident against me. Waiting for the storm to pass was my only option. It probably gave my parents a few sleepless nights.

Perhaps I had missed something. Maybe we weren't even invited to the wedding, and I had only presumed we were, since I was family and all. Our turning-up must have caused anxiety or something like that. The matter was never resolved or brought up again. It was conveniently swept under the carpet.

Mitch was a great dad—the kind of dad every kid wants. He never lost his sense of kid-like wonder. He had a knack for dreaming up the best ways to have fun. He created adventure from the mundane, and nobody was better at building things, discovering things, and coming up with wacky antics for added effect.

His pride and joy were his four daughters. He doted on them, and the girls loved him for it. Mitch was the fun dad who pulled out the face paints, draped the girls with plastic capes, and transformed their faces. He taught them how to throw a ball, ride a bike, draw a picture, program a computer, bathe a pet, do math, play cards, and cheat at playing cards. And sometimes, when they needed help dressing and getting themselves pretty, he picked out their outfits and fixed their hair—in ponytails, curled, straightened, or crimped. He mastered style and flair for their sake.

Mitch's girls inherited his originality. They filled their days working on creations and innovations, designing new looks, new projects, new spins on fun. Nothing about them was dull. They never rode a bike in a way that was ordinary—they rode with grandiosity, bedecked with glitz and sparkle.

"Look at the camera," Mitch instructed one of his daughters. "I want you to ride your bike over the ramp again, so I can get a picture this time."

He captured meaningful moments of his girls at play. The camera loved Mitch's girls, and it never caught one in an awkward pose or weird facial expression unless it was deliberate. If photos could capture a generation, their camera snapped scores of lifetimes. The images revealed a picture-perfect family, and I discovered a window into their stories by simply leafing through photo albums.

When Mitch and his wife were away out of town, I sometimes babysat for them. I either went to their home to look after the girls, or the girls came to my place. During their stays, my house rocked with activity, fun, and sometimes clashes.

"I want my mom. I want my dad. I don't like this."

"Well you got me for now, so eat your broccoli."

"My mom doesn't make me eat broccoli, or do dishes. Don't you have a dishwasher?"

"We are the dishwasher."

"I'm not a dishwasher."

"You are while you're here."

I was out of my element fostering girls. I had spent too much time with boys, doing guy things and playing sports. Dressing up, putting on makeup, and fussing with your looks only brought out my awkwardness. I couldn't afford all the accessories and trinkets girls seemed to need. Besides, how would I decide what to buy? I had no fashion sense, which was sadly obvious to my with-it nieces.

Sunday mornings were a gong show as I struggled to help the girls get ready for church. They had high standards for the look of the day, and helping them attain that was stressful. Alex groomed himself. Fortunately, our drama didn't curb his progress. Since I wasn't a miracle-worker or economical with time, we typically arrived at church late. The girls paraded in with flair—whereas I stumbled in looking like I had been flung off a hay wagon.

The girls returned home after a stay at my place, happy to resume their normal way of life. They gladly waved goodbye to my simple ways. I couldn't match their lifestyle on my salary, and perhaps it was hard for them to understand that. I hadn't been employed long enough to earn job security, and I watched my pennies closely. With a somewhat unpredictable future, I couldn't afford to splurge on costly fun. Mitch was a good provider for his family, and they benefited from his success. I often envied their seemingly easier existence. It had me believe that some were blessed and others were not—and I was *not*. But that was only my perception.

Mitch and his wife worked hard to establish a good home life. No two parents put more into giving the best to their children. Free time equated to family time, and they filled vacation days and holidays with fine adventures for their girls. They made big plans to do cool stuff, like travel, go camping, and check out the latest attractions. Everywhere they went, they chalked up new and exciting experiences.

They brought home souvenirs to remind them of notable moments spent together as a family. A hearty slice of recreation included hunting down merchandise. Shopping was a fun distraction for Mitch's girls to explore—a pastime that became easy to fall into. They chased deals, browsing for hours. Perhaps time spent at the mall was tiresome for Mitch, so he came up with fun ways to escape the agony of shopping. On one occasion, he disappeared into the crowd, and the girls soon found themselves without their male escort.

It put a stop to their excursion, at least until the lost could be located.

"Where's Dad?"

"He was just here."

"Maybe we should put a leash on him."

They scanned the mob of shoppers, and one of the girls spotted him. He was standing in a display window, his body rigid, his demeanour stoic, his eyes locked and staring forward. A few mannequins shared their space with him, but they paid him no attention. People passed by, oblivious to the storefront invasion. Even the store clerks were fooled by the trespasser.

One of the girls moved close to the window and pointed to her dad. "Should we leave him? He looks like he's having fun."

Mitch was good at imitating lifeless figures, and he used that know-how to derail other masters of the skill. One day, Mitch came across a busker who was using his talent to masquerade as a statue—not just an ordinary statue, but a bronze statue of a famous dead guy.

It's not hard to sympathize with a guy trying to make a living off the kindness of passersby—busking to pay rent can't be easy. Even so, Mitch couldn't resist a challenge, and he put himself eyeball to eyeball with statue guy. Mitch was being a blatant nuisance, pointing his finger in the busker's face, causing him to lose composure. Statue guy probably wanted to knock Mitch's lights out, so Mitch backed off. Mitch's game might not have been all that nice, but people thought it was real damn funny.

Shopping expeditions with Mitch were more entertaining than productive. Perhaps his motive was to get his daughters' minds off spending money, to keep some of the greenbacks inside his wallet instead of inside the cash register of big-box stores.

His role as man of the house was many times challenged by the females who outnumbered him. Claims for closet space, bathroom time, and phone privileges might have resulted in a few clashes. But family life didn't come without reward—he loved his girls deeply, and they loved him back.

The fun and allowances helped make up for some of their trials. Diabetes was epidemic in their household. In their family of six, three were type 1 diabetic, insulin-dependent— Mitch and two of his daughters. Trips to the drugstore were like shopping sprees at Bulk Barn or Costco for normal people. For Mitch, it meant stocking up on insulin for himself and his girls.

The disease played a huge role in their lives, dictating what was allowed and what wasn't. The limitations put a lot of pressure on girls trying to grow up and fit in. No one else in their circle of friends had to be so mindful of their diet, activities, and schedule. Blood glucose tests, syringes, and vials of insulin used up their time and stole their normalcy. They worried about serious and even life-threatening complications associated with the disease. A slight miscalculation in a dosage or too long a span between meals could bring on an insulin reaction and another trip to the hospital.

The stress level was sometimes epic, yet they faced it with boldness. Mitch's wife carried most of the load, managing daily dosages and nutritional requirements. The family thrived because of her efforts.

"Here's how you load the syringe."

Mitch's lessons in self-administering injections became too common in their home.

"Take this here grapefruit and poke it with the needle. Then push down on this thing—it's called the plunger. You know, like the thing beside the toilet? You push down on it all the way, and all the insulin gets pushed out into the grapefruit, which is like your skin. Now, get this system down pat, and we can all shoot up together."

Since it had to be done, they went about it as a team, and threw in fun for good measure. The strength of their family unit was in their ability to face things together. It was a good strategy for moving forward.

One other significant force that kept Mitch anchored was his trust in God. Early in their marriage, he and his wife began to mould a life built on scripture. They held each other up with prayer and leaned on faith for support. They would need it to face trials that were surely to come.

Our extended family endured the 1990s bearing a flood of losses—*bang, bang, bang* . . .it felt like a myriad of attacks. No sooner had we caught our breath following one loss that we were bracing ourselves to manage the next. Brothers, parents, grandparents, uncles, cousins . . . I lost count at fifteen. By the time the final decade of the millennium ended, funerals had become normal for family gatherings. What a way to approach Y2K.

I sensed the heaviness Mitch carried after John's death, because I felt the same. Mitch didn't talk about it—he more or less danced around the subject. And I didn't force a dialogue, since I was just as closed. We couldn't share any of the good memories. It was like a wall had been erected between the past and present. Somehow, the past got stuck on the other side of the barrier. I tried to clear it from my memory and scrub the tape clean so I wouldn't have to bring up the pain.

During the days leading up to John's funeral, the house was a hive of activity. My family handled arrangements with mechanical dissociation. Plans were made and carried out, but there was no escape from the numbness.

There was an issue with John's car. It was parked outside the back door, like a badly situated crypt. Then someone moved it to a location behind the garage, at the far end of the yard. I suppose the police had done their best to clean up the area, but beneath the car's undercarriage, they had left what looked like blood-soaked earth and small, unrecognizable fleshy fragments. Something had to be done, quickly. We couldn't risk my parents coming out and noticing the detritus.

It wasn't the kind of day to be outside; cloudy, windy and rainy, which was good for keeping spectators away. I stood on the back step with Mitch, assessing the dirt-packed driveway. A few fat raindrops pelted the top of my head.

"I know it's bad, but I need to do something about this right now." Mitch's words were strained and shaky. He closed his eyes and exhaled loudly.

"I'll help you." I didn't want to, but the situation put me in the condition of *have to*.

He asked, "How are we going to do this?"

I opened my mouth to speak, but I stalled, trying to make sense of the job we were about to tackle. I faced the cold wind and answered him with a nervous chuckle, to let him know I wasn't being a bitch. "Do I look like the answer lady?"

"Yeah, you do."

"OK, then. I guess . . . we should get a shovel and something to put . . ." I had to take a moment to think of a word. Then it came to me: ". . . the stuff . . . in. Does that sound sick or what?"

Mitch shrugged his shoulders and hid his face from me. "We don't have time to come up with a better plan. Let's just get it done."

I went to place my hand on his back as he started walking away, but I was too slow. He lumbered across the yard to the garage, and I followed. We avoided going near John's car. We'd had enough dealing with objects related to trauma for one day. Inside the garage, we found a spade and a used grocery bag.

I mentally distanced myself to carry out the task. It wasn't right that anyone else be saddled with the responsibility. We worked hastily, as if covering up a crime scene. In a warped sense, it was the last collaborative effort between the three of us. Mitch and I disposed of the few remnants of our brother, and I tried hard not to think about the thing we were doing.

My family was operating on borrowed fuel, and masking their devastation. We couldn't immediately process the reality of John's suicide. It took weeks, months, even years for some of us to absorb his loss. We went back to our lives keeping busy with work, focusing on what was in front of us instead of what lay behind. We did what we had to for the sake of sanity. I kept the pain hidden, because talking about suicide was taboo. People might think it was contagious, and they'd look at me like I should be put away. Shutting up was better.

It could easily have been the same after Denis's memorial, but the atmosphere there was different. We grieved the loss of our brother without feeling the stigma, and we were able to remember him in the company of people who had these things figured out. In the real world, the subject of suicide caused too much discomfort. So, on the inside and the outside, silence was our preferred method of dealing with John and Denis's deaths.

There was an accident on New Year's Day, only a couple of hours into 1993. It was a cold night—minus thirty-nine degrees Celsius. Ice crystals hung like tinsel off a coal-black ceiling. And it was eerily quiet except for the ladies cleaning the dance hall after the New Year's Eve bash. The band was packing their van as the women locked up the dance hall and began walking home in the cold.

Home was merely a block away for the women, who lived across the street from each other, but they had to cross a highway to get there. Snow crunched beneath their boots like the sound of teeth chomping down on dry crackers. They each carried a container of food leftover from the banquet. With her free hand, one of the women pulled her hood tight to keep the chill out. The frigid air stung, and she squinted into the cold. A large tear leaked from the corner of her eye and froze on her cheek. The brutal cold made it hard for her to negotiate the night.

The women arrived at the intersection next to the church. To get home, each would cross the road on opposite sides of the street. The van leaving the dance hall rolled to the street between the women, who waited on separate corners of the intersection. The van turned onto the highway, billowing exhaust from its tailpipe, forming clouds of smog. The cold was extreme, the haze wouldn't lift, so it hung like a veil, giving the night a ghostlike quality.

The van travelled west and met an eastbound vehicle that was coming into town. One woman waited for the car to pass. The other didn't notice its headlights through the dense fumes, and the driver didn't see the woman enter his path.

Mom's injuries were serious. The right side of her mangled body required multiple surgeries to repair bone and joint.

But somewhere in the chaos, there was a miracle—she hadn't sustained a head injury. The downside was that she was cognizant of the suffering, the trauma, and the pain.

She never complained or showed her discomfort. She kept negativity to herself, not wanting to burden us. Mom considered this huge hardship only hers to bear. One day, I walked into the hospital room and found her sitting up in bed. She was the essence of regal. Even at her worst, she carried herself with poise and dignity. I considered her strength, and how gracefully she manoeuvred through hardship. She had shown us how to walk with and overcome misfortune, and to not display adversity like a merit badge.

Meanwhile, three years of dealing with catastrophe had caused a major decline in Dad's well-being. He had stood through two sons committing suicide and his wife suffering a serious accident. The stress was nearly unbearable for him. He was aging at what seemed an exponential rate. There were days during Mom's hospital recovery that I questioned whether Dad's declining condition was surpassing the magnitude of hers.

I wore out a set of tires on my car travelling the road from my home in Alberta to collect Dad in Northern Saskatchewan, to bring him to the hospital in Saskatoon where Mom was recuperating. This is what four months of tending to aging and ailing parents looks like . . .

> . . . travel north to home and make sure Dad is OK. Manage his home. Consider meals (buy groceries, prepare and freeze a week's worth of portions). Deal with laundry, safety (get MedicAlert), mobility (get scooter from Veterans' Affairs), house maintenance and repairs (defrost frozen water pipes and the intake

to the septic tank). Make sure Dad doesn't burn down the house trying to do repairs himself (whole 'nother story there). Look after Dad's social needs by arranging for visitors to drop in, or get Dad to the Seniors' Centre for a game of cards, a cup of coffee, or maybe even a potluck. Write out a new TV schedule because the satellite programming changed—find out show times for *The Price Is Right, Little House on the Prairie, Gunsmoke,* and *Highway to Heaven.* Shovel snow. Look after paperwork (income tax, prescription applications for reimbursement, Veterans' Affairs applications). Consider Dad's health (make doctor's appointments and freak out because he travelled by bus by himself to go see a specialist). Visit Dad in the hospital if he's been admitted, and arrange home care and visits from a nurse for when he gets discharged.

Travel north, pickup Dad, get him prepared for a trip to go see Mom. Get his car road-ready, because he's more comfortable in his own vehicle. Travel south to the hospital in Saskatoon. Get to the hospital parking lot and look for a wheelchair. Wheel Dad in to see Mom and watch as he bursts into tears at the sight of her. Get them to chapel, since Mom wants some worship time. Somehow manoeuvre Mom's rollaway bed and Dad's wheelchair into the worship area, which puts them a fair distance apart. Scurry between the two, ensuring their comfort instead of listening to the sermon (the chaos is not lost on the minister, who at least doesn't seem too peeved by the disruption). Plan a shopping trip to purchase goods Mom needs. Ask hospital reception if we can borrow a wheelchair for downtown errands (they say no, but we stash one in the trunk anyway). Get lodging for an overnight stay. Consider calling a tow truck when the car won't start after a night parked out in the cold. Examine the battery and clean the posts. Fix the issue and avoid mechanic costs, thanks to those repair lessons from Dad. Go back to the hospital and visit all day again. Drive north, drop off Dad, go west, and make it home on time to get a bit of sleep before the start of the work week . . .

. . . that was the condensed version. It still makes me tired thinking about it.

I worried about Dad. I had never seen him so vulnerable. He needed his routine and the familiarity of home. That was his best chance to manage, so I committed as much time as I could to help him through the ordeal of Mom's lengthy hospital stay.

One day, the nurse came to assess him. I sat with her, and we agreed he likely wouldn't get through the week without being readmitted to the hospital. He was at his lowest when it came time for me to leave. He asked me to stay longer, but I had already used up all my time off from work. Leaving him that day was tough. I drove home feeling like shit. I called him every day to gauge his well-being. By some miracle, he rallied—and came through the fourth month like a trooper. Then Mom came home, and that settled him the most.

She had spent four months recuperating in the hospital—sometimes in the ICU, sometimes in the burn unit, and several times on the operating table. She received new parts to replace bones and joints and skin grafts on her legs like quilt patches. She was discharged from the hospital in May, and was finally able to come home.

Mitch, Gus, and I got busy helping her settle in at home. She couldn't navigate stairs anymore, so the living room became her new bedroom. Residue on the walls, from years of smoking, begged our attention. Mom had been a non-smoker since the accident, and we wanted to remove cigarette stink from the house.

The scum came off like thick soup, and we joked about its grossness. Years of accumulated smoke-gunk explained why our kids regularly came home sick following a stay at Grandma and Grandpa's. The grandchildren were loyal to their grandparents, so it was out of the question to discourage visits—and we were still somewhat oblivious to the effects of smoking on health.

Throughout Mom's recovery, distance made it difficult for my siblings to make themselves available. They helped out when they could. House repairs had been neglected for years, and delaying them further was out of the question. I didn't have the skills to rebuild Dad's bathroom floor, so I let my brothers handle that. It's a good thing Mitch was a handy kind of guy. The spongy floor boards could cave in at any time, and someone taking a comfortable dump might find themselves finishing the job in the cellar.

For a couple of years, Mom's and Dad's well-being improved and they were able to maintain their independence. They functioned well in their own home, within a community of friends and family. But then things turned bad again. Dad's health deteriorated. He grew tired and didn't have the strength to keep fighting. He died in March of 1995. There was no known cause, but I think he died from the heartache of too many losses. Mom found the courage to go it alone after that.

By midsummer, Mom had started having pain in her stomach, and it wouldn't let up. Doctors took forever to run tests and determine the cause. The diagnosis came. My siblings and I were there when the doctor revealed his findings.

We were in the emergency wing, where the hospital staff did triage. EMS brought Mom by ambulance to the University Hospital in Saskatoon. They kept her in the ER for two days without admitting her. The room was cramped with about a half-dozen beds holding people in similar distress, each separated by a curtain. Nurses and doctors tended to patients. The space filled with the din of instruments whirring and beeping a broken rhythm. The smell of disinfectant clung to everything.

The doctor stood at the foot of Mom's bed, between two of my brothers. "I wish there was a better way to put this. It's cancer, and it's very aggressive. Terminal. There may not be much time . . . a week to ten days, perhaps. I'm very sorry."

Then he left us to absorb the news.

His cruel words pushed hard against my chest, hurting my ribs, making it hard to catch my breath. A terrible cramp seized my stomach. There was nothing I could do but endure it.

Sound escaped the space around me and my family. It swirled a deafening buzz on the other side of the curtain. We were stunned and numb. We each held our own silent resolve, our deadpan stares giving no hint of the tumult inside. No one had the courage to look Mom in the eye. We felt like we had let her down. We stood paralyzed, stalling the imminent comprehension of her dire sentence.

We needed a distraction from the grimness of the situation. On the other side of the curtain, a nurse pried information from an uncooperative patient.

"Sir . . . sir . . . can you please tell me how tall you are?"

She waited for a response, but received a bloated lull.

Our eyes fixated on the floor, so we wouldn't have to watch if emotion overtook one of us. We pricked up our ears for something else to grab our attention—anything to detract from the doctor's news and the beating it was giving us.

The quiet broke with a whisper, like a nervous wound . . . a faint blather from somewhere within our circle. Rod spoke, perhaps on behalf of the tongue-tied patient.

"I don't know . . . I'm lying down."

He jarred me sober with the absurdity of his response. I stifled a laugh and wept silent tears instead.

The nurse kept pushing her patient for information. "Sir, please answer my questions."

We let our minds wander to the conversation next door rather than focus on our own situation. The developing drama between the two provided a welcome diversion.

I suppose we could have ignored what didn't concern us. But always there was a challenger to outdo, and Mitch was the comic who simply couldn't stand down. He volunteered a response to her next question: "Sir, can you feed yourself?"

He hammed a jerky, robot salute, mashing an imaginary ice cream cone on his forehead.

Again, I was caught by a brother's ludicrous reaction and this time, the laughter was even more difficult to suppress. It competed with the grief I was trying to conceal. I couldn't ignore the duel between the two comics, who were also struggling with inner conflict. My cheeks were drenched with heartbreak, while my hand clamped hard against my mouth to keep the meddlesome mirth inside.

A deep, raspy cough resounded from a bed at the far end of the room, and Mom floored us with her own contribution to the lunacy: "Is that a horse over there?"

We couldn't hold back anymore. We spontaneously erupted in cackles and chortles, stirring up a disturbance in the ER. Our weeping competed with our laughter, and soon the two converged. It was hard to tell which emotion was front and centre, but it didn't matter. What mattered more was the shared outpouring of our unadulterated grief. I remembered Denis's ill-timed guffaws, and somehow, they didn't come across as inappropriate anymore.

Our exuberance caught the nurse's attention. She entered our space and offered assistance: "I can find you somewhere more intimate. I'll have the orderly bring your mother to a private room."

"Thank you . . . that would be nice."

Mom died on a Saturday morning in late November 1995. Her death triggered another family reunion, the kind I wished wouldn't have to be arranged so damn often. This one bruised me worse than all the previous ones put together. The ever-expanding row of graves was dismal. Their growing number unsettled me. I was bothered that family funerals might become the new norm.

On the day of the funeral, winter granted us a reprieve from the worst. The sun managed to shine for a while, and we reaped the benefits of its warmth. Inside the church, we whispered a collective goodbye to our beloved mother. Pallbearers carried her casket outside into the crisp air, and we followed behind, marking her final exit from a place that had known her consistent loyalty.

She left us, and we discovered a new kind of heartache. It's like jumping into the deep end without a tire tube to keep you afloat, or taking the training wheels off your bike and almost colliding with a fence—only I think it's much worse. I learned what it felt like to be an orphan—abandoned, lonely, and afraid.

My siblings and I scattered like spores to the wind, detached and unsure where we fit anymore. It's funny how the influence of one person had kept us grounded. Once she was gone, we began to lose each other.

We didn't make the effort to get together as often. If and when we did meet, our conversations were safe and didn't dig up too much of the past. Getting too close might scorch us like a red-hot poker, so we kept our distance. Perhaps we used fear to justify our growing apart.

My sister's husband died, so we attended yet another funeral. Pauly wanted—needed—us to be there. I came, and so did Rod and Mitch, along with their wives. Pauly was the one who could best express grief. She allowed herself to feel sorrow in the moment. Unlike me, she didn't lock it inside to fester.

Pauly lived in Missouri. She and her sons opened their homes to us. The first thing we did was embrace. Then we marvelled at the wonderful character and decency of our two grown-up nephews. They charmed us with their generous hospitality. It was a long overdue homecoming—or at least that's what it felt like.

Reminiscent of old times, we huddled around the kitchen table, catching up on news. Picture albums were opened to validate bragging rights or give cause for a good ribbing. It felt good to fall back on the way things were.

We traded memories about our brother-in-law, Ernie. He was the American invasion who joined our family. When our sister brought him home to meet us, we took an instant liking to him. We shared stories to remember the moments we spent with him.

In 1970, the early days of Pauly and Ernie's relationship, Ernie worked on scoring points with our family. He volunteered to take the four youngest kids camping. We'd never gone camping before, so it was a new experience for me, John, Mitch, and Gus. Ernie had modern camping equipment that functioned better than the amenities we had at home.

We helped Ernie pitch his tent at Dad's farm. He found a good spot in a small clearing, protected from the wind. There were enough sleeping bags if we doubled up, which was a good idea, since it was September and cold. It snowed during the night, but we were snug and warm in Ernie's tent, which was heated with a propane burner.

Ernie wanted us to have the benefit of the full outdoor experience, so he arranged a hunt for us. He brought all the gear we needed to catch snipe. He gave us each a paper bag and told us to wait in the bush while he scared them out of hiding. We'd never heard of snipe before. Our instructions were to keep the bag at ground level so the snipe could run into it. We held our position with grit, determined to catch the little critters.

It's just sad that Mitch was the only one to catch on. He played Ernie's game and faked a near-catch of a snipe. He held up a bag with its back-end blown out, which gave the rest of us incentive to keep up the hunt.

They were fast little buggers, too fast for us to spot. I still have no idea what one looks like. I suppose our tender youth and inexperience were to blame for the skunked hunt.

Snow snakes were as hard to find as snipe. Apparently their pale, stretchy bodies blend in perfectly with snow. Ernie said that if we looked hard enough, we could recognize their pink, beady eyes peeking out from snowbanks, but I never saw any of them either. Maybe it was because I had such poor eyesight when I was a kid.

We revealed to our nephews the tricks their dad played on us. They weren't the least bit surprised, although they were amazed at how gullible we were. Mitch told them, "You have to be born in Saskatchewan to inherit hick ignorance. You can't just learn it."

It felt good to remember my brother-in-law in a way that brought him back to life. I hope the stories eased the loss for my sister and her family.

The funeral provided us a glimpse of Ernie's early life, the part of his history that happened before he met my sister. He was an ex-serviceman and a proud veteran.

The US Armed Forces gave him military funeral honours. Servicemen in full attire set a tone of reverence and respect. The rifle party of the Honor Guard fired a three-volley salute. Two of the servicemen folded a United States flag and presented it to my sister. We watched as she and her sons embraced the flag and then each other.

The trouble didn't start until after we got home. I'm not sure why shit gets stirred up at funerals and weddings, but it seems like it's a common thing. When one strong personality makes a claim, everything goes sideways. The best response I know is to take a wide berth around the issue and hope it blows over.

But sometimes the trouble stays in your face. I didn't want to walk on eggshells to appease someone's fragile ego, and I couldn't understand why anyone would allow such an insignificant comment upend them. I cared for both my sisters-in-law, but sometimes they could get carried away with bullshit concerns.

One took a rigid stance on an implied slight and another tried to apologize for the unintentional offense. In my opinion, it wasn't an issue warranting a big upset between them. I was baffled. One drew a line in the sand, which put a wedge between two brothers, though Mitch and Rod didn't allow the situation to sever their fraternal bond. Even so, my little brother's spouse needed to be placated.

Pride destroyed any chance of a reconciliation—my sister-in-law's arrogance occupied the centre of the matter, ruining any chance of future get-togethers. We could easily have put the issue behind us, gotten on with life, and maintained peaceable connections. But stubbornness kept the conflict alive. Opportunities to mend fences came and went, and none were capitalized on. Years passed, and the gap widened. And then it seemed like it was too late.

Mitch was determined to advance his career in the oilfield. Working rigs was a foot in the door to the oil industry, and he set his sights on moving up the ranks. He pursued higher education. Between work shifts, he studied and completed technical courses. With hard work and determination, he became a power engineer. And then he kept learning, achieving higher class levels until he became Power Engineer, 2nd Class.

The distinction opened new opportunities for him. One option was to work overseas. The take-home pay was good, and the experience would be exciting. He was keen to learn about different cultures, and what better way to do that than by immersing himself in one? When he received an offer to work in a foreign country, he decided to accept the challenge.

The change was stressful for his family. In the past, they had adapted, pulled up stakes, and followed Mitch wherever his work took him. They often relocated—mainly to different towns in Alberta where the energy sector was booming. They even moved to a remote northern town near the border of the Northwest Territories. Rainbow Lake was their home for a few years, until Mitch found work that brought him south again.

When Mitch and his girls reminisced, they talked about their life in Rainbow Lake the most. They spoke of the closeness among residents, and how everyone looked after one another—which was necessary considering the remoteness of the locale. The village was surrounded by wilderness, and kids had to be careful walking alone—bears were common in the area. And wolves.

Isolated is one way to describe the community. Rainbow Lake had one road out for travel by automobile, and an airport for quicker getaways. Winters were harsh, and summers were plagued by swarms of blackflies, whose bites were particularly nasty. Many residents vacated Rainbow Lake for the summer to get away from the blackflies.

The road trip to and from Rainbow Lake was exceptionally mundane, with miles of bush and the occasional wildlife sighting. It was hard for kids to sit through such a long trip. When they got antsy, the teasing and the whining started, which disrupted the drive. Mitch bluffed a threat to curb their bad behaviour.

"Before we leave home, I'm going to line those girls up and give them each a good spanking. Then, when we're on the road and one of them acts up while I'm driving, I can just tell her, 'See, that's why you got that spanking.'"

But he never did follow through on the plan.

The first foreign country Mitch worked in was Ecuador. There was serious trouble brewing in the area at the time— Canadian oilfield workers had been kidnapped in September 1999 and kept for ransom in the jungle. He stayed in the same compound the men had occupied before they were taken. The Ecuadorian army boosted security to keep it safe. Even so, the situation made family at home nervous.

In mid-November, the hostages were still being held in the jungle. Armed guards escorted Mitch and his co-workers everywhere they went. Mitch got used to the boys in camo, who carried M-16s slung over their shoulders and shadowed his every move. He sent home pictures of downtown Tarapoa, a squalid little community situated near the Columbian border. Tarapoa was a dangerous place to hang out, especially for anyone who wasn't a local.

The hostages were released on the hundredth day of their captivity. Canadians had been waiting with bated breath to learn of the liberation. The whole country felt the relief of the long-awaited homecoming of their brother-patriots.

Mitch's family weren't relaxing until he was home again, but that would be awhile down the road yet. They tried not to worry about the possibility of more trouble. The memory of the hostages in captivity would sit for a long time.

The instability didn't dampen Mitch's optimism about his new post. He wanted to learn the language, understand the culture, and respect the people whose country he was occupying. It wasn't enough for him to simply pass the time earning money. He supported local vendors buying wares at fair prices. And when he came home, he gave everything away to his family and friends, pampering them with gifts.

Mitch made friends wherever he went. His easy charm and perpetual grin drew people to him. They called him "Smiley." After Ecuador, Mitch took extended work assignments in Kazakhstan and Yemen. He gave each new post the same consideration. He learned to speak Kazakh and Arabic. Languages came easily to him.

Another kind of culture competed for his attention, though—the kind that occupied inside the walls of company compounds. Workers tried to keep their minds off missing home. They acted shamelessly on impulse, and sometimes disrespected the locals. Companies took steps to keep indulgent behaviour outside the camps, but cooperation was limited by the willingness of employees to comply.

Overseas work and travel constituted a different lifestyle. For Mitch, it was continuous readjusting—to home, to work, to family, and to leaving home again. The constant rallying made it hard to maintain balance. Before long, the pressure of two conflicting worlds began to leave a mark.

Mitch's personality changed. Each time he stepped off the plane, he was less like the husband and father he used to be. Habits from the road didn't adapt well to family life. He found the transition increasingly awkward. He struggled to give his family the best version of himself, but kept falling short. Perhaps in years past he had set the bar too high.

There was an anger inside him that hadn't shown itself in years—not since he was a boy. It resurfaced a couple of times, with alarming consequences. He began to live fast and hard, as though trying to make up for time spent as a husband and father. He seemed to want the kind of enjoyment that gets you in trouble and destroys your faith.

Sometimes he arrived home agitated, putting his family on edge. Nervous tension hovered in the space around him, leaving them unsure of what to expect. His mood shifted randomly. Drastic and intense, only occasionally did he linger near normal.

Mitch's marriage hung on the brink as his personality continued to shift. His girls were baffled at their dad's strange behaviour. His life was becoming a mess—at least, that's the way it looked to those closest to him.

The reveal of what was happening to him and his family hit me like a paintball pellet between the eyes. I couldn't understand his actions, why he would knowingly devastate his family. I picked a side, made my opinion known, and pointed out his irresponsible conduct. I gave him no opportunity to explain himself. I couldn't hide my disappointment in him. I suppose I thought my job as the older sibling was to steer my brother straight. But it only drove a wedge between us. And then he couldn't trust me anymore.

I was the one who drove that wedge into our relationship. I didn't give him a chance to let me in and show me what was going on with him. I heard bits and pieces of his misdeeds, and refused him a voice.

As adult siblings, we had drifted apart somewhat. We were busy, each surviving and looking after those who depended on us, though we stayed in touch even when distance separated us. I assumed there was nothing on earth that could sever our bond, but perhaps I had taken our relationship for granted.

Many times, he acted like a big brother toward me. If I needed help moving into a new home or fixing my car, he was always there, the first to offer me a hand. We didn't spend much time together during our teenage years, though we attended the same parties on occasion. I was always after some boy. It was no secret that I was easy, so guys gave me little respect. If Mitch heard a guy shit-talk me behind my back, he would steer me away from him. He didn't want me to get myself mixed up with boys who were only after self-gratification. But I didn't always listen to him. I got myself in fixes anyway. He knew all the bad things about me and still he loved me. He gave me more than I could ever hope to repay him, and I should have listened to him. And when we were adults, I should have listened, but he was on a strange new journey that didn't fit the norm, and I couldn't work out the cause of it.

If I had paid attention, I would have considered our family's history, but I had wiped that slate clean a long time ago. The past was behind us, and I didn't want to look at it. We didn't need excuses to defend current behaviour. We were smarter now, and better able to work through problems. We had developed an immunity to old tapes from the past—ones that kept trying to replay themselves inside our heads. Above all else, I wanted to believe we weren't plagued by mental illness anymore.

But then, he was diagnosed: bipolar disorder.

There was a time when I almost got it right, when I faced my first big challenge at being a proper big sister. I was four when a situation arose. I needed courage and determination, and I stepped up to the plate.

My big brother Denis was in the hospital, healing from head trauma. Mom and Dad tended to him there, so Mitch and I were sent to live with our aunt. Our temporary home was something else—lots of space, plenty of forest, close to the highway . . .and it had a nice sandbox for our enjoyment.

I had a cousin who, at that time, was the only child of my aunt and uncle. He was older than me by about four years. I'm not sure if I was yet mature enough to realize my envy toward him. In my opinion, he had a privileged lifestyle—a new bike, the best toys, his own room, an indoor toilet and bathtub with running water—comforts that were beyond my parents' means. Plus, there was an elegant mural on a feature wall in the house and a live houseplant that folded in on itself when touched. I thought it was all so exotic.

My sister and older brothers lodged elsewhere, at another aunt's home in town, which was close enough for them to walk to school. It was odd not having them around. The only sibling substitute close at hand for Mitch and me was my cousin, and he wasn't particularly fond of sharing his abundance.

My aunt gave him the job of watching us while we played in the sandbox. His idea of watching us was to make sure Mitch didn't touch any of his toys. That killed any chance of the fun I was looking to have. I grew angrier by the minute while he put my little brother through what I considered an ugly ordeal. If eyes could be fierce, mine would have ripped my cousin a nasty wound. I wanted to throw rocks, chuck them at his head, fast like a slingshot, but I was helpless. I could only watch as a spoiled, arrogant eight-year-old picked on my toddler brother.

After a while, my cousin grew tired of the game and left us unattended. Ideas of how to ditch the shitshow barreled through my head. I considered that, on my own, I could be quite capable of looking after my little brother. It couldn't be much worse than the care he was getting here. I devised a plan to deal with our predicament.

I scoped the yard for any sign of posse looming. No one was watching, so I decided to make a break for it. Adrenaline coursed through me. I gripped Mitch's hand and led him down the curvy driveway, toward the highway. I was taking him home. I could feed him, shelter him, and protect him without anyone's help. And I would do it the correct way.

We reached the highway and I turned us eastward, toward town. His little legs couldn't keep up with my haste, so I slowed to match his gait. I didn't want us to get caught, so I urged him on toward liberation, which was a quarter-mile away.

My four-year-old intellect gave me the notion I was in control. We kept moving, and it felt like we were in the clear. It was our first experience of life on the lam, and it seemed to fit our renegade selves.

We kept walking toward town. Boreal chickadees sang to us, and we relaxed a bit, enjoying the trek. Tall trees on both sides of the highway made our path look like a tunnel. The hemmed-in effect of it made me feel small and insignificant, so I adopted a cocksure composure.

We were halfway home when a fuss uphill made me turn and look back. Up the road, my aunt was waving frantically and calling after us. My cousin raced toward us on his bike. I took a firm hold of Mitch's little fist and told him, "Run!"

I half-dragged and half-carried my little brother, but I couldn't make enough headway. My cousin sped past us and swung his stupid bike into our path. We ground to a halt and he mocked us with a smirk. I wanted to push his ass off that bike, but the best I could muster was to stare him down with a snarl.

Before years began wearing away at my spirit, I was plucky. I had gumption. My attitude could and did change outcomes—sometimes for the better.

For a while.

Then things got complicated.

Life worked on me, changed me . . . changed Mitch, too.

CHAPTER NINE — THE SEX TALK

Breathe life into this feeble heart, lift this mortal veil
of fear
Take these crumbled hopes, etched with tears, we'll rise
above these earthly cares
Loreena McKennitt
"Dante's Prayer"

Tuesday, March 2, 1993, 9:47 a.m.
I'm busy, don't bother me. Things don't get themselves done, you know.
If it's broke, I fix it. If it's empty, I fill it. If it's dirty, I clean
it. If it's garbage, I chuck it.

The to-do list keeps growing faster than I can make it
shrink. I don't remember what free time looks like anymore.
It's a rare thing to stop and just sit.

It was a hell of a start to the year. *"Happy New Year … your
mom's been mowed down by a car. Have you made any New Year's
resolutions? Maybe you should put those on hold for a while."*

I'm with my dad, and he's a little less stressed because I'm
here. I see fear in him. It makes his step less sure, it interrupts

his sleep and lingers long in his space like a stench. Anxiety is out to conquer him.

It's hard to see him vulnerable. He used to be so large in life. He had authority. He was the parent. But now, he's showing me a look, the kind he might have given his parents a long time ago. The look of a small boy, lost and afraid.

I don't know how to turn this around. I fumble, and sometimes add to his worry instead of take away from it. I think he can sense my defects and wonders how the hell he got strapped with such an incompetent caregiver.

Today, he volunteered to make breakfast.

"That's a great idea, Dad. I sure could use a taste of old-time normal."

I had been working on him, trying to help get him out of his funk, and this small gesture of cooperation was the tiny light at the far end of an uphill tunnel.

He's no stranger to the kitchen, he's made meals before. He adds his own unique flavour to a dish. Pepper is his preferred ingredient. If meals had a label showing a breakdown of food content by volume, the second item on the list would read "rolled oats" or "brown sugar"— rolled oats for filler and brown sugar for the palate.

When Dad was in charge of fixing meals, which wasn't too often, the menu included porridge for breakfast and hamburger patties or baked beans for all other meals. Dad claimed that pepper brought out the best in porridge and that hamburger went a lot further to feed a family when cut with rolled oats. He added extra pepper and sugar to baked beans to make them tangy and candied.

My siblings and I had our own opinions about ample zest, and the rock-hard of what we called, puck-burgers. Our palate preferences rarely aligned with Dad's, but we knew better than to voice ours. We could always fill up on bread in a pinch.

This morning, Dad prepares breakfast following his usual standard. I don't complicate his menu with suggestions. The meal is easy for him to make and that's the whole point—build up confidence for him to become his own caregiver. The peppery sweet porridge tastes best when he serves it with a dash of independence.

He's ingesting a small measure of accomplishment with every spoonful. Breakfast is a feast laid out to celebrate a win. It raises us above our immediate concerns and chases away worry.

We are filled and at peace—the two of us at the table, taking a breather from uncertainty. I watch Dad in amazement. There is determination in him yet, though circumstances keep chiselling at his resolve. He hunches because it's easier than straining weary back muscles grown tired with age and creeping osteoporosis.

Dad's arms, which once rippled with hard bands of muscle, are feeble now, their tone languid and spent. His bony-thin arms are like two cornstalks propped at the edge of a lonely field. They dangle from slumped shoulders that have carried sorrowful burdens for too long.

I survey the top of his head while he studies his coffee cup. His hair is wiry-thin and the skin at the roots is waxen, and I'm thinking I can press my thumb there and leave a print. There's a line like the edge of a shadow on his forehead where the tanned part starts. He used to wear a hat to block the sun, but it didn't protect his face from catching rays. His skin is leathered where the sun touched and carved creases into a frown.

The skin is pleated at the rim of his upper lip, and his cheeks are sunken where the absence of teeth shapes his jawline. It gives his face the look of an elongated oval, like an alien's silhouette. But Dad's eyes aren't empty like alien eyes. Dad has sadness and love and a deep yearning in his, though he often wears a lost and rankled look.

The frustration of getting old and feeling useless sometimes gets the better of his mood. It's hard for him to be patient with himself while remembering how easy it once was to get things done. The mechanics of his limbs and digits have failed, slowing his attempts to a stall. And then, trying became too much of a bother for him.

He misses her... my mom. He can't think of her without an ache welling up inside him. They didn't always use hugs and kisses to prove affection, and saying *I love you* was awkward for them, but facing life's challenges together solidified the bond between them.

Their history wasn't always a flower garden. More than once, they arrived at the brink of calling it quits. Many indignities tested their limits, and they each pulled punches to salvage what was left. But seeing her in a state of near-annihilation knocked him on his ass, and he remembered the little French farmgirl he had fallen in love with in his youth.

He sits at the head of the table, because that's where Dads sit—right in that place of authority. He's so quiet, I have to lean in to make sure he hasn't fallen asleep.

"Dad, would you like some more coffee?"

He perks up. "Sure."

I serve us both a refill, and we resume our hush at the table.

The lull gives me a chance to remember a long-ago moment shared between Dad and me. It was a different time, and his embrace had been enough to give me comfort. I was a teenager again, feeling the sting of disappointing him. He draped his arm around my shoulders and kept me close as I cried. I was afraid of the daunting challenges looming in my future.

I was eighteen, unwed and pregnant. It's not the path he had envisioned for me, but it was the one I was travelling down. I'm not sure whose heart was more broken—his or mine. I suppose I had a romantic notion that being in this state would guarantee me the support of a mate. Instead, I was joining the expanding population of single mothers—and I was scared.

I remember sitting with him, side by side on the couch, watching a television show. I was in the final weeks of my pregnancy. My teary breakdown interrupted the program, and Dad cradled me and simply let me cry.

Sometimes a good bawl with the support of a loving parent is all it takes. I hung onto the resolve it helped me foster. I had made a pact with my young self that I would get us through this. I'd find a way to survive. I'd rely on my wits and hope that my efforts were good enough. And I'd be shrewd and badass to protect what was mine—especially my child and my spirit.

Seeing Dad now aged and worn, I hope that I've measured up to his expectations. Actually, he told me recently how proud I had made him. I cling to that. It helps me to know that I can add *good daughter* to my short list of honourable traits.

He lifts his head to look at me with squinty eyes like he's studying me, seeing me anew and considering my confidence. He puckers his brow, as though a question is itching to wriggle free of his thoughts. His mouth gapes open, but nothing escapes. There is a sense of vulnerability about him, and I recognize that, at this moment, I should remain attentive.

There was an incident that happened decades ago, and he's trying to tell me about it.

Some things you need to know about my dad:

> He was a good, practising Catholic.
> He was a member of the Knights of Columbus.
> When I was small, he used to come to church
> with us all the time.
> Then he didn't.

I watch him struggle to get words out. He's focusing on his coffee cup, perhaps expecting it to give him a cue. The first attempt at sound comes out as garbled gibberish. He clears his throat and begins again.

"One time, I went to a conference in Prince Albert for Knights of Columbus. Four of us went."

He pauses to take a sip of coffee and stares into the cup. It mustn't have been syrupy enough, because he picks up a spoon and adds another scoop of sugar. After he's stirred in the sweetness, he takes up the yarn again.

"There was me, two other guys, and the priest."

As he catches his breath, I say, "That sounds like it would have been a good experience."

"No." He spits the word, as if it's gone sour in his mouth. "We had to stay overnight. It was for two days."

More stalling.

"We had to get a hotel room. Our room had two beds, so two of the guys took one of the beds."

Dad's tone is taking on a bothersome edge, like a growl and a moan competing for the same air.

"I had to sleep with the priest in the other one."

I'm starting to feel nervous, and I want to interrupt him, but words refuse to come out of my mouth. My eyes won't blink, and I am held captive, waiting for him to go on.

"All night long, he kept putting his hands on me, and I had to keep fighting him to stop it . . . the cocksucker."

He draws a quick breath, like a hiccup. He shudders for a brief second and goes quiet again.

And now my guts are quaking.

There's a tune by the late Jim Croce called "I Got a Name." The song played on the radio and lingered near the top of the charts during the 1970s, so I heard it often. I never paid attention to the words before, but now a couple of its lines shout out to me:

> *I got a name, I got a name*
> *And I carry it with me like my daddy did*
> *But I'm living the dream that he kept hid*

I suppose the words could mean the good dream or the bad dream. The lyrics send chills up and down my spine, and the reason my innards are doing a twist and flip. I can't help but wonder if this priest did more than simply molest my dad. Something tells me there is more to the story, but the trail has likely gone cold, and fact-finding will be difficult. Too many years have passed, and not enough witnesses remain.

Sunday, May 16, 1965, 9:45 a.m.

When the church bell rings, it's time to get to Mass. Sunday mornings are a ruckus of primping and fussing. Boys have their hair slicked smooth with Brylcreem, women cap their lids with pretty bonnets, little girls wear tiny white gloves, and Dads shine their shoes.

My family walks from home to church, which is only half a block. We fill the third pew from the front on the left side, facing the altar. Mom and Dad sit at each end of the bench to keep us hemmed in. The rest of us cram in the middle, except for whichever brother's turn it is to serve as altar boy.

After Mass, Mom rushes home to make sure the chicken in the oven isn't over- or undercooked. The priest is coming for dinner. She sets the table with nine plates, one more than the current number of family members.

The house is clean and tidy. Mom spent the previous day scrubbing and waxing floors to a shine. Pauly and I dusted furniture with polish that smelled like antiseptic lemon. Rhubarb pies, waiting to be served for dessert, sit on the counter.

Mitch and I follow Dad home from church while the rest of my siblings linger with friends in the churchyard. It's a beautiful spring day, and we want to ride the tire swing.

With one free hand, Dad helps us gain elevation on a rubber doughnut. With the other, he raises a smoke to his lips. I have an image of him still—an almost-dandy, leaning casually near the base of the swing, cleanshaven, wearing pleated trousers and a dress shirt, with a fedora cocked on his head. I think I saw that figure once before, in a movie on TV where the star catches the leading lady's eye.

Pauly walks across the yard toward the swing and joins Dad to keep us airborne. Mitch lets out a squeal and tightens his hold on the ropes. He relishes the thrill of flying. I hear Rod, Denis and John cavorting from down the street as they make their way home. Soon, they want a turn on the swing, too.

No one notices him arriving. There's no sound to alert us, except perhaps the gentle rustle of his robe over the grass. I look up and squint my eyes to see a dark figure looming over me, blocking light from the sun. A dark, towering silhouette without a smile or emotion. I quit picking dandelions, the boys step away from the swing, Pauly holds the ball that Mitch wants to keep kicking, and Dad stubs a cigarette between his thumb and forefinger. Play stops, and we are sombrely attentive when the priest shows up.

Dad ushers Father into the house, where Mom is busy with dinner preparations. She is startled momentarily, wipes her hands on her apron, and welcomes the priest. Dad leads him to a chair at the end of the table, the place normally reserved for the head of family. Dad chooses a seat right of the priest, which also happens to be the server side for altar boys. Perhaps it's a force of habit.

Mom brings them each a cup of fresh coffee. The priest reaches for the mug and brings it to his lips. They discuss church business while Mom pulls food from the oven.

There's no need to ring a dinner bell. We know, almost by instinct, when the food is ready. We file into the house and take our seats at the table—except Mitch, who's place is taken by Dad. There's an empty chair beside Mom, and he doesn't seem to mind the switch.

Various details are stranger than most, and the notion of Dad being less than the boss at the table doesn't sit well with me. Something's amiss trying to fathom the priest's posturing. He appears larger than life. The harsh angles of his face framed by wire spectacles don't help soften his persona. A row of buttons run the length of his garment from collar to floor. Perhaps the black uniform is deliberately tailored to convey authority, even though the chain and crucifix hung around his neck imply servitude.

The priest touches his forehead with the fingers of his right hand and makes a sign of the cross. We follow his lead and bow our heads as he prays a blessing over the food. The prayer comes out like mumbled chatter, perhaps in Latin, because I can't make out the words. He could be delivering the punch line from a Bob Hope joke and we'd never know. We cross ourselves again and respond, "Amen."

The priest gets first dibs on the food. His is the only physique at the table that's portly. I watch him pile his plate and wonder why Dad hasn't barked, "Are you gonna leave food for the rest of us?!"

I know bread's purpose is to fill the void, and I forgive him for the oversight, but it doesn't stop me from giving Father the stink eye. The priest doesn't notice that I'm bothered. He's too busy shovelling roast chicken into his maw. That's understandable, because Mom is the best cook in the Catholic Women's League.

I don't recall many more dinners that my parents hosted priests. There was a shift in the way church life influenced our family. Dad stepped back from participating, and it may have caused friction, but I didn't particularly notice. Perhaps I was too busy shovelling bread into my maw.

Dad became grumpy. He didn't want to play with us much anymore. I used to pester him to play catch with me, which was something we both enjoyed. Perhaps age was making his body hurt, so I found other ways to sharpen my game. Even his social life stalled. He and Mom had friends who came to play poker once in a while, but not the same men who used to talk church business. I only saw those during Mass, and they didn't pay us much attention.

Mom held up the torch, leading us to church every Sunday. She doubled down, helping to run lay-led liturgies after the last priest moved away. Our church became a mission post. One priest served several missions, so Mass was held only once a month. But that happened about fifteen years after the dinner that I remembered.

I didn't feel ostracized, though people might have wondered why Dad stopped going to church and they used it as an excuse to give us the cold shoulder. No stories circulated, no heads rolled, and there were no threats by church authorities to keep him from spilling secrets. Dad may not have felt we were at risk, so he didn't utter a peep. But I would wager that humiliation and shame played the biggest part in maintaining his silence.

I have no idea whether that particular priest tried molesting others, and I suppose I may never find out. I only know he didn't do anything to me. I'm not saying the thing was never done to me—just that it wasn't done to me by a priest. In retrospect, I had a hunch that something did happen to my brothers. There were signs and slip-ups and too much knowledge about things that shouldn't be known by young minds.

You can tell when someone is trying to cover something up. They try to disguise a lie with too much detail. They keep going on and on, attempting to convince others with elaborate strings of flap. You don't have to say a word, just let them speak and they keep digging themselves deeper and deeper. Some people eat up whatever is told them, because they can't discern the truth from a hoax. It's a comical thing to witness.

I saw cover-ups, but there was nothing comical about them. They were chinks in armour, and I knew how to spot them. When you build your own means of protection you learn to recognize tiny flaws in others' designs. Secrets are meant to remain hidden. You may not see them by looking directly at them. You need to look beyond where the light shines on them, to notice the thing they cast. Heat radiates off a hot surface, and you can't see heat, but you can see its shadow. You can verify the proof of a thing by following its shadow trail, and perhaps arrive at its source.

If it were easy to interpret actions, I suppose someone would have wondered about the progression of our inappropriate behaviour. Self-mutilation with cigarettes, excessive drinking, promiscuity. and causing trouble weren't part of normal for healthy kids, even in my generation. No one offered help, understanding, or fixes. Instead, we were shamed into toeing the line. I suppose it worked—there was no other way to right it or deal with it back then. We didn't totally self-destruct... yet.

John, Mitch, and I had more in common than just being from the same family. I believe all three of us were prey, but we didn't know this about each other.

Anger was one way we acted out, and we used it mainly between us. I didn't want to be the one left standing on the lowest rung of the ladder, and neither did they, so we fought each other for better ranking. We couldn't defend ourselves against predators, who outweighed, intimidated, and overpowered us. It was easier for us to fight amongst ourselves. We thought we could elevate our own status by keeping the other's dignity stunted. But in the end, we were all like rats, exposed and scurrying for cover.

I'm not sure if it had anything to do with gender, but it always seemed to be me against the boys. Maybe it was because I was the most stubborn, as I was told on more than one occasion. I fought viciously, and rarely succumbed. The unwritten rule was to get back up and never let them see you cry.

I imagine it was difficult for my parents to watch us become so bitter toward one another. We spent our teenage years chipping away at ties that once bound us together. It's sad to recall, but during that time, I think I hated my brothers.

I guess we were trying to prove something to the world and to ourselves—that we weren't losers.

Perhaps I wouldn't have fought so hard had I known that winning was going to feel this bad.

Tuesday, March 2, 1993, 10:52 a.m.
I continue watching Dad from across the table. He's nursing his coffee, and doesn't look up. I'm trying to think of how to respond, to take the edge off our conversation. I want to somehow give him peace.

His words sure have shaken me.

I play for time.

I neglect to drink my brew. I'm insulating the mug with my hands, but the contents grow cold anyway.

I wish Dad had a pet, so I could pretend it needs feeding or maybe the plants need watering.

I stall some more.

I can't simply not speak. But at the moment, I'm struck dumb. If I give myself a chance to recover, it's possible a word will come to mind. I could follow a script from discussions I've been having with myself for years. There were points I tried to make myself believe, like justifying actions with excuses and rationalizing secrecy for the greater good. I'm kidding myself. But perhaps there is something in there to console or help him.

Nothing comes to mind. So instead, I'm not going to think hard. I'll let my heart do the talking. I open my mouth and these words come out: "It wasn't your fault."

Letter to God:

Dear other Dad,

I know everybody ever born is your kid and all, but it seems to me you could have tried harder to be a less absent parent. I think you gave us each a little too much room to freewheel. Some of us aren't cut out to take on the responsibility, and do the right thing with all that freedom. Obviously not everyone got your memo about following the golden rule.

What's up with all the kid-bangers running churches and schools? You think maybe you could have intervened there . . . a bit? Would have been nice and maybe saved some kids a lot of bullshit.

That one guy in particular, he really did a number on my dad—and maybe my brothers, too. He's dead for sure now, and I hate to imagine him living the dream somewhere in your nice house. It makes me wonder about the fairness of it all. It gets me to thinking—that if this guy is there, way up there, celebrating shit, it should be really easy for me and my family to wriggle our way in. We didn't do anything remotely close to the bad that dude did.

So, the logic doesn't compute that you should ever refuse us access.

I'm thinking that everything there will be shiny, mellow, kissy-faced, and blissful. But just so you have a heads-up, I'll be on the lookout for him. I don't much care that I should be behaving myself inside your perfect realm . . . I will punch his fucking face in anyway.

luv,

Your other favourite kid (ha!)

CHAPTER TEN — REUNION

Bring the wind to carry me over
Lead me home to my town
Tell me when that breeze is blowin'
Takin' me home to my town
Glass Tiger
"My Town"

Margret was a friend to me, though I don't think I was ever one to her. A good indication of friendship is to invite a friend to a birthday party—but I deliberately didn't do that.

Margret and I started school together in Grade 1. We shared the same teacher and the same classroom. Sometimes we shared the same textbook because there weren't enough copies to go around.

We didn't exactly seek out each other's company. At recess, I played sports while Margret, who wasn't athletic, hung out somewhere quiet. She lived on a farm, so the only time we saw each other was at school. Mostly we competed for best marks in math and spelling.

Then I got distracted. I was almost thirteen. My mind was on boys, looking good, and growing boobs. I obsessed over clothes and hair and whatever else might snag a boy's attention.

I had a plan . . . a good plan. A birthday party kind of plan. There would be decorations and food and music and dancing. I worked out the details and decided who should come. There'd be the same number of boys and girls, so each would have a dance partner.

I announced the plan to my classmates. Just before the start of summer break, I told them, "I'm having a birthday dance in August. I'm going to send out invitations. Just wait."

I drafted the list of invites, and every name fit my idea of a party-worthy guest. Unfortunately, not all classmates made the cut, including Margret. She talked funny and was kind of nerdy. I didn't think any boy would want her as a dance partner, and I didn't want a wallflower hanging out along the perimeter. That was how I justified not inviting her.

School let out at the end of June. I filled my days with work and play and forgot about scholastics. Summer flew by, and birthday party plans never materialized. The idea lost its appeal and I didn't give a second thought about how to celebrate.

There was nothing symbolic or special about my birthday that year. I was away for most of the day. I arrived home and found that a present had been dropped off for me. The package was gift-wrapped, and included a card. I tore off the jazzy paper, and inside was a box of pencil crayons. I opened the card. It was from Margret.

Happy birthday
Hope you like the crayons

I held the gift in my hand and felt its weighty burden on my ego. Dancing and birthday parties weren't so appealing anymore, and I was relieved that my lame idea had hit the skids.

It never came to light that I had been such a jackass, but it gave me pause to think and evaluate my conscience. I felt conviction in my spirit. My vanity had just taken an ass-kicking. I recognized that Margret had gifted me twice—once with crayons and the second time with a lesson. I put aside the first gift and went to work on the second.

I made a new plan . . . a better plan, one with a higher purpose. I made it my mission to show Margret my gratitude. I'd go full bore on building a relationship with Margret and become her worthy friend.

I waited for school to start up again. I didn't remove the crayons from their case—I was saving them. I wanted to use them in art class, with Margret.

Margret never returned to school that fall. I looked for her, but she wasn't there. It took a while for me to figure out what had happened to her. I learned the schoolboard had decided to redraw boundaries for bus routes. And because she lived halfway between our town and another, she was bussed to a different school.

I didn't see her again for decades.

Every ten years, a group of volunteers from my hometown planned, promoted, and hosted a school reunion. Hundreds of former residents showed up, and the village's population swelled during the few hectic days of a summer celebration.

It was that time again: August long weekend 2004, time for another reunion.

Organizers put together a celebration that consistently topped the previous one. They managed hospitality with impressive panache. In a community with no shopping facilities, restaurants, or overnight accommodations, the task was daunting. But organizers were the descendants of people not intimidated by lack of conveniences. The spirit of small-town Saskatchewan was rooted in fortitude, so the people built and improvised.

I liked reunions and I didn't like reunions.

It depended on certain matters.

I liked that all my siblings came. I liked returning to my place of birth. I liked visiting relatives. I loved the lakes, the bush, the open countryside and the north.

I didn't like getting rock chips on my windshield. I didn't like that the ball diamond was turned into a hayfield. I didn't like how rundown some of the houses looked. I especially didn't like that Saskatchewan no longer felt like home. I kept returning, though. And I kept searching for that old familiar feeling.

There is a persistent urge to return to one's origin—migrating birds do it all the time. Something is programmed in the code that ties us to our beginning. I wasn't alone in that. Each reunion drew more than nine hundred home-comers. People came with their families, their pride, and their bragging rights. They packed all that into an RV, anticipating a great celebration.

A crowd gathered at the entrance to register for the reunion. Excitement was mounting, people were mingling. Friends became reacquainted amidst shrieks of recognition. Histories were exchanged, and some poor sap was cornered by a guy touting a litany of accomplishments implying urban-supremacy.

Then I saw her. She was standing in the throngs. There was no mistaking Margret—her visage hadn't aged a day. She was a taller version of her kid self.

It had been more than thirty years since we had last spoken. I pushed through the crowd and nudged to get her attention. Her eyes lit up with instant recognition, and we tripped into a clumsy conversation. We quickly got reacquainted, and found plenty of common ground to keep our discourse lively. I learned her history, and I was intrigued. It isn't that she'd achieved notable feats—just that she was exceedingly successful leading a good life.

Time hadn't changed her. She carried herself in the same way she always had—unpretentious and dignified. She was unique and slightly offbeat, and she talked in the way a deaf person voices words. She was tall and lanky, and looked at the world with eyes that only saw good.

I carried a memory of the gift she gave me for the birthday that was long past. She had probably forgotten about it, but I remembered the crayons clearly. It's one of the reasons I sought her out. I kept my gratitude secret, so she wouldn't think it weird that I'd hung on to it all these years.

We wandered into the common area of the community hall while sharing more of our stories. Tables were set up with displays offering glimpses of the past. A local seamstress had crafted a beautiful patchwork quilt sewn with cloth images of old buildings. The showpiece was featured nicely on the back wall. I recognized several of the images—the school, the grain elevator, the general store, and other structures that had long been torn down.

Margret pointed to a particular square on the quilt. "Say, isn't that your house?"

"Yeah, I guess that makes our home part of Makwa's history, too."

It was strange seeing a black-and-white image of our house displayed so prominently. The picture was blurry, but I recognized the sign hanging on a pole outside the front door that read "Government Telephones." In the centre of the sign was the Saskatchewan coat of arms, bearing a lion and wheat sheaves. Memories flashed through my mind of the switchboard's influence throughout my youth.

Margret brought me back to the present. "I don't remember Mom and Dad going there often to make calls. Imagine that, we lived on the farm without a phone. How would we get along without one now?"

"It's called progress. Whether it's a good thing or not is debatable."

"Is the house still there? I haven't been down that street to notice."

I said to her, "It was demolished about eight years ago. Mom found a buyer for it a few months before she got cancer. Dad and her were planning to move into a new place, but he died before it was ready. So, Mom moved in and lived by herself. Then she got sick and passed away shortly after. Meanwhile, the people that were living in the old house abandoned it. In the spring, the house was condemned and torn down."

"That all happened within a year?"

"Yeah, it was quite the year. Lost our home and the folks."

"Sorry to hear that."

"It is what it is."

I didn't want to make light of the details—only to move on from unpleasant memories. We refocused on the quilt.

Margret noted another of the images.

"What's this other place? I don't recognize it."

"I think it used to be a café. I vaguely remember getting bubblegum from a dispenser there. It was the first time I'd seen a gumball machine. The place must have closed down when I was still very young."

More people gathered at the quilt. Nostalgia was spreading faster than juicy gossip. We gave up our place at the front of the queue for others who were craning their necks to inspect the patchwork.

I asked Margret, "Do you recall the old curling rink, the mushroom factory, and the dance hall that was used as a movie theatre for a while? I'm not even sure if the mushroom factory was a real thing or if it was just an old livery stable. It was barely standing when I was a kid. Maybe they called it that because of the piles of manure inside, which probably made it ideal for growing mushrooms."

"No, none of those places ring a bell. We didn't get to spend much time in town."

A woman I recognized as Margret's sister approached us. "Hi, how are you?" she asked me.

"I'm great. Nice to see you here."

"I'm going to have to steal my sister away." To Margret she added, "You're needed for a family matter. Follow me, please."

Margret turned to me, "Can I catch up with you later?"

"Sure, see you then."

I regretted missing out on a deeper friendship with Margret. We could have been close. I'd had plenty of awkward moments coping with my own peculiarities, so it would have been easy for us to relate to one another. Perhaps if I hadn't been trying so hard to fit in elsewhere, our friendship could have grown. Some people might not have considered Margret polished enough to suit their ideal, but I saw her for what she was: a kind soul with great potential as a best friend.

Saturday, August 2, 2014, 9:15 a.m.

It's reunion time again. Déjà vu hits me, and I'm giddy with anticipation. People are assembling in small groups, recalling old times. They rekindle friendships, and jubilation pervades. Ten years has been generous to most. I'm hopeful, and eager to resume where the last reunion left off—and I'm not alone in that sentiment.

Organizers launch the weekend with a morning buffet. Excitement radiates off people as they wait in line for breakfast. I join the queue and stack a couple of pancakes on my plate. I slather them with Mrs. Butterworth's sticky-sweet syrup. The smell of bacon sizzling on the grill draws more people to merge into the buffet line. I find a spot at a picnic table and sit down to partake in the meal.

The seating area is located where the school building used to be. A steel wire fence encloses the cement base of the old foundation, making the space look caged. A crowd assembles inside for breakfast. Decorative solar lights are wedged into openings between the chain links on the fence, and each light displays a flag inscribed with a name to remember someone who will never again attend a reunion.

Across from me sits Margaret's sister.

"Nice day if don't rain."

Saskatchewan conversations always start with the weather. An early morning downpour had caused rainwater to pool in the low areas, and the likelihood of "nice" wasn't in the forecast. For now, the sun is beaming down, causing me to squint. I try hard to focus attention on Margret's sister. She grins, knowing the weather will decide itself.

"How are you?"

"I'm well. How's the family?"

"All here . . . or almost all here." I do a silent roll call of my family.

A woman, I don't recognize, cries out in excitement to an old schoolmate. In her zeal to embrace him, she bumps the picnic table, sloshing a bit of my coffee. I hang onto my cup in case anyone else saunters by and spills it.

"Were you at the campfire last night?" she asks.

"No, we were at my brother's anniversary celebration." The memory of the festivities is still fresh in my brain. "I heard people say they had a good time at the sing-song."

"It was a good time . . . and well attended. Too bad you missed it. So which brother was this for?"

"Mitch." I didn't want to share any details, so I drop her a question instead: "Is all your family here?"

"For sure. We wouldn't miss this."

"Is Margret close by?" I turn my head to scout her out.

She hesitates to respond, and I fail to associate her pause with one that happens before a person dumps bad news.

"Margret died . . . about nine years ago now."

The news hits me hard, like a sucker punch. I feel my enthusiasm plummet, as if it were a clumsy raft nosediving off a waterfall.

"She had . . ."

I don't hear the rest of her words, the details seem to fall off somewhere. I watch her lips move, and it looks like she is pushing out sound, but my ears catch nothing. So I'm not exactly sure how Margret died, even though I was just told.

I keep my upset hidden. I don't want to make our exchange uncomfortable, so I try to remain attentive. I nearly choke on a mouthful of pancake. More of Mrs. Butterworth's syrup

CECILE BEAULIEU

might help with the dryness in my throat, though I don't think it's the pancake that's causing me to choke.

We move to the topic of other family members, and we exchange details of our own lives. People are socializing all around us, sharing histories. Excitement is mounting and people are getting louder, making it hard for us to have a normal conversation. The party seems to be gaining momentum. But then, the sky suddenly drops a torrential downpour, and everyone runs for cover. I make a beeline for my RV.

The world outside is grey and wet. Rowdy clouds are knocking overhead, and the smell of ozone lingers in the air. I watch the driving rain from a window seat. The scene holds me captive and softens the blow of bad news. A sudden bolt of lightning flashes nearby and it startles me. A shiver grips me and I pull my sweater tight, nestling my chin in its warmth. I'm thankful to be sheltered and dry, so I can deal with Margret's death. Sorrow is not a strange affliction for me, but coping with loss is becoming a habit I'd rather like to break.

Twenty minutes later, the rain lets up, but I hesitate to venture outdoors. I sit for a bit to tend a wound. Losing Margret doesn't make sense. I surmise that there's been a mistake, she shouldn't have been allowed to die so young. There is no logic to her loss—especially since, in my opinion, there are other people much more deserving of getting deep-sixed.

I have no tears, just heaviness. What feels like a blockage in my airway must be the place where the heartache is stuck. It'll be with me for a long time, and I'll get used to it . . . again. The ache will settle in among all the other sorrows I cart.

After a bit, I recover, so I get up and carry on. I go to find the stand where they sell the solar lights and buy a few—one each for Mom, Dad, John, Denis, and Margret. I write their names on the flags and shove the stem parts through link openings in the fence. I linger on the one I pen for Margret. It reads:

Margret
Thanx for the pencil crayons

July 2013

Mitch bought a Harley. He named it *Harley* and took it on its first road trip travelling from Golden, BC. He planned to meet up with us in Kamloops, where my son, Alex, and I were staying for the week. We rented a cabin on a mountain lake, and Gus joined us with his children. The kids played in the water while we unpacked and waited for Mitch to arrive.

The day was sunny and very warm, and we were pumped about our last-minute throw-together of a mini family reunion. Our location was excellent. We had an unobstructed view of the lake and a small stretch of shoreline for our exclusive enjoyment. On the deck next to the cabin, Gus pitched a tent for him and the kids to sleep in. They wanted the open-air feel of camping and to catch night sounds coming off the lake. A staircase with wooden railings led down to the beach. The dock had a covered sitting area, jutting out into the water. A breeze rippled the lake surface while water fowl bobbed in the waves. We noticed the kids were trying to build a sandcastle with their hands, so we grabbed plastic pails and shovels, and joined them on the shore.

We sat on the dock, dangling our feet in the water, when we heard a distant thrum of pistons firing. There was a long, low growl and a rumble like thunder pummelling pavement. All heads turned to watch as Mitch and Harley crested the hill. A squirrel on the side of the road, spooked by the commotion, scurried up a tree to take a better look. Mitch rolled his mechanical beast past neighbouring cottages to the front of our cabin. We abandoned the beach to greet him.

Mitch waited at the top of the bank, straddling the bike. He looked like a biker gang member, which might have caused worry for some of the neighbours. Within moments, an SUV towing a bike trailer pulled up behind him. Inside were Mitch's wife and two daughters. They were Mitch's backup for the journey, travelling with him from Golden. They parked the SUV alongside the cabin and joined us near the beach. We formed a circle around Mitch as he steered our attention toward the finer features of Harley.

If Mitch was seeking attention, he found it. He was badass, and we loved it. I felt the vibration of the bike's power pulsate on my chest. Harley thrummed like a majestic lion restraining itself and Mitch was the skilled trainer taming the beast. It could be fierce when Mitch triggered the throttle, and that's what made it so exciting.

The youngest among us, two-year-old Ben, stood transfixed with admiration. Harley was the kind of toy that awakened in him a love for all things large and loud. Mitch saw his nephew's rapt expression and motioned for us to bring him closer.

Mitch leaned in and asked him, "Would you like a ride, Ben?"

The little guy responded mutely with a shudder, his mouth agape. Mitch held a bike helmet out for him to touch. Ben patted it with his little hands, as if to discover a new texture. We placed the helmet on his baby-boy head and lifted him to the bike seat.

Rather than risk contact with the hot head pipe at the front, Mitch instructed us to place Ben on the seat behind him. Ben was too agog to hang onto his uncle's vest, so we supported him and trooped alongside as Mitch walked the bike. The drive wasn't engaged, so Mitch revved the engine for added effect. There was sheer bliss on our baby nephew's face. His gaze was fixed forward, and he made no sound in his euphoria.

Ben remained close to his Uncle Mitch to make sure the bike wasn't going anywhere without his notice. He became Mitch's little shadow, a new role model to emulate. Gus directed our attention with a whisper, "Look . . . look at Ben."

Baby boy had a thumb hooked into the topside of his diaper. He was leaning back on one foot and toe-tapping with the other. The stance was a little odd and off character for Ben. But then we noticed Mitch, whose thumb was hooked through a belt loop of his leathers, leaning back on one leg and toe-tapping his biker boot in time with the music. It was one of those moments when I wished I had a camera close at hand.

Most of the clan went to explore the waterfront. I stayed behind to fire up the barbecue and cook supper. Mitch and Gus withdrew to a corner of the patio to engage in private conversation. Ben followed them and climbed onto his Dad's lap. I tried to imagine the subject of their talk, but watching them stirred a tinge of envy in me with regard to the closeness they shared. I loved my brothers, and I knew that a sister couldn't easily infiltrate the bond between them, but it sometimes felt like a brush-off when I was left on the outside.

The two men were striking as far as looks go. They carried a certain measure of confidence, and were both successful and ambitious—and I couldn't make those claims for myself. So perhaps we had little in common, and I shouldn't have been concerned with fitting in. I was who I was and they were themselves, no more and no less appreciated.

We filled our bellies with tasty barbecue, and afterwards, we drove to the city of Kamloops. At Riverside Park, there were live bands setting up to entertain the crowd. We found a space on the grass large enough for our group to sit together and enjoy the show. Mitch and Ben toe-tapped to the music while the older children went to find a playground. Alex, along with Mitch's two girls, who were of drinking age, went looking for beer. The band played a mixture of country and rock, which satisfied all our appetites for music. The tunes quit soon after dark, our cue to vacate the park.

Gus had left earlier to put his kids to bed. Mitch and his spouse were spending the night in town. The beer-drinkers wanted to party at the cabin, so they climbed into my truck and I played chauffeur. We stopped to buy cigarettes, because alcohol apparently causes cravings for smokes. My small caravan of fun-lovers was feeling no pain when the girls began serenading a back-and-forth harmony to the tune of "Love Shack." It was quite boss.

The road to the cabin had several sharp curves. Tall grass grew along both shoulders. I kept expecting a small animal to run out into our path and become roadkill. We travelled up the mountain, ushered by a full moon. Its beacon painted the topside of plants pearly white. We lost the moon's light when we reached the tree line. The beam off the headlights disappeared into blackness above the road grade, as if the trail was leading us into a tomb. It had been a long while since I had travelled back roads. I felt boxed in by the forest, and I was edgy driving through it. The sensation lasted until we arrived at our temporary home on the shore of Paul Lake.

We piled around the picnic table beneath the full moon. Gus joined us for a drink and Alex opened a round of brown bottles. We toasted the night, the lake, the water birds, and the stars. Gus and I kept shushing the three partiers, so the kids in the tent could get some sleep. But the kids weren't in favour of missing out on the fun. We heard the giggles, and didn't have the heart to discourage their amusement.

Jokes yo-yoed across the table like a competition between comics. We embellished each other's stories and applied no limit to the drivel. My laugh muscles ached and begged for a timeout. Then, when a certain topic hit too close to home, the girls went quiet. They focused their eyes on a lit cigarette in the ashtray, as though it held the answer to a thorny puzzle.

My niece pursed her lips and turned her head—perhaps to hide an emotion. "I remember when Dad was doing weird shit."

The mood around the table turned sombre. No one else said a word. She paused before continuing, "I was there . . . you weren't . . ."

We let her talk, because it was safe for her to do that.

I recalled her smiling face in family portraits, how her wholesomeness could incite envy, and how the images could move me to believe in the possibility of genuine content-ment and fulfillment. What the photos didn't reveal was the flip side of lives turned upside down by mental illness. There was no caption suggesting a family at risk. I wished the girls didn't have to bear this burden, or keep up appearances for the sake of pretence.

Gus and I were on the same page, feeling the weight of our nieces' sorrows.

"There are always going to be bad days," Gus whispered. "Hang on to the good ones, like today."

"My dad, your grandpa, did stuff that made me wonder about his mental state," I said. "He was getting old, and I think that had something to do with it. His behaviour was bizarre sometimes, but I can laugh about that now—so go easy on your dad. We're all going to get old, and I hope you'll still respect me after I use your favourite sweater to wipe my butt."

"Or when she urinates in your kitchen sink," Gus added.

We stayed up late. More stories circulated around the table while water birds crooned a requiem in the background. The lake rippled the colour of molten silver where moonlight kissed the surface. Choppy waves slapped against the dock, as though applauding our company. Each story triggered a new memory, which sparked another anecdote, which ate up the night.

It was long past midnight when Gus rose from the table and headed for bed. I tried shutting down the party, but the rest didn't want to give up that easily. I left them on their own and called it a night. Within minutes the noise level escalated, so I emerged as the hard-ass.

"You guys are going to wake up the neighbours and make trouble for me! Shut 'er down! Now!"

I expected resistance and drama, but to my astonishment, they quietly filed inside and went directly to bed. I fell asleep . . . once the awe of my newfound authority wore off.

May 2014

An accident happened about six months before the reunion. I was in a dispute with a truck over rights to a crosswalk. The truck won. The truck suffered no damage, and I sustained a broken elbow.

It could have been much worse. The truck could have run me over completely, but I think there was divine intervention. Someone was looking out for me, and I think it was my mom.

Three months later, the elbow hadn't healed properly. I couldn't manoeuvre tight spaces without my stiff, stuck-out arm catching something, so I went under the knife for another fix—and then immediate rehab to get my wing flexing again.

I received a phone call while I was in rehab. I picked up my cell, and a voice I didn't at first recognize spoke: "Hi, Céc, how are you?"

There was care and concern in the tone. I paused for a second before responding. "Hey, Mitch . . . Wow, so good to hear from you."

I missed him. Months had passed without a word from him. I knew he wavered in and out of depression and perhaps that was why the silence. His words provided balm for my hurt and something like reconciliation or a homecoming for my heart.

"Céc, I'm making plans for summer. Are you coming to the reunion?"

I heard optimism in his voice, and I sensed his smile on the other side of the line. "Yeah, for sure."

"Good. I want to bring my bike and trailer and build a float for the parade. I want it to be about our family. I'll need help. Are you in?"

"Of course."

His enthusiasm was infectious. He wanted ideas. A visual from 1967 came to mind.

In 1967, Canada's Centennial, Canadians observed the hundredth birthday of our nation. Every community held a grand celebration. Our village planned a fantastic picnic and an impressive parade. My mom designed a float for the parade.

She devised a clever way to showcase our family's contribution as telephone operators in the community. She decorated a cardboard box with tissue carnations on all sides but one. On the blank side, she punched holes to anchor telephone plugs that were cabled together, making the box resemble a switchboard. A large teddy bear wearing a headset worked the phone cables. She had us help decorate the car with pink tissue carnations and twisted streamers. She placed the teddy bear and the switchboard on the roof of the car and secured them to the cab.

Mom may have intended to pass down her creative talents to her kids, but I wasn't on the receiving end of them, so it's a good thing Mitch was. Mitch and I discussed a float plan for the reunion and parade, even though my input wasn't necessary. I couldn't hold a candle to Mitch's creativity, so he worked out the details on his own.

The other important event at the forefront of our minds was celebrating his thirty-fifth wedding anniversary. Mitch and his wife were renewing their wedding vows on the same weekend as the reunion.

"You're coming, right? It's on the Friday night."

"Yes, I'll be there."

"It's going to be a great weekend. There'll be so much to catch up on. I haven't seen some of my old friends in years."

I knew exactly how he felt, and for the first time in ages, I was looking forward to going home to Saskatchewan.

Friday, August 1, 2014, 1:30 p.m.

I roll onto the school grounds in my truck early Friday afternoon of reunion weekend. A field, where the schoolyard used to be, serves as a parking area for RVs, so I make my temporary home on the exact spot I used to play softball, volleyball and soccer. I join my brothers, who are also spending the weekend in their campers. We are parked together, except Mitch, whose accommodation is set up on an acreage in the country, where the anniversary celebration will be held.

The venue for the anniversary party is rural and private, and about a twenty-minute drive out through back country. My sister, Pauly, and I hitch a ride with Rod. Our kids and spouses aren't attending this part of the weekend, so the three of us are the sole representatives of our families.

"Are you sure it's OK with them . . . that I come to this?" Rod worries about making things awkward by attending.

The conflict between my sisters-in-law is an unresolved issue. Reconciliation attempts were ignored, so the dispute following Ernie's funeral was never settled. Five years should have been plenty long enough to bury the hatchet, but it remains a sore spot.

I had posed the question for Rod's sake and been told there wouldn't be a problem. "Yes, I made sure of it. They said it's OK for you to come. It's about time she got over it. But don't expect an apology." I assure him that I have his back.

I still think it would have been considerate for Rod to receive a personal invite, like I had. It was high time to let bygones be bygones, but pride has a way of keeping people from facing their own weaknesses. It's shallow to allow a minor conflict to stew for such a lengthy duration and cause unnecessary division. I feel bad for both my brothers, and want the bullshit to come to an end.

We drive past our dad's old farm. Pauly and Rod bring up memories of the few years they spent living there. There isn't much left of the yard that's familiar. The buildings have been removed, the trees downed, and the yard tilled to make more field. The part of the land that used to have life and character is gone. I suppose that's what happens when profits trump sentiment.

The road is washboard-rough in places where gravel is sparse. Recent heavy rains have pelted the road and caused fill to drain into ditch. In the low spots, the surface is soupy, like thin porridge, which further slows our progress.

Our navigation sense is put to the test when we encounter a washed-out bridge. We double back to use an alternate route. It's been years since either of us have driven the area, and we combine our recollections of the layout. The redirection sets us back ten minutes. If nothing else, we're becoming reacquainted with the old neighbourhood.

We arrive at a second washed-out bridge, another casualty of the unusually wet summer. We scratch our heads, wondering how we're supposed to get to the other side of the waterway. Route options are dwindling. We backtrack again considerably, extending our drive. It's becoming apparent that we won't arrive in time to witness the whole service.

The ceremony is nearing its halfway mark as we pull into the farmyard. We join a gathering of about fifty people, just in time to catch the renewing of vows between husband and wife.

The crowd looks small relative to the large farmyard. Tall spruce and poplars stand guard at the perimeter. A bright border of pink and green shrubbery separates lawn from garden. Rose blossoms against emerald foliage provide a pleasant background to an elegant celebration.

The minister's back is toward us. She is addressing Mitch and his bride. Members of the bridal party flank the couple on both sides. Guests stand nearby watching the ceremony. A few children play quietly at the lawn's edge, and the sun competes with the clouds for an unobstructed view.

The event is classy, with an air of sophistication, and obvious that meticulous planning went into making preparations. We could hardly expect less from a family who possesses such good taste.

The bride and her daughters look beautiful and elegant. Mitch is striking in his less formal attire. They are picture-perfect, and a photographer's camera captures flawless photos. The celebration has the air of a first-class garden party, with the props, ambience, and prestige of a storybook wedding.

"Did you see the ring he gave her?"

"See it? I was almost blinded by it. Remember the last time we checked out the rock he gave her, and we put on sunglasses as a joke?"

"Wish my husband would buy me bling." She says it in jest, within earshot of her unruffled mate, who grins and rolls his eyes.

It's as if the sky, the elements, and the sun have made a pact to cooperate for the affair. The only thing missing is a trio of musicians providing background music. The production is flawless, and I think there must be a hitch. But there isn't. It's a special day for my brother and his wife. The limelight is with them and on them.

Maybe I'm envious of the whole picture. Perhaps I can't help but behave as the outsider who lingers at the fringe. Visits with Mitch are spectator sport for me. His family interacts naturally and lovingly, and I want to fit in with them. But that kind of harmony evades me, it's always beyond my reach.

There must be something wrong with me, because everyone else is obviously mesmerized and enchanted by the display. It's too much show for me to be comfortable, and I can't help but feel like I'm the square dance caller attending a ballerina convention. Something is off, and I can't put my finger on it.

It should be enough that my family are all together in one place. I need to relax. I neglect to appreciate the moment. Instead, I balance on the edge of a fragile nerve. So I hang back, and opt to observe more than participate. Maybe I just don't want to get burned again.

Frankly, it doesn't matter that I'm awkward with the pageantry. It's their day, not mine. That's something I need to get right with. This celebration is proof of the pledge they make to one another, a promise that will carry them the rest of their days. I need to honour that, and focus on their union.

With the formalities over, the guests break rank and line up to congratulate the couple. The volume of laughter rises as people gear up for festivities. We slowly migrate to a nearby country hall that is equally festooned. Servers are busy laying out a hot meal, and everyone takes their place at a table. I sit beside my sister, and we are joined by more family.

I gradually loosen up to enjoy the gathering. Our hosts treat us to an evening of good food and goodwill. We partake in a few libations. There are speeches and toasts to the couple, along with jokes and sound advice on what it takes to build a loving relationship between husband and wife. The party lasts until near midnight. People start leaving, so Rod, Pauly and I join the convoy of vehicles going back to town.

I reflect on the evening and surmise I wasted much of it being uptight. The celebration played out according to a well-orchestrated script, without a hitch and without drama. I recognize that there was so much jubilation to appreciate and share in, and that perhaps my family was starting to get it right.

Saturday, August 2, 2014, 12:45 p.m.

It's Saturday afternoon and I'm on my own. The reunion is well into its second day, and the rest of my family seem to have found somewhere better to be.

Despite the setback at breakfast, I am moving forward with plans to make the best of the weekend. The news about Margret upset me for sure. I'm trying hard not to get spooked about omens and shit. I resolve to shake off that notion. There is still plenty of time for the weekend to redeem itself.

I pulled through the previous night's anniversary event without causing any damage, and I am hoping to be just as successful today. So, I wait to hear from Mitch. He is supposed to let me know when and where to go to help prepare the float for the parade.

The rain stopped just before noon, and the sun is drying things off. It's getting hot, and turning out to be a great day for a street show.

I text Mitch and wait for a reply.

Nothing.

If we are going to get this thing done, we need to get on with it.

The parade is set to start soon. I walk to the main corner of town, where everyone is flocking. From this location, I shouldn't miss anyone coming or going.

I text Mitch again: "Hey where are you? It's getting close to parade time."

People are gathering, bringing lawn chairs and settling down for a good view of the parade. Kids are excited, and parents keep them curious about what's to arrive. A few men put up blockades at both ends of the highway leading into town. Somewhere behind the church, a lineup of floats, decorated vehicles, horses, and people wait to file onto the street.

I go inside the hotel café to buy bottled water. It's packed with customers I don't recognize. I realize I am fast becoming a stranger in my own hometown.

There is still no word from Mitch.

Maybe he has enough help making the float and doesn't need me.

And then I remember something. I check my phone. No bars. I am too far from a digital tower to get decent cell phone coverage. My messages aren't likely to get through at all today.

A police cruiser comes into view, leading a procession. I surrender to the obvious—the parade is going to start without my help. I sit on the curb and resign myself to being an observer.

Other families have come up with plans similar to Mitch's. Vehicles file by, some decked out, some pulling trailers loaded with representations of their family, business, or accomplishments. I recognize surnames and keep a lookout for familiar faces.

The air is charged, and spectators become as much a part of the parade as the players. People run into the street on impulse to embrace long-time friends passing by in the procession. Kids collect candy tossed from a supply that never seems to run short.

With each passing exhibit, I anticipate seeing my brother's project. I strain to get a glimpse of floats to come, searching for a clue about where the rest of my clan is.

After the parade ends, I head back toward the school grounds. I am one in a throng going on a stroll, moving like a wandering carnival. A girl dressed in glitter is passing out stickers and tiny flags. A decorated horse wagon stops on the road to pick up passengers. Somewhere behind me, people are singing the old theme song from our school.

I need to solve a puzzle—what is the deal with our family float? I am trying to figure out what happened to our plan. I arrive at the heart of our camping spot and find Gus.

"Did I miss something? Were we supposed to meet somewhere?"

"I don't think they made it to town yet."

They referred to Mitch and his family.

"I suspect they might have had a late night and a slow start this morning," he adds.

People are forming into groups at almost every camper location, and our own little circle is beginning to draw a crowd. More out-of-towners arrive, and before long, a couple of Mitch's girls wander in to the centre of our party.

"Where are your parents?"

"They're finding a place to park the bike hauler so Dad can ride the Harley in."

"What took so long?"

"We sat up talking until about four this morning. Nobody had the energy to get going."

Someone hands them each a beer, and they find a place to sit down. The drinks start flowing, conversation becomes lively and yarns are spun. The scale of laughter measures high, and our numbers continue to climb.

We're jammed into the open area between our campers. Some kin occupy lawn chairs, while others stand or sit on the ground. There are people of all ages, from great-grandparents to toddlers. We have a connection to one another and a yen to rekindle old ties.

"Give up that lawn chair for your grandma, please. I'll share a corner of this seat with you."

The kid does as he's told, surrendering the perch. He drops to the ground and resumes playing his Game Boy. Grandma takes the seat, places a hand on the little guy's shoulder, and gives it a gentle squeeze. He kind of likes the feel of her touch, and moves in closer for more.

The ground is somewhat damp from the morning's rain, and humidity hangs in our space. The weather is the opposite of the area's normal aridness. White, bulbous clouds move across the sky, giving us intermittent relief from the hot sun. Some of us bask in the heat, but most prefer to stay cool. Shade spots are the popular picks, but harder to claim, so we keep our party hydrated with a liberal selection of beverages.

A familiar rumble rises above the din of our festivities. The beefy rhythm grows closer, coming from the other side of the field. Within moments, machine and man emerge just beyond the perimeter of our clan circle. All eyes focus on the wondrous pair of them, bike and biker. Like a scene out of *Easy Rider*, Mitch rides in on wicked Harley.

Mitch has a star quality that everyone notices, but he doesn't see it in himself. He can't exactly pull off *badass* because of his benevolent nature. He manages to play tough for a short while, until he cracks a smile with eyes that radiate compassion.

Mitch props the bike on its kickstand, leans back against the seat, and folds his arms. He's taking in the family with a big grin, and is obviously having a good day. We widen our circle to include him. The kids approach to admire his bike.

"I forgot to bring this last night." I hand him an envelope. He pulls out the contents and laughs. Inside is a Christmas card stuffed with a gift card. He's amused by the cartoon of Santa riding a reindeer.

"It's not an anniversary card, but the closest thing I had to one. I was in so much of a hurry to pack that I forgot to get a proper card. I thought you might appreciate the joke."

He does.

"Merry Christmas, then." He gives me a hug.

I am playing hostess for the afternoon, serving snacks and stocking coolers with ice and drinks. Our party keeps growing with the arrival of more family members. By this time, we are numbering almost thirty. It's exactly how I imagined a reunion—one giant, warm embrace.

The wind starts to pick up. I'm concerned about the awning on the RV tearing, so I attempt to roll it back. Mitch recognizes my ineptitude at the task and takes over.

"First you disconnect the doodad at the thing-a-ma-bob and slip the flange over the gear socket . . ." He starts a ridiculous monologue to amuse us. He is in his element, performing bland gestures and voicing flat instructions. All the while, his smiley eyes expose his game.

"Line the spigot to the ball bearing and turn the wingnut counter-clockwise. Slide the shroud on the elbow side toward the bushing and remove the cotter pin. Once the metal rod is level with the hinge, spin the wingnut until the hex bolt drops into the harness."

Somewhere in all the distraction, he rolls back the canopy into its protective cover. The crowd laughs and claps.

It's getting late, nearing suppertime. Slowly, the mass of us forms a front, moving toward the hall, where a hot meal is being served buffet-style. Our numbers mix with the mob as old friends join us, and we stroll as one to the banquet.

After supper, a trickle of family members returns to our camp area. By the time I arrive, there are few stragglers left.

Mitch's Harley is gone.

"Where'd your dad go? Is he coming back?"

"They went to put the bike away since it looks like it'll rain again."

We are reduced in numbers, though no less fun. There's a steady stream of passersby, and some pause for a chat. It reminds me of how people used to visit when we were kids.

There were no door locks on most houses. The rowdy thwack of the screen door closing was our cue that visitors had come calling. Most simply dropped in without knocking and stayed for a cup of coffee or a game of cards. It was a common thing to do back in the day.

Beer garden, live music, and dancing are on the to-do list for the rest of the night. A din rises out of party central, promising fun. We don't want to be left out, so we drift toward the noise.

We form our own little clique, Alex, my two nieces, and I. It's a do-over of a bygone night in Kamloops. I speculate whether I fit in with these three as a peer. Perhaps I provide them with stability, like an anchor—or they just like having me around. Truth be told, I think they keep me close for the wad of beer tickets I'm packing, knowing I'm not likely to redeem them all for myself.

The rain that held off for most of the day decides to drench us, though it doesn't hamper anyone's mirth. We dance in the water streams forming at our feet. We hoist the tempo and stomp in puddles, getting everyone soaked.

Old, familiar songs blend with the night, the rain, and the thunder. The overhead clatter adds a glorious modulation to the music. There is synchronicity of motion—bodies swaying to a slow, hypnotic beat. Time fades into darkness, and we rock to the rhythm.

We linger inside the embrace of family and friends until last call. We reconvene at our own party central. The sky starts to clear, the clouds shove off. Our resolve is boosted to keep celebrating instead of going to bed.

The rain has soaked the seats of our lawn chairs. We prop up the cloth ones so they can dry off. Gus and I towel off plastic benches and create a small circle. We anticipate gleaning more amusement from the night.

About ten of us are left, playing overtime. The sky seems to recognize our stubbornness and decides to give us a new show. Dark clouds part to the west and to the east, like the spreading of fine drapery. We receive a backside view of Mother Nature's best as thunderheads shoot jagged fire-bolts in the distance. We remain dry, beyond the storm's reach. Above us, the dark dome is speckled with stars, which shimmer like rhinestones against black velvet.

The storm leaves us alone for awhile. Then, Mother Nature gives us more. We are blown away by the lightshow. Splashes of green, blue, and pink, like coloured icicles, hanging off the ceiling. Northern Lights span the skyline, giving us a rare glimpse of nature's finest.

The last time I witnessed this kind of fantastical display was in August 1995. On that particular night, I was told, "Come quickly. Come to the bedside of our mom. You need to be here."

Rod wouldn't give me any details. His tone troubled me, and I quickly prepared to travel to Saskatchewan. I remember the anxiety in his voice and how it weighed heavily on my spirit.

We sped eastward on Highway 16 toward Saskatoon. During the drive, we were flanked on the left by neon cascades lighting up the expanse of a charcoal canvas. Any other time, the night show of Northern Lights would have amazed me, but I couldn't appreciate the wonder of nature for the sickness in my stomach.

We rallied to our mother's side that night, and the doctor gave her little hope. His words went against my dream for her to beat the cancer. I had thought the lights were a sign—an assurance that she could rise above the sickness. Instead, the outcome was dark and ominous, with no silver lining.

But on this reunion night, I take in the full splendour of the lightshow without impending pain and loss.

Pauly rises from her seat and moves toward open field, away from artificial light. Her arms are hoisted in a gesture of praise, like an enraptured evangelical. Her body sways in time to the undulating light beams. Pauly is taking in the scene, like a child receiving a gift. She reminds us how easy it used to be to appreciate simple pleasures. We couldn't be more content. None of us want the night to end. It's peaceful here. We find tranquility and a sense of home—comforting, like a warm hug.

Yet . . . something niggles at my thoughts. I'm bothered. It's been lurking most of the night.

"Did anyone see Mitch after they put Harley to bed?"

CHAPTER ELEVEN — CRASH

Now the sun's gone to hell, and the moon riding high
Let me bid you farewell, every man has to die
Source: Dire Straits
"Brothers in Arms"

Wednesday, September 10, 2014, 8 p.m.
The rest of the story unfolds as though plucked from a modified version of the popular tale *A Series of Unfortunate Events*. It, too, follows a predictable outcome—one where shit happens.

Was it dramatic?

Yes and no. It depends.

Was it devastating?

You bet it was.

It bypassed logic, that's for sure.

Logic is my preferred means for working out conundrums, but logic doesn't always sink in at the right time. There were details I wasn't privy to—details that could have been helpful to know beforehand. But then, I think not knowing was a gift. Details couldn't give me solace, which was what I really needed.

There was the freefall. Then the almost-recovery. Then the other slow, steady, deliberate, calculated... plummet. Mitch's psyche was travelling down a one-way road in the wrong direction. I suppose his actions could be solely attributed to mental illness. I suppose there could be other ways of seeing it, too.

Choices.

Living well comes down to choices. And with choices come consequences, which many people don't often anticipate.

There are obvious choices, and there are less obvious choices. We make them every minute of every day. Some provide fulfillment, some lead to over-indulgence, and others are made to ensure survival.

What does it take to maintain a healthy lifestyle?

It depends on the individual's definition of healthy. My health thrives on simplicity, because that's what I need to sustain balance. Others may fill their lives with business, competition, appearances, extravagances, or achievements. Each follow their own path toward maintaining their semblance of health.

Does the quest add stress?

It could, if it follows unrealistic expectations for . . .

> stuff you need, stuff you have, stuff you don't have, stuff you want, stuff others want, what's expected of you, what you expect of yourself, the goods you buy, the toys you value, the competition to have more, the spectacle you must portray, the attention you

must attract, the places you want to go, the people you want to impress, the job you must have, the salary you need to make, the credit cards you rack up, the bank loans you take on, the house you mortgage, the vehicle you drive, the trends you aim to follow, the status you strive to achieve, the image you seek to maintain, the delicacies you hunger to taste, the entertainment you yearn to experience, the functions you attend, the clothes you wear, the style you chase . . .

It makes me dizzy.

I can't imagine the burdens some people place on themselves to reach a higher standard. Especially ones trying to make ends meet on an adequate but not limitless income—all to support a disproportionate lifestyle.

I can't imagine upping the challenge with a physical impairment, such as Crohn's disease or cancer—or diabetes.

Add another complication, like a serious mental illness, and you have the makings of a perfect shitstorm.

Cause and effect.

On the night we danced in the rain beneath a kaleidoscopic sky, a tempest erupted at a secluded farmyard twelve miles away. Mitch was out of control, raging against opposition to his free will.

There must have been a turning point in Mitch's demeanour, which I suppose became obvious to someone.

What triggered his upset? What sparked the rage?

There was a decision made, and it must have been based on reason—one of when to come, another of when to go. Did he decide to leave, or was it decided for him? Did the decision cause the mania, or did mania cause the decision?

For a guy so strongly anticipating the reunion, it made no sense he gave the event a scant few hours of his time. There was a whole other night and day and other night for him to attend it. His actions followed no form of logic.

Was it mania, or a reaction to something else?

Nothing had happened earlier in the day to lend us a clue.

There is a picture in my mind still—Mitch, leaning back on the seat of his Harley, casual, easy, even content. He's flashing the killer smile, the one that draws people—and they can't help but smile back at him.

It's in Mitch's nature to give his full attention to every person he encounters. He focuses with care and concern. When he sees me, his eyes show me kindness. It's as though he's letting me know I am valued and loved. He has a gift for connecting with people.

He looked happy to be home. He was enjoying our company, and we delighted in his. He showed no hint of anxiety, conflict, or desire to leave. Mitch was simply there, with wonderful presence. And I can't figure out how he switched from serene to volatile in the time it takes to load a bike onto a trailer.

If there was something hokey happening to his mental state, his actions would have given it away. He would have kept things hidden by avoiding eye contact. Someone would have noticed he was agitated. So it doesn't make sense that he connected actively with his eyes, smile, and easy manner, then suddenly became manic.

I didn't see fear or turmoil in his eyes that afternoon—only contentment and joy. He was showing his truest self, in the spirit of the fun-loving boy he used to be. In the short time we had together that day, I hope he recognized how much I valued and loved him back.

That was the last time I saw him.

Mitch took charge of his own destiny. He answered only to himself.

He left. Went home. Went back to work.

He spent a month working shifts and going home to an empty house. He maintained contact with a few people, but I wasn't one of them.

I regret that I didn't push harder, that I didn't impose or force myself into his space. I allowed obscurity and distance to ease my guilt and free me of my obligation as a big sister. I assumed the situation was under control and was convinced those closest to him could better handle it. Knowing he didn't trust me made it easier for me to give him room to work things out on his own.

I was so fucking stupid.

No one wanted to cause the situation to escalate. We loved Mitch, and wanted him to have great joy. He conveyed peace and contentment that day, and we were blind to whatever menace lurked in the background.

Can you love someone too much?

Mitch's wife did everything she could to protect him. She loved him as completely and capably as she could. She set safeguards for his benefit. She took measures that may have felt restrictive and controlling, but Mitch's own actions sometimes eliminated other options. Perhaps it was her influence that sustained him so we were able to see him one last time.

Many times in the past, he had acted irrationally. Mental illness caused him to navigate a horribly fragile path of eggshells with his family. His mind played awful tricks on him, so maybe it wasn't always clear when to impose rules and when to relax them.

Ultimately, he made the choice. Him alone. He kept the secret hidden, and then he acted on it.

One day, he didn't go to work.

He didn't go to work the next day, either.

They found his body.

I got the call, and the news crushed me. It made me hate things, like phones and sound and mornings. It made me hate life and people.

I hated time, because it never stopped. It just kept moving forward, regardless of my will. It paid no mind to the huge loss weighing me down. It half-carried and half-dragged me along a dark, bumpy path, like rolling me down a highway wrought with potholes. I especially hated that I arrived at another roadblock.

How could I have let this happen again? Hadn't I learned anything from the first time? The second time?

The clamour inside my head boomed—Why this? Why now?

I tried hard not to sink, but I was losing the battle, hard and fast.

Mitch left a note, but it didn't give much consolation. He said he was sorry and tired and that he loved us, his whole family.

I was sorry and I was tired, too, but I wasn't able to find any love in his message. I wasn't able to find love in anything.

I could find pain. I could find rage, and I could find darkness. But I couldn't find love.

So I hung on to the things I could find, which were toxic. I allowed those things to remind me how I had failed my brother.

What I should have been able to mend, I didn't. I had failed as a protector, a confidante, a sibling. He couldn't confide in me, and that is the regret I will carry for the remainder of my days.

In the morning, I wake up and I am the same person I was the night before, which is one not worthy of being called a good sister. And the next day, that truth will not have changed. And in three years' time, the sun will rise, I'll face another day, and I will not yet have cast off the weight of my guilt. I will grieve all my brothers as intensely as the day I lost them. I will be the same pathetic person I have always been, only more alone.

In the meantime, I build a wall. Not one made of bricks and mortar or chain links, but a wall built of grief, guilt, and rage. It serves two purposes—one to keep things in, the other to keep things out. I am not exactly sure if I build it to protect myself from the outside, or to protect the outside from myself. Either way, my space is empty . . . just like my soul.

CHAPTER TWELVE — RELEASE

> Oh dear Dad, can you see me now
> I am myself, like you somehow
> I'll wait up in the dark, for you to speak to me
> I'll open up, release me
> *Pearl Jam*
> *"Release"*

Every Morning, September 2014 to February 2018

It's quiet now. There are no voices. There is only white noise. It's as though my ears are bunged up and have forgotten how to hear—but somewhere, there is a muffled murmur, or a hum, like the drone of a last armoured tank quitting a levelled battlefield. Beneath the war zone's cratered surface, a stifled moan emerges. Battle smoke and toxic mist sting my eyes, and I stand alone amidst the rubble. The stench of death is everywhere.

From afar, a woman's mournful cry crosses the expanse. I feel it more than hear it, as though its source has the power to shred a grieving heart. Her lament bleeds and booms, and

I awake with a start to recognize her wail as my own. I taste the salt from tears I've shed as dawn's new light transforms battlefield to bedroom.

Each morning I realize anew what I've lost, and the grief bites me with the savagery of a rabid dog. I bear an ache that is hardened like stone, and my soul is dark like the space between stars on a moonless night. I long for the day when grief's impact will soften.

Loneliness, sorrow, and anger are my constant companions, and questions occupy my every thought. I ponder things that confound me. I strain to make sense of the senseless, to understand what is incomprehensible, to mend what is beyond repair, to find the tools to break down the barrier separating me from love.

It's been more than a few years now.

Too many seasons pass, and still too few. Time crawls with sluggish forward momentum, heavy and without purpose. I dig in my heels in a pathetic attempt to turn back the clock— perhaps to somehow make things right. God owes me a do-over, and I would make it count. I would be a better sister.

I remain locked inside myself, inside my home. If nothing else, the refuge within is safe and provides me a modicum of comfort. It's not an unfamiliar space—just another rag room filled with remnants of the past. There is no path to before, no reconstruction, no re-fusion of atoms, no miracles. Every day is a repeat of the previous, and I learn to be still.

I study shadows. I watch the steady, slow progression from light to dim as the shadow line skims across a surface. The distraction offers more than distant recollections—it consoles me and provides me something other than pain. But it also exaggerates the silence.

I spend time reading, researching, and trying to devise a plan—something to stop the ground from caving in around me. I won't be venturing out anytime soon, joining hands around a campfire, singing "Kumbaya," but I know I must eventually return to the world.

I came across a term that made me reconsider my relationship with the idea of suicide. For people like me, who keep suicide open as an option, the experts call it "premeditated." This bothered me. I didn't like the sinister and diabolical undertone it implied. Suicide had always been a logical solution to stop the pain, nothing more. The term *premeditated* suggests a crime of hatred planned against someone else.

I have to rethink, relearn, and abandon an old belief. I need to move things in a new direction—one that leads toward living instead of toward dying. I need to embrace each day as a gift given, not a curse imposed.

I'll make a new plan—a better plan, one that educates and gives hope. I'm going to kick despair to the curb, so it doesn't gain any more ground. There is a better solution, and I'm going to find it—because this family deserves a break. They have been through enough.

So this is my strategy:

> Stop feeding the suicide monster and the anger it breeds on.

> Let go of the past and allow peace to heal the wounds.

> Forgive myself and those who have hurt us so much.

Change the pattern and stop the pain.

Honour the memories of those who have passed and grieve for them respectfully.

Be thankful for the time we were given together.

Aim to restore the truth of their humanity and dignity.

Don't forget God's gift of the loved ones who still remain.

Resolve to reach deep into this self-imposed world of silence and allow pain-tainted words to flow like rivers of ash. Pour the words into form, whisper traces of life back into the emptiness, and always, always . . . *remember them . . . and remember also, to live and to love and to learn.*

I have learned one other absolute truth:

Suicide is very, very painful.

> Now we see dimly as in a mirror;
> then we shall see face to face.
> Now I know only in part;
> then I shall know fully,
> as I am fully known.
> —*1 Corinthians 13:12*

ACKNOWLEDGEMENTS

Thank you to the many individuals who helped move this book from the trash heap to the book shelf.

Without the expertise and keen eye of editors and reviewers from FriesenPress and the Writers' Guild of Alberta, I couldn't have fine tuned the prose and story content. Many thanks go out to you.

I am grateful to the many Authors in Residence at Edmonton Public Library who took the time to sit with me and review pieces of my work. You gave me a tremendous boost in confidence as a writer.

Thank you to the 'critters' at Critique Circle who helped me to develop better writing and editing skills.

I owe deepest gratitude to my close family and friends who took the time to read through some of my early drafts. You've provided me excellent feedback, answers to questions and kind words. Thank you to Pauline, Roger, Rose, Gerard, Shelly, Chris, Lindsay, Chaz, Simone, Rachel, Delia and my bff Joanne.

Thank-you John Bach for giving me the space, time and tremendous encouragement to stick with it. When I was down and broken, you picked me up and helped me heal. You became my closest friend. And then we got married in Aug 2022. Life just keeps getting better.